ANTLER DUST

ANTLER DUST

a novel

MARK STEVENS

PAANDAA
ENTERTAINMENT

Boulder, Colorado

ISBN Number 10: 0-9774188-1-2
ISBN Number 13: 978-0-9774188-1-7

Library of Congress Control Number: 2006909080

First Edition: March, 2007

Cover and interior design by NZ Graphics, www.nzgraphics.com

Printed in the United States of America

Published by Paandaa Entertainment, Boulder, Colorado

Visit our Web site at: www.paandaa.com

for Jody, my creative cowgirl

1

Allison Coil stroked the soft neck of the massive bull elk. The skin was still warm to the touch. She felt the smooth fur on the animal's head, looked at the crimson dot on its skull that leaked blood, then pressed her index finger against the spot where death had found an opening.

Death in a flying cylinder, she thought.

"This is the point in the process where none of us really knows what to do," said Vic, one of the three hunters who had led Coil to the site of the kill. They had just returned to camp for their quartering tools when she showed up, making the rounds to check on clients.

"He was still struggling when we got here," said another of the trio. "We were forced to finish him off."

The three young men seemed appropriately respectful. Too many hunters treated animals as little more than bull's-eye targets.

"Is this your first kill?" she asked.

"First kill, first shot, first day," said Vic, the man bearing the least amount of equipment—jeans, boots, and blaze-orange vest over a heavy winter jacket. "Beginners' luck all the way."

"How did it feel?" she asked.

"Feel? I don't know. It all happened so quickly."

Coil stood up. The four of them were gathered in a grassy clearing a half-mile from their camp outside the main bowl of Ripplecreek Canyon.

"Good lung shot," she said. "Too bad he didn't die instantly."

Allison had guided these men into the wilderness three days earlier. She was a rarity in the Rocky Mountains, a female guide in macho land.

Her job was to escort hunters on horseback into the high country, to help them set up tents and prepare for the hunt. This group was a welcome break from the greenhorns who tried to pretend that they had never worn a silk tie, drunk a three-martini lunch, or driven an SUV with a cell-phone sprouting from one ear. This group had an earthy, genuine feel. She remembered taking note of Vic's good looks on the day she had loaded them in, and she took a second to study them again: trim sandy-blond beard, a surfer-like shock of blond hair, square shoulders, strong hips and a solid demeanor.

"If I hadn't come back today to check on you boys, which one of you would have taken this puppy apart?" she asked.

"I was going to wing it," said Vic.

"So . . . do you want a hands-on lesson, or do you want to watch me have fun by myself?" Coil asked.

"A lesson, please," said Vic. "You might not be around to hold my hand the next time I bring down an elk."

"You've taken your kill for this season, mister," Coil said. "If you learn how to do this right, you can hold one of your buddys' hands." She looked over at the two other men, who took a small step away from each other, laughing.

Coil showed Vic where to make an incision in the white belly, a straight line from anus to heart-high, and how to avoid puncturing the intestines. She used a small handsaw to cut through the pelvis, then splayed the rib cage back. The hunters peered warily at the guts open to the wide sky. Like a doctor in an outdoor operating theater, Coil admired the animal's clean, shiny innards. White intestines, beet-red liver, pale-pink lungs—nature's color-coded diagram. She cut the corrugated esophagus, a windpipe like a vacuum cleaner tube, from the animal's throat. The discard pile grew as the animal was parted out. Vic took over as they emptied the viscera from the elk's cavity.

"We admire your guts," said one of the others. "So to speak."

"I don't know why they call it field dressing," said Coil. "Seems like the opposite to me. Think how much work it would take to put this elk back together, if it was possible to reassemble a dead animal. Say, for instance, if it was a kit you might buy in a hobby shop."

"An odd thought," said Vic. "But I think I know what you mean."

"A surgeon could stitch it all back together, but the pieces wouldn't bring life, wouldn't mean you could kick-start the heart or refuel the brain."

She was getting curious looks from her audience as she worked around the ribs, still cleaning.

"If you see enough of these, it's something you start to ponder," she said. But she had begun pondering it almost as soon as she had survived the crash of the jetliner. Prior to that day, death was just a word repeated endlessly on the nightly news.

Neither of the bystanders seemed as eager to help reach in and scrape, to get their hands bloody. This made Coil wonder why they could come all this way, spend all this money on a guided hunt, and not want to see the inside of an elk. But then again, it was probably just a game. Death was a talking head on CNN.

She helped them fill water jugs in the nearby creek, wash out the carcass, and cut off the legs. She showed Vic how to scalp the antlers and leave enough nub to show evidence that the kill was male, in case the boy-men were stopped on the way home by a forest ranger.

They quartered the animal, strapped the hindquarters to Bear, her Appaloosa, and walked back to camp. She and Vic hoisted the pieces up with rope, so the meat dangled from a branch well off the ground. Dangling meat attracted all kinds of wild creatures—raccoons, mountain lions, and flies. Coil peppered the meat to discourage the flies.

As they worked side by side to complete this last step, Coil decided that Vic fit all of the criteria that she looked for in a man. He stirred her up, no question about it. She wondered exactly which organ fluttered inside her chest at such moments. It was a heart-lung combination that went light and limp and left her a bit breathless.

What did the space in her chest cavity do the rest of the time? What did she look like inside? How close had an ambulance crew come to learning that after the plane wreck? There were other bodies floating in the water for them to study that day, ejected and discarded. What the medics did see was her superficial exterior. She was short and slender, a hundred and ten pounds after a big meal. She had cropped, functional, straight brown hair that was easily covered, quickly cleaned, and more manageable than it had been during her city days back East, when a stylist took care of the externals. Her face was narrow and small, with reddish-brown eyes, a solid nose, high cheekbones and bright white teeth, the product of a milk-fed youth combined with strong Midwestern genes.

As Coil cleaned her knife with a jug of water and paper towels, Vic sidled over and started asking questions, making his move. She could read him like spoor. He asked how long she had been a guide, how long she had lived in Colorado, asked if all the "guy stuff" and macho posturing bothered her. These were questions that he did not really want answered, she knew. She had heard it all before, but what woman hadn't? Anthropologists had a phrase for it: mating ritual.

Vic told her about the three of them, even though she had not asked. They were co-workers from an advertising firm. Of all things, Coil thought. Her former career when she had lived in the East, prior to the accident. Vic quizzed her about how her life was set up, how long she had been out of the city. She offered vague answers, and did not give any indication that she was nailed down to a relationship, because she wasn't. Not officially.

Bear was hitched to a nearby tree. Coil went up to him and began tightening his cinch and breast collar. The long haul back from this spot in the wilderness meant it would be difficult to reach home before nightfall. She would probably end up riding in the dark, which made her wary, because the air smelled like it was gaining weight. Snow for sure. Blizzards and horse rides in the darkness were something that never concerned her when she lived where the mountains were brick, the open plains were asphalt, and she traveled in birds made of fragile steel.

"The question is, how did a woman like you end up here?" asked Vic, as he sliced off a chunk of tenderloin.

"Why is that the question?"

"Okay, it's one question." He cut the steak free and bound the rest with twine.

Vic reminded Coil of an old college girlfriend whose blunt questions were delivered with earnest eyes that demanded sincere answers, whether the subject was the meaning of life or missing socks.

"The answer is that I needed a break from the world of big machines, big highways, big buildings, and big news."

"In other words, all the intensity," Vic stated.

"Yeah, I suppose. I used to be in your line of work, as a matter of fact."

"No kidding?"

"Griffin & Good," she said, knowing it would prompt a response.

"One of the biggest agencies there is."

"They thought I knew what made for great slogans. Toothpaste, amusement parks, grocery store chains, toilet paper. Tag lines were my thing, little words trying to mean a lot."

"You're a long way from that world. What happened? Did you run out of steam?"

He was sitting cross-legged on the ground, no longer working, just talking to her. His brown eyes bore through her, but his questions did not feel invasive.

"I needed to touch things again, real things."

No, that wasn't it. Besides, it sounded corny. Everything is real. The answer had something to do with stoplights. Or voice mail. Or email. Or $20 hotel breakfasts.

"It seemed like I was part of the clutter—TV, billboards, radio, whatever," she said, after a pause.

"Tangible, but not real?" he asked.

Somewhere amid her ramble she had stopped, and now found herself sitting next to him on the cool ground. The tenderloin rested on a piece of tin foil at her feet. It was raw, red, supple, and looked very much alive. As she gazed at the meat, Vic put an arm around her.

"Can you hang out tonight?" he asked.

"Nope, I'm due back," she said.

"Are you, may I ask, involved with someone right now?"

The thought of a quiet, groping roll in a tent, a loving siesta, a one-night stand on a mountaintop, had its appealing aspects. But Coil knew it wouldn't work.

"Yes, you can ask and the answer is sort of—well, yeah," she said. "And that goes with one of the other things I don't miss. Big confusion. Out here, it seems the only things that go haywire, get messed up, are the things you want to go wrong. The rules are your own."

"I can respect that." His hand moved gently away.

"Thanks," she said. "Not that you don't seem to be a complete sweetheart. Truly."

She thought she heard him smile.

The moment passed.

She went back to being a professional guide. She packed up Bear and her giant, black mule, Eli. Vic and his buddies started building a fire and discussed meal preparations. Coil mounted her horse and turned to survey the camp one more time before heading Bear toward home. Vic held up his hand in a way that she saw as a combination of wave and smile that might communicate "maybe another time." It was a little signal trying to mean a lot.

Coil pointed Bear straight up through the scrub oak and the main trail that would take her down to Ripplecreek.

* * * *

Dean Applegate lay prone in the snow. The distant ridge that he had been relying on for bearings had vanished in low clouds an hour ago, about the same time he had popped open a can of cold beef stew and called it breakfast. Through a pair of binoculars braced against his eyes,

Applegate panned the facing hillside as carefully as the master had taught him. The twin lenses delivered a jittery view of the landscape, a phenomenon he had never seen discussed in hunting magazines. But at least he was going through the motions, doing what he had read and what he had been shown by other sportsmen.

From down Ripplecreek Canyon, he could hear a distant clatter, the alleged cacophony orchestrated by animal rights protesters to frighten off the deer. The noise of those meddling buzzards blended in a staccato clamor, fading in and out. The clouds were sinking and the racket seemed to bounce at him from different directions.

There. Something moved.

The plodding shape was near the bottom of the slope where he was perched.

It was moving toward him.

The creature was at least a hundred yards away, so Applegate could not tell for sure whether it was elk or deer. It's moving too slowly, he thought, and it occurred to him that it might be wounded. It might be an outcast or an orphan, but that didn't matter.

I am an assassin. No pity.

He tried to remember all the things a good hunter would do at this moment, with prey in his sights. The list came slowly: check the wind, stay low, watch your step. But all of that was garbled with one notion: *Shoot.*

The animal turned to give him a good butt view, then it turned back and continued to move steadily, relentlessly, as if *it* were the one doing the stalking. But Applegate didn't think he had been spotted. Camouflage was key. Applegate felt at one with the scenery. He was dressed to kill from cap to boot. His face was caked in olive and black greasepaint. The tree-and-leaf pattern on his parka, pants, gloves, rifle, socks, backpack, binoculars and sunglasses all matched. The pattern was known as *ambush* and that was his theme: *Surprise and destroy.*

Applegate imagined how his friends' faces would look when he came back with the trophy. He knew they didn't think much of him as a hunter, but their opinion of him would be transformed on the spot. There was no doubt.

He aimed and waited. The animal poked its nose around a large tree. *Deer.*

Applegate swatted away creeping doubts. Wild animals never looked very big at a distance, but the animal in his sights was too small to be an elk.

He squeezed the trigger and the world exploded.

The brown shape dropped.

Rifle still up around his shoulder, Applegate stumbled down the slope, through the scrub and thorny bushes, ready to fire again if the animal decided to get up and limp off.

He knew his kill would be no match in size for whatever George Grumley might bring down today. A whale underwater turns into a minnow once it's in the boat, he thought. But at least this small animal was something to show for his hunt. Something, he told himself.

It was dead, a clean shot. The brown heap did not budge. From where Applegate stood, the animal appeared bisected by the thin trunk of an aspen sapling flecked in quaking gold leaves.

Applegate kept the butt of the rifle tucked into his shoulder and cocked his eye square down the barrel as he stepped to the side of the aspen, a bit hesitant, fearful even, to invade the space where an animal had just died. Alas, it was more a yearling than a prize buck. It was *something*, though. It was a kill, anyway.

He eased the rifle off his chin and studied his victim. He did not recognize it. What the hell was it? The fur was smooth, much too smooth for a wild animal. Perhaps it was a new species? This would be a second feather in his cap, something to show the men back at camp. He had not only proven his ability to kill, he just might have discovered a new form of wildlife. He couldn't see the head, though, and thought it must be tucked underneath the body. Maybe the animal had broken its neck in the fall.

He stepped around to the side of the baby aspen and squatted slowly. His knees cracked unceremoniously. He hated the way his knees cracked when he squatted near the fire back at camp, like the pop of burning sap. He could always hear the muted chuckling of the other hunters.

A hand poked out from the fur where there should have been a hoof. There were fingernails, too, clean and white. Four fingers. There was no need to look for a thumb.

It all stared up at him, human as guilt.

* * * *

Rocky Carnivitas heard a muffled *pop* off in the distance. It gave him reason to smile. Someone was taking another animal off the planet. The echo of the rifle shot was a like a satisfying growl that resonated deep in the woods. He waited for another, but it didn't come. The shot was either a one-bullet drop, with no need for a finishing shot, or a miss. From the sound, he calculated the shot was at least a mile away, down Ripplecreek. You could never be too sure, given the echoes and funny way mountains absorbed sounds, kicked them around. He hoped the bullet had found its mark, hoped a hunter would soon be dragging a carcass down to his truck so all the granola-crunching protesters would gape at the corpse, get angry, and make more of a stupid fuss than they were already generating. Maybe the evidence that their protest had not worked would make them give up, go home, and get haircuts.

Rocky crouched next to a smooth boulder high up in Ripplecreek Canyon, a few hundred yards above where the taller trees in the forest gave way to irregular clumps of scrubby bushes scattered among vast, open stretches of loose rock. At his feet, a big bull elk lay on the ground, alive but unconscious. The huge animal took furtive breaths as Rocky gingerly slipped the collar and GPS unit around its neck. He worked carefully to avoid bumping the valuable rack, trophy antlers destined to one day hang on the wall of a hunter's den. Some fat cat would pay ten Gs or more to stand in the woods and kill him later. It was odd how the elk's eyes flitted about, nervous and fearful. The animal was probably wondering if it was dying. The collar, as thin as a shoelace but made of leather, snapped together.

Rocky gave the elk a puppy-dog pat on its chest, then stood up next to him.

The air over the upper bowl of Ripplecreek tasted wet. He was lucky to be doing this work during the morning's relative calm. At least he had hiked far enough up the valley that the mayhem from the protesters had faded away. None of them would venture this high, especially with the sky turning into a snow-sopped sponge. There was a storm coming. The damned hippies had better have skis.

Rocky stepped over to his backpack, dug out a small grease-stained notebook, and jotted down the GPS unit number and a note about the location, time of day, and size of the animal.

The elk was theirs. Tagged. Marked for death some elk day down the road.

"Nice work, as always," said a voice too close. Rocky whirled around. Grumley.

Rocky's boss was dressed for a weeks' worth of icy air, goose-down pants over his legs, beaver-skin mittens dangling from his belt. He was holding a rifle casually in his right fist. A rusty Eddie Bauer watch dangled from a leather lanyard around his neck. There was a story to that watch. Grumley treasured the timepiece and insisted he would take it to the grave, would be buried with it around his neck. The watch had been taken from the stomach of a bear he'd shot. The bear had invaded a Boy Scout camp up near Meeker. None of the scouts had been hurt, but the Scoutmaster had been mauled to death. It had taken Grumley three days of tracking through rugged high-country terrain to catch up with the bruin. When he had hoisted the bear from the branch of a tree for bloodletting, the watch had fallen from a slit in its belly. Grumley tried to bring the watch back to the Scoutmaster's next of kin, but they wanted Grumley to keep it as thanks for his efforts to protect others. The watch was still ticking.

"Take you by surprise?" Grumley asked.

This was a loaded question. It was never smart to admit to being taken by surprise in the high country, but there was no advantage in lying to Grumley.

"Fuck, my heart's pounding. Jesus, don't ever do that again." The note-book quivered in Rocky's hand.

Grumley had a peculiar look on his face.

"Is that the bull we were after?"

"Has to be," said Rocky.

"Good," said Grumley. "A bonus."

Grumley wiped his beard and lips with the back of his hairy hand as if he had eaten something sticky. Grumley habitually scratched or twid-dled at the thick, three-inch tuft of gray-white beard on his chin.

Rocky didn't understand what Grumley had meant by "bonus." Maybe he was supposed to know, but he didn't ask. Grumley was not the kind of man who liked being pestered with questions.

The elk began pawing at the dirt, starting to come to.

Both men gazed at the animal as it recovered. Grumley watched it with professional interest. He owned the hunting guide operation and this elk was money in the bank to him. Rocky Carnivitas, on the other hand, watched the elk with apprehension, hoping he had done everything correctly. Rocky didn't like people looking over his shoulder. But then, who did?

"How the hell did you sneak up on me?" Rocky asked. "I thought you were with your buddies. And, say, did you hear the damn protesters?"

"I've been thinking about your . . . whaddya call it?" Grumley's hand made twirling motions as he tried to find the right word. The gun swayed in his grip.

"Proposal," said Rocky.

"Right."

Rocky felt a rolling earthquake sensation in his gut. How the hell had he missed being followed? What was his boss doing here?

"Let's review that proposal, shall we?"

The last time they talked, Rocky had been able to screw up the courage to confront Grumley by knocking back a couple of double Wild Turkeys, and then describing his proposal during the brief gap of time between being lucid and stupid. After spelling things out, Grumley had looked at him intently, thoughtfully—as if Rocky was simultaneously delivering a well designed business plan *and* relieving Grumley of a chronic tension headache. That session had taken place in the barn a week ago. Since then, Rocky had wondered when and how the subject would come up again. He had hardly suspected it would happen here and now, up in the high country, with a gun right *there*, flopping about in Grumley's hand.

"Okay, you want me to give you twenty grand," Grumley said, "or some such healthy amount like that. Right?"

"That's just a *for instance* amount," Rocky said, squatting down next to the elk to check the collar again, trying to act casual, as if this whole sordid scheme was no big deal.

"What do you mean by 'for instance?'" Grumley asked.

"The ballpark," Rocky replied. "Not necessarily the final number."

"So the amount of money might go up from there?"

"Or down. Depends on the situation."

"Okay, the ballpark," Grumley said. "The fucking ballpark. And all of it is my money. Hard earned, I might add. This buys me freedom from my wife and it buys me some sort of protection, because you are going to sit tight and not discuss my business operation with the authorities. Have I got it right? Is that the rough idea here?"

When Rocky had first conceived of the plan it had made sense, the kind of sense incubated in a bottle of Wild Turkey. But now he was not so certain of its wisdom. Rocky stood up. The clouds had thickened in the past few minutes and the air carried a fresh whiff of pine. He tried to ignore the erratic twitching of the elk's hind legs. It made a scrabbling sound on the rocks.

"That's more or less the idea," Rocky said. "But if you want to talk—"

"Good. Because I have a question, Rocky. Have you been fucking my wife?"

Rocky froze. "What the hell do you mean?" he asked, but the pause had given him away.

"You little fuck," growled Grumley.

"She . . ."

"She what?"

"She wants—"

"Oh, so you know what Trudy wants too, huh?" Grumley scoffed. "Fuckin' beautiful." He held both arms out as if he could hug the hillside. The rifle dangled loosely in his hand.

Rocky spoke quickly. "Trudy just wants enough money to make another start."

"I can't believe I'm talking to a guy who's fucking my wife."

Rocky swallowed hard. He kept an eye on the gun. "It's just seed money to get her going," he said.

"Seed for two fuckin' birds?"

"It would only put a dent in your stash," Rocky said. He knew this with certainty.

"Who put you in charge of my books?" Grumley grunted. "You screw my wife and you fuck with my business too, is that it? Did you hear what I said? My business. Think about it."

"It's just a drop in the—"

"Says who? Fuck you and your miserable little plan." Grumley pointed the barrel of the gun at Rocky's face, then let it drift away. "How does a nobody like you figure he's gonna snap his fingers and make himself a somebody?"

Snow began falling. It was sudden. No advance troops. The storm started in full battle mode.

"Well—"

Grumley took a step forward. Rocky backed up to where the elk lay scraping rocks with its hooves. Grumley's fist came up gripping the gunstock like a brick, and Rocky felt his cheek burst in pain. He lurched backwards and reached out to clutch at a rock, any rock, to brace his fall.

"You fucker," Grumley said. "You goddamn fucker."

Rocky crawled toward his backpack, coughing, spitting blood, disoriented. He shook his head and struggled to his knees, knelt over his pack, and dug quickly into it. There was one shot of xylazine left. He swung around and pressed the barrel of a dart gun against the elk's still-quivering neck, a nice soft spot. The overdose would be as effective as a bullet behind the ear. The elk would die fast.

"What the hell are you doing?" Grumley asked.

"Trying to get your fuckin' attention."

Rocky cocked the dart gun.

"Okay, okay," said Grumley. "You're a miserable fuck."

Rocky felt a surge of relief. The situation was coming under his control. He still felt woozy from the sucker punch, and the wound on his scalp was going to be a humdinger, but that was a minor problem.

Grumley walked away. He made fifteen feet, then turned around.

"Goddamn," he said. He raised the rifle and pointed the muzzle at Rocky. "My business is my fucking business!"

But Rocky fired first. He pulled the trigger, sending the dart into the soft flesh of the elk's neck. There was nothing Grumley could do now to stop the elk from dying. Rocky looked up at the muzzle of the rifle pointed at his face and realized too late he had used the weapon on the wrong beast.

* * * *

The hour it took to get to the top of the mountain was given over to a thousand "what ifs" as Allison Coil contemplated the constant flurry of choices the world offered. The elk's choices had led him to a bullet. Her choice had left Vic's tent less crowded. With the sky dropping, her decisions now might turn out to be critical to surviving the remainder of the day and night on the long journey down to the canyon. The gathering storm would no doubt quickly curb the zeal of the protesters.

A group of animal rights protesters had set up tents at the base of the mountain that morning. She had not given much thought to them until now. She imagined that most of them were like the men she had left back at the hunter's camp, city dwellers out on a lark. But with the coming snowstorm, they just might learn the hard way that Mother Nature was indifferent to the rights of everyone and everything on this planet. You might as well protest earthquakes, fires, floods, and falling airplanes.

A rifle shot interrupted her thoughts.

She yanked the reins, halted the horse, and instinctively rose in the stirrups to get a fix on the sound. She was at the top of Black Squirrel Pass, the summit of the ridge that formed the west wall of Ripplecreek. Sounds traveled strangely in the mountains. It was hard to get a fix.

She waited and listened. She reached for her binoculars, tucked in a front saddlebag. Bear peered around inquisitively, then lowered his neck and chomped on a stray tuft of meadow rue. The pack mule, Eli, seemed to be asleep.

The scrub ahead was vacant, but the chest-high brush farther on could hide a large herd of deer or an army of hunters.

The upper bowl of Ripplecreek was nearly a mile across. Through her binoculars, the falling snow at the top of the pass was compressed into a porous white whirl that turned distant clumps of trees into little more than dark blotches with undefined edges, vague shadows.

She saw something move. It was so small in her field of vision that it did not register at first. A tiny shape was moving near a cluster of rocks, off the trail, near Lizard's Tongue. Somebody was struggling with something.

The shape disappeared, down behind some trees, and was gone from sight.

Coil lowered the binoculars and squinted, saw nothing but swirling snowflakes, and raised the lenses again.

She could see nothing but fuzzy whiteness now. Nothing on the ground moved. She replayed the mental movie: four or five seconds' worth of film, a man pulling something through the snow. Dragging a deer? A lone do-it-yourselfer using a sled to haul a carcass? Perhaps.

She put the binoculars back, cinched her hat down against the chilly wind, gave Bear a cluck, and dug into her jacket pocket for a Fig Newton. The trail would take her past Lizard's Tongue, where she could get a closer look at what she had seen through the binoculars. There had been something about the man's body language that did told her one thing; he was in a bit of a scramble, hurrying as if the clock was ticking. She looked up at the oncoming storm. Perhaps it was.

2

At the mouth of the canyon, Dawn Ellenberg sat in base camp with a walkie-talkie while two reporters with notepads stood nearby, chatting with each other. Maria Nash was the poorly dressed, slightly nervous cub scribe from Glenwood Springs. Robert P. Calkins III was a more seasoned reporter, a brash young man from the *Vail Trail*. Neither had taken a note in over an hour.

Ellenberg had poured countless hours into her PR campaign, pumping the event as having Woodstockian dimensions, but Maria Nash and Robert P. Calkins III were the only two "journalists" she had managed to muster at the scene of the protest. Not one television crew. No Denver newspaper reporters. No *USA Today*. No *People* magazine either, even though she had bought lunch for the Denver-based correspondent and had extracted a "we'll see, maybe" over curried chickpea tofu. No one had even bothered to drive over from Aspen.

Maria Nash and Robert P. Calkins III. There she was; there they were. That was all. The word would go out from her mouth to their pencil tips and through their meek little computers to their editors. Ultimately, it would just be another little after-thought in the big, flying sweep of worldwide news. Maria Nash had asked her fair share of questions, but nothing out of the ordinary.

"What is the size of the army of protestors?" she'd asked.

"About 500," said Ellenberg.

"How many did you anticipate?"

"There was really no way to know, but we're thrilled with the turnout."

"Is it enough to get the job done?"

"You bet."

Robert P. Calkins III had laid back, letting Maria do the nuts-and-bolts dirty work, then weighed in with, "Is the big meat-eating public out there really with you? Have you studied the meat-eating statistics lately? The numbers are up, I've gotta tell you."

Ellenberg responded with a long pause, then offered this reply: "Every great cause starts with somebody somewhere saying 'enough, enough.' We need to educate the public, we need to enlighten the public, and that's why we are here today."

Dawn Ellenberg was the founder and lead piper of FATE, which stood for Fighting Animal Torture Everywhere. She was the star of the show—well, actually, mini-show at this point. A strong wood fire burning a few feet away helped beat back the growing grayness and the cold. She hoped the glow of firelight cast her apple cheeks and long, full hair in an earnest light. Even if there weren't photographers, as she had fully expected, she still wanted to look the part. She scrunched up her knees, planted her boots flat on the ground, and rubbed the heat from the fire into her legs.

Whenever team leaders radioed in to her by walkie-talkie, Ellenberg could hear the bizarre bits of drone in the background. The faithful had brought drums, snares and bongos. They had dragged up cymbals, whistles, wood blocks, bells, horns, and boom boxes that played everything from rap to Beethoven. There were yellers, barkers and howlers. They were scattered throughout the canyon, making their presence known. But when her radio was silent, the effect was not as impressive. She wanted a pervasive sense of bedlam that would send every mammal scurrying out of harm's way.

Next year, she would recruit from the entire country, draw them all in for a seminal bash that would define the word "protest" for decades to come. It would be like Burning Man, only with purpose and results. The 1968 Democratic Convention, G8-Summit, and European Anti-Nuclear Marches were all known for their massive protests.

She would put this canyon—and FATE—on the map.

The storm was unwelcome. Had the TV cameras been there, it might have appeared to the viewing audience that the protesters were committed troopers—real warriors, not city wimps—willing to take on the hunters in even the toughest elements. But there were no cameras, and if it wasn't on TV, as she knew all too well, it was no revolution.

"Give me your wrap-up thoughts," said Nash, coming alive. "I've probably gotta get out of here. Success or not?"

Nash had a slightly husky voice, something of a rushed look about her jumpy eyes, and absolutely no style to her stringy black hair.

"This is a miserable day for Colorado hunters," said Ellenberg, with all the gravity she could muster. Nobody respected whiners. "Anyone who has ever loaded a rifle in the name of wholesale slaughter has to be nervous. They're on the run now. They're scared. The wholesale slaughter has *got* to stop, *will* stop, *can* be stopped."

It was the speech she had rehearsed for this moment, for a gaggle of reporters and cameras. But by the time she looked up, Maria Nash had already stopped writing. Robert P. Calkins III hadn't budged, or so it seemed. Maybe he had a secret digital recorder and was getting it all.

"This is hell day for hunters," she said straight to Calkins. "Things do change. Americans used to smoke at work. Americans used to drink and drive, or at least not care when we did. But society made changes and it will soon make another. This is hell day, the beginning of the end, for hunters. Not only in this pristine Colorado canyon, but in every hollow, in every field, and along every stream where the hunters' holocaust takes place. They have heard the noise today. Believe me, they have heard. From now on, it's *their* days that are numbered."

She gazed solemnly into the fire as she spoke. Maybe one of them could describe the scene with flowery prose.

"How will you know for sure this worked?" asked Maria Nash.

"If I know in my heart that one animal has been spared from the wholesale slaughter." She paused for effect. "One. That would do."

Maria Nash clicked her pen.

"Praise the animals," said Ellenberg, her cheeks baked in the fire's heat. "We are at one with them today."

* * * *

Coil slowed Bear at the base of Lizard's Tongue, a distinctive spire of rock like a castle turret with an open gap. The snow fell with intensity. Down to the right, where the slope dropped quickly, was the rocky scree where the man had disappeared.

If the deer was already dead, no hunter in his right mind would have contemplated negotiating such a steep pitch. On top of that, a deer would not drag well in one piece, unless it was a fawn, and no one could have cut it into pieces so soon after the shot. For whatever reason, the man might need help. She could not glide on past the scene without seeing if he would resurface.

She turned around in her saddle, trying to spot Black Squirrel Pass and reverse the line of sight in her mind. She could barely see three hundred yards. Whatever she had seen through the binoculars, it had happened between Lizard's Tongue and a distinct stand of trees. The man had moved, however briefly, right here, in the open.

She gave Bear a pat on the neck and climbed down. She squatted at the trail's edge and peered down across the tops of the rocks. Each rock seemed equally coated with a fresh, white stocking cap on its featureless face. She wrapped Bear's rein around a rock and headed up to Lizard's Tongue.

From the rock bunker at the top, Coil could see further down the slope. There were more rocks and snow. There was also a broader view of an empty landscape, which she scoured with a thorough look-around through the binoculars, her elbows securely propped. But the man or men had vanished.

She brushed off the inch or so that had accumulated on Bear's saddle and climbed on. The entire world was turning white, except . . . an elk. It was lying there, not quite all white, a couple of dozen yards off the trail.

It was a beauty, too, judging by the sizable rack.

Out of instinct, she looked around for the hunter who had shot it. Prime elk did not just lie down and die in the open.

"Stay here, Bear," she said.

Down the slope a bit, she eased up beside the animal. There was no need to check for signs of life. The antlers, about as large as she had ever seen up close, were like a miniature, smooth-boned forest. The fifth point was snapped, but the main beams were intact. The wound that brought him down could be on the opposite side, underneath, but there was no trace of blood.

She brushed some snow off his hide, checking him, and cleaned his face. His eyes were open, mouth slightly ajar. This animal had not been dead for long.

"Where the hell are your elk buddies?" she asked him. "Or your hunter?"

He was much too big to have been dragged by any one man, *couldn't* have been dragged by any one man. But this was in the vicinity of what she had seen. The guy in her binoculars would know; there had to be a connection.

She sat back from the elk's head, looked off at snow-coated Bear, and patted the elk's haunch. It was remotely possible the elk's killer would return with a team of helpers to quarter the animal. But it did not seem likely that anyone would be venturing back into the teeth and jaw of this storm. *Here* was something for the protesters to get sick over—the sheer destruction of an animal for no apparent purpose. The elk had not been tagged. He had been treated like garbage and he would rot. It was an utter waste and against all the civilized rules, what few existed, that defined the line between hunt and slaughter.

Coil stood up and pondered the scene one more time, estimated her distance and bearings from Lizard's Tongue, and climbed back on Bear. The wind howled, as if to warn her she was running late. She tucked her kerchief tightly up over her face and pulled down her hat.

Her bones ached, but so did her head, as she tried to put it all together in a way that made sense. Right now, nothing did.

* * * *

Two miles back down Ripplecreek, Grumley forced his mind to cover the issues and think. He had stepped out of routine, but a return to routine would be so much better without that little fuck. It felt like it would snow for a week. Mother Nature was taking care of business.

Carrying two rifles had been distracting. His own rifle was in his sling, and Rocky's dart gun was in his hands.

After dumping Rocky's body, he had covered a hundred yards before realizing he should go back and retrieve the GPS collar. The dead elk, not far from the main trail, was a problem. Maybe he should have stayed to quarter the damn thing, but he didn't have the tools. Hauling Rocky off and away had been exhausting enough. Rocky's last act, as a dead weight, was one of his most cruel. Dead bodies handle about as well as a bag of wet sand.

Grumley kept moving. His burly and muscled body was fashioned by years of rigorous hiking. He moved like a fullback, always ready to head-butt a moving truck. He wore the outdoors—nicks, scars, and dings—on every scrap of his face. He would have to work on a story to tell the other three. He already needed to come up with something to tell Applegate: why he had skipped off without joining him on his hunt. Or crusade. For Dean Applegate, probably the most unlucky and least talented hunter George Grumley had ever known, every trip out of the tent was a frightening cocktail of raw emotion mixed with zero stalking skill.

Trudy kept flashing through his mind. He wondered what she knew about Rocky's attempted extortion. In reality, Grumley figured, the whole thing was self-defense. More than likely, Trudy had no idea Rocky would make the threats. There wasn't a challenging bone in her body.

A slight pounding in his temples told him it was time for a drink. Water searches would be impossible after dark; staying on the trail would be challenge enough after dark in this storm.

Grumley veered off the trail and picked his way through a tight stand of aspens to the streambed, which was relatively flat through this stretch. He put his boot down through a few inches of fresh powder and pressed with all his weight on an older, crusty layer beneath the fluffy stuff. The amalgam of snow and ice creaked for a few seconds and then gave way. His boot landed in six inches of cold creek. Lying prone, Grumley dipped his lips in the water. He sucked slowly, steadily. It would be impossible to drink too much.

"George?"

Grumley flipped over like a cat on fire.

It was Applegate, ten paces away, already waving both his hands to show him they were empty.

"What the fuck?"

"It's me."

"You little—"

"I spotted you back in here."

"Jesus H."

Grumley stood up. Applegate stepped closer, a fucking Gomer Crockett in head-to-toe catalog camouflage. While Applegate had never been the human equivalent of a rabbit's foot, his tentative posture and bug eyes suggested things were worse than ever.

"You been following me?" asked Grumley.

Applegate shivered badly. His jaw was not solidly connected to his head. The cotton parka would be okay for the mountains in July, not October.

"I think I killed a guy."

"*Think?*"

"A guy, one of the protesters. I think it's one of them. It wasn't another hunter, anyway, because he wasn't carrying a gun. Unless he fell on it. You gotta come help. We gotta tell somebody."

"Where?"

"Where what?"

"Where did this happen?"

"Back up the valley, straight up the spine here. Not far."

"When?'

Applegate looked around to the right and then to the left as if study-ing the aspen would help him remember. His face was a picture of fear. He was not thinking.

"I don't know. Twenty minutes, maybe thirty. I've been sitting, think-ing, wandering around. I made it halfway back to camp, then wasn't sure which way to go. I found the main trail here, sat awhile, then, you know, thought I'd try to find him again, the protester. I've been thinking . . . he might not be dead."

"You said you killed him."

"I know, I know. But he might be in shock. I didn't really, you know, check. I didn't feel for a pulse or anything. But he's probably dead. He was there, draped in this brown thing. Like a cape, only bigger."

"Cape?"

"Like a big piece of drape or something."

"You can find the way back to this guy. There's no question? Sometimes it's not so easy. Everything all starts to look the same," said Grumley.

"I think so." Applegate stood up.

"Be sure so."

"I am."

Grumley stepped over to his rifle and the dart gun, both propped against a tree, ten yards from the creek. Grumley stood between them and Applegate, who surely had been too confused to notice, and tapped Rocky's dart gun off its prop on the tree. The rifle cut its own grave on its way down slope through the fluffy powder.

* * * *

Applegate hunkered down for a second as they came down the slope and held his palm above his eyes like a golfer shielding the sun to read the grain on a putt. But there was no sun, only steadily falling snow.

"There," he said, pointing to a clump of buckthorn, not too far from where Grumley guessed the creek bed was located.

The body was wrapped around the base of the bush, in the windbreak, spared from being buried too much.

"Aw, Christ," said Applegate, keeping his distance and starting to sob.

Grumley started brushing away snow, trying not to disturb the body.

"If I was the coroner, which I'm not, I'd say he's dead. What is this brown thing?"

"It's like a big curtain."

The brown thing was large and neither shaped nor stitched like regular clothing.

"You shot him where?"

"From up the slope," said Applegate. "Hundred yards or so."

"No, where in the body?"

"Christ, I don't know. I thought it was a deer."

"I believe that's what you were supposed to think."

The cape, or whatever is was, completely surrounded the body. Grumley had found an arm and could feel the legs, but he wasn't particularly keen on rolling the guy completely over to see much more.

"We've gotta carry him out," said Applegate, "tell the authorities, you know, whoever. Somebody."

"You want the hassle? Cops?"

Applegate did not answer.

"Of course not," said Grumley. "You'd be a fool. You're the guy they want."

"They?"

"The animal nuts. This dude was trying to get shot. Well, maybe shot, but not killed, exactly. But you did the trick. You're looking at time, buddy. Negligent homicide or something. It wouldn't matter how much remorse you'd spew out."

Applegate swallowed a mouthful of fear.

"Is that the rifle?" Grumley asked, studying Applegate's Sako, with its beautiful wood-grained craftsmanship.

"Yeah."

"You gotta lose it."

"Lose?"

"Give it to me," said Grumley. "I'll take care of it. Anybody asks, you put it down somewhere and forgot it. Lost it."

"Okay," said Applegate.

"If you walk out carrying this guy on your shoulders like a sack of potatoes, especially the way you're dressed, what you're looking at is media frenzy and your butt on the barbecue."

Grumley could not believe Applegate hadn't disappeared on his own, pretending that nothing had ever happened.

"You ever build a snow cave?"

"No."

"You don't want to. Tonight would not be a good night for you to try your first."

"Right," said Applegate, starting to focus.

"If you admit to anything here, you're going to drag yourself down and they'll probably get me, too. We do not want that. You with me?"

"Yeah."

Grumley took a step closer to Applegate.

"I got fucking too much to lose if my name is so much as whispered in connection with any of this. You'd be the dumb out-of-towner with the inability to distinguish a deer from a human. Since you were part of my hunting party, I'd be fodder for the local mincemeat factory. This guy's dead, he's not going to get any better, and judging by the looks of things it's a condition he was after, for whatever crazy reason. You fucked up once. You don't fuck up twice. You gotta pretend it was a *real* bad dream."

It was not far from Lizard's Tongue to Rocky's frozen body. If Applegate got stupid on him, trouble could be piled on misery.

"Now," said Grumley, taking two steps closer so he was smack in Applegate's face. "We're going to walk back to the main trail. We're going to hope the snow falls until Groundhog Day and covers every one of our goddamn tracks. We split. You head down to safety. I'll go back to camp. You don't have too far to go, maybe an hour or two at the most, depending on your pace. You never fuckin' saw me."

"Okay," said Applegate, appearing more like the meek farm-boy-gone-to-college than he had looked for years.

"You can make it okay? You're gonna have to use your wits a bit, to stick to the main trail. At least it's not snowing as hard down here as it is up on top."

"Agreed."

"You'll get cleaned up and wait at the barn, right?"

"Whatever."

"What happened to your rifle?" he asked.

"Lost and forgot," said Applegate. "Right?"

"Right."

Sending Applegate down alone carried huge risks. At the very least, he could have a tough time staying on the trail, given all the snow and the night. He could have a change of heart and blubber it all out to the first person he saw. But it would spare the obviously weary guy a steep hike back up to camp.

"Can you start a fire in the snow if you get lost?"

"You showed me once."

"Can you do it now?"

"Think so," said Applegate.

Grumley dug in an inside pocket for two packs of fire starter gel. "One should do it, but you've got a spare in case you screw up."

"Matches?"

"Got those," said Applegate.

"You got any food?" asked Grumley.

"All gone."

Grumley eyed the body.

"Aw, don't," said Applegate.

"Why not?"

"Leave him. I'll make it."

A canteen and a quart of water or some food were worth the risk. They could both use something. He had seen how thirsty Applegate was, too. Grumley dropped to his knees, next to the body. The brown cape was a pain. It seemed wrapped every which way and around, all tangled up.

"Jesus," said Applegate.

"Got it," said Grumley, wrapping his fingers around a bottle of some sort that sat in an inside pocket. It was one of those squeezable plastic bottles used by bicycle riders. He probed around some more and found a rectangular, sandwich-sized Tupperware container.

"Bingo," said Grumley.

The water was cold but the dissipating heat from the body had kept it from icing up. Grumley figured there was a pint or so inside and passed it to Applegate.

"Don't get your lips on it," he said.

The Tupperware held chunks of cheese and crackers. Everything was gone in a minute. Grumley jammed the Tupperware back in with the body and handed Applegate the jug with instructions to toss it somewhere when he was done.

Dead guy, Grumley thought. This was the day for dead guys. It was a total coincidence. Two fucked-up deals, no question, but more than anything it was important not to let one get tangled up with the other. And it was really fucking important to get out of this valley, with all the damn protesters and everybody crawling around, before anybody else spotted him.

* * * *

Coil kept seeing the hunched form, struggling desperately with the load. The vision was shadow-like, but clear enough.

An hour to go. Bear seemed eager and anxious; Eli toiled along like a weary, worn-down soldier. Coil's eyes widened and she took a bit of relief from the decreasing intensity of the snowfall.

Jet noise always seemed particularly distinct in a snowstorm, as if the roar was passed from one flake to the next. The blunt bawl from this jet had a deep, droning wah-wah quality to it. At first it seemed like a distant reminder that jet traffic even existed, a subliminal message from the world of technology. Then it was as if the jet was swooping along the treetops of Ripplecreek. The sound bounced down and around her and she glanced up, half expecting to catch a glimpse of a silver belly.

She caught herself wondering if the jet was bound east or west—New York or L.A., Denver or Salt Lake. Perhaps it was a short-hopper on the way into Grand Junction, the passengers lined up in neat rows, elbow to elbow, heads bouncing in unison like puppets all controlled by the same puppeteer, all rocketing along through the skies. Alcohol for the travelers, jet fuel for the engines, and tons of good faith to keep the whole thing aloft.

At cruising speed, of course, the jet engines did not have the same straining quality they did at takeoff. Coil wondered if anybody realized how fast a plane was traveling on a runway before liftoff, or whatever they called it. Liftoff was for space shuttles and things like that. Planes *took* off. Whatever one called the means of getting airborne, it did not make a lick of difference when it came to human beings surrounded by hunks of metal rocketing through the thin air. Not all things that were supposed to go up managed to make it. Some flopped. Some nose-dived. Some came to a terrifying juncture—halfway earth-bound, gravity-happy, man-made structures that weighed thousands of tons, fancy-free mechanical things that used air, of all things, for power and opportunity. Coil had been on a jet that arrived at that juncture and couldn't make the transition. Gravity won, or flight lost: one of the two.

Coil pictured a businessman sleeping in first class, an empty glass of Sauvignon Blanc on his dinner tray, a paperback thriller propped open on the synthetic blanket draped over his swallowed-a-basketball gut. His mouth drooping, slightly ajar, making the snoring even more irritating for his seatmate. She had been there, oblivious to the dangers.

Two years now in the mountains, and she was beginning—barely beginning—to consider the notion that she had, in fact, been lucky. Another few seconds further *down* that runway and the drop would have been an exponentially greater slam to reality. A few seconds more and 31 dead could have been 119 dead. Not just would the bordering-on-boorish computer parts salesman next to her be dead. Not just would the family of three across the aisle, who had barely made their connecting flight, be dead. She, too, would have been gone, and the millions of moments she had experienced would have been dead, too. At least, the moments wouldn't have existed, which was as good as being dead.

Death, she had learned, is simply a corpse you carry around underneath your skin. Until one day it pops free.

* * * *

The snow caught the FATE followers off guard but not off their game. A few came back early to warm their hands by the bonfire at base camp, but most trickled back in small, elated bunches and the spirits of the camp began to soar.

The ones returning were greeted with a wave of applause, some of it generated by bare palms, freshly warmed, and some of it generated by the soft, puffy, repetitive *whomp* of two mittens coming together. There were smiles all around. The two lame reporters were long gone, off to meet their deadlines and their bar appointments.

"People!" Ellenberg shouted over the general din. Everyone stopped immediately. "We've got a pot of vegetarian chili and corn muffins almost ready. If anyone thinks they don't have enough warm blankets or clothes for the night, please let us know."

There was silence all around.

"Good. Again, congratulations. Let's sound off, to make sure."

"One," said Ellenberg.

"Two," came a male voice across the fire. The count climbed quickly to fourteen, and then stopped.

"Fifteen?" asked Ellenberg. "Fifteen? Who is fifteen?"

"He was behind me in line yesterday," said a husky woman whose head poked out from a turquoise blanket. "Little guy, struggling with the hike. Had trouble breathing or something."

Ellenberg remembered him, all too well. He was kid-like, hadn't said much, and stared at her from a seat near the front of the bus during the entire bus ride. He was the frail looking one with the Red Sox cap. He could have been twenty-five; he could have been twelve. What showed of his scalp was hairless. His nose was a button and his cheeks puffed hard, pink and frail. On the hike in, he had sputtered and coughed much more than the others, and she had asked him, directly, if he was going to be able to make it. The answer was "yes" and the smile that went with it said *don't worry*.

"Does anyone know where he pitched his tent?"

"There was a tent forty or fifty yards off a ways, down in a small aspen grove. That way." The man pointed off. "I was talking with kind of a small guy who was putting it up yesterday."

"Anybody claim that tent?" she asked.

Nobody.

"Could you show me?" asked Ellenberg. The chatter had come to a distinct halt as Ellenberg passed the man a flashlight, and the two headed off.

They bumped around for three or four minutes, in the dark, plunging through snow-soaked bushes, until they found themselves standing next to a tent that sagged in on the sides from a build-up of snow.

"Hello," said Ellenberg. Please be there, she thought. "Anyone home?"

No answer. The man was searching for the zipper to the front flap.

"We can't barge in," said Ellenberg. "That's private. We don't have his permission."

"You're right," he said, a touch chagrined.

"Did you see him?"

"I saw him putting the tent together and asked him why he put it here. He shrugged and said something about being a light sleeper. Nice enough guy."

The group headed back to the warmth of the bonfire, where the concern and fear draped over them like a bad cloud. Maybe he had headed down on his own. It was only an hour or less back out to the road. Maybe he would turn up at any minute with a good story to tell and none the worse for wear. Ellenberg said a quick prayer to the public relations gods.

3

I t was fatigue all bound up with worry and weird thoughts. Coil had a
hard time connecting the images from the day in her mind. She had
put Bear away in the barn with a small sack of his own oats and had
unloaded Eli, then sent him out to the corral. They both needed a good
scrub and once-over for nicks or other damage, but that would wait. It was
almost midnight.

There was no one around to help or even talk to. Somebody sleeping in the barn would have at least demonstrated some concern for her
whereabouts or well-being, but Coil had to remind herself not to look
for such civilized touches. She was either safe, dead, or struggling.
Three choices. Take your pick. Had someone been sleeping in the
barn, Coil would have at least felt like she belonged to a family. Loose-
knit, for sure, but still a family. But the barn was empty. So much for
sentiment.

Coil walked the last stretch home, carrying the backpack from Lizard's
Tongue. David would already be there, or would be soon. Sometimes he
took some time to unwind from his shifts, and then there was the drive
up from Glenwood Springs. She wanted to curl up and wrap an arm over
his broad back, have him not say a peep, and conk out. But now she was
torn between wanting to avoid the long talk in order to maximize sleep
time and wanting to discuss the day with somebody who might be able
to drape the scene in logic.

Coil followed the road until the fence ended at the edge of Pete

Weaver's Ripplecreek Ranch and she cut diagonally through an open field that was the marshy edge of Owl Creek in spring and summer, but just another snow-covered field in winter. Within ten yards of the creek bed, she snapped on a flashlight and found the footbridge, slightly off to the left. It had snow up to its underbelly, snow nearly up to its rails. She couldn't quite get her legs out of first gear, but that was a common sensation after a day on a horse. The strides felt minuscule; the earth slowed.

She crossed Owl Creek, followed the creek bed down along the opposite bank, trudged through the unblemished snow to the top of a small ridge and spotted the dim shape of her cabin. A weak porch light cast enough watts to offer a bearing, but it looked as if David Slater had not yet arrived. Otherwise, the whole place would be ablaze.

She stopped on her porch, kicked the snow off her boots with a gentle tap against the threshold, and opened the door to her small A-Frame. The kitchen corner faced south, so sun poured through two tall, wide windows. The bedroom, though there was no *room*, was on the opposite side, tucked back in the corner. A heavy, wood-frame couch and a couple of old sitting chairs framed a living area around a wood stove at the front, and a too-long table made for an eating space next to the kitchen. The only closed space was a closet-sized bathroom stuck off the back. A spiral staircase led up to a set of twin beds in a loft area where Coil liked to sleep because she could wake to a view of the peaks of the Holy Cross Wilderness, off to the east.

Coil lit a candle on the dining table, grabbed a beer from the refrigerator, and headed straight to the bathroom to start the shower steaming. Continuing to stand up would at least delay sleep, and it might keep her perked up enough to wait for Slater. She was sure sleep wouldn't have its way with her until she told somebody what she'd experienced, and surely it was worth telling to Slater. He would have some ideas, anyway, and telling somebody, anybody, would make it seem more real. She lit newspaper and kindling in the wood stove, took a long draw of Coors, and undressed. The can of beer served as friend in the now-steaming stall, and she let the water blast her from behind. The fizzy drink reached beyond her mouth as the liquid replenished a thousand drought-ridden streams and rapids in her chest. She expected Slater to call out any second, to let her know he had arrived.

There was no Slater as she dried off, stuck a few large pieces of wood in the stove, and stretched out on the couch. She finished the beer and thought about making some tea, something that would keep her moving and doing until Slater came. She watched the flicker of light from the vent in the stove and realized that making tea might be a bit much, a touch too complicated, for this particular moment.

* * * *

She felt a kiss on her forehead, light enough for a baby.

"It's six," he said. "Try not to cry."

"I'm late."

The schedule had her heading back up. She couldn't remember where or what for.

"I've got breakfast ready," said Slater. Coil recalled the gentle clinking sounds from the kitchen during the last half-hour, as she wormed her way to the surface of reality. And then, from even deeper down, she remembered the sensation of him dropping the quilt over her as she slept on the couch, sometime in the wee hours.

"What time did you make it in?"

"One-ish. You could use an answering machine."

"Yuck," said Coil.

"You were down for the count. Hard. Not that I even tried to wake you. Something about the look on your face said *done*."

"You're working too?"

Coil crawled off the couch and tried to convince herself that the getting moving part would not cause any physical pain. At least she wasn't hungover. That was one small blessing to count.

"Wasn't supposed to be," he said. "But we've got a problem."

"Problem?"

He was all duded-up in his green, slightly rumpled uniform. She liked him best in blue jeans and old sweatshirts, sitting in an aspen grove in a high meadow, splitting a six-pack and slicing summer sausage to go with crackers, mustard, and cheese. This wasn't bad, the official dress of a National Forest Service resource conservation officer—once known as forest ranger. But Slater looked uncomfortable in the uniform.

"Missing people type problems. One of the protesters," he said. "Probably dead type problems, given the storm. It's one of them all-hands-on-deck things. The sheriff has already called his troops together and made it clear he doesn't want anything that would keep the publicity rolling."

"Missing where?"

Coil had pulled on a fresh set of Wranglers, an undershirt, and a green and black checked flannel shirt that deserved to be washed, but would have to do.

"Somewhere up the canyon."

"Do they know who?"

"Don't think so."

The storm would have been rough enough if you were prepared: brutal or fatal if you weren't. She had not heard the protesters, but by the time she'd come over the top of Black Squirrel Pass, the storm had probably chased them lower.

"You must have had a rough one," said Slater. "Snow pretty hard?"

"Like the end of time."

"You get hung up?"

"Not by the storm."

"Huh?" he asked, stopping as he put butter and orange marmalade on two pieces of black toast.

"I was late as it was, dawdling a bit, as always," said Coil. "Then I heard a gun shot. A minute later, I saw somebody dragging something, *big* something. From a fair distance, but I saw it," she added, more to reassure herself than anything. "Then I went to the spot where I'd seen him, or them, and I found nothing but a dead elk. Only the elk hadn't been shot. There were no wounds."

Slater stared back, mouth full of toast, concerned. "Holy *guwbuh*," he said.

Coil tried to compose herself and discovered her stomach was uneasy.

"He was an angry man, the way he was dragging that thing."

"How long between the shot and when you found the elk?"

Coil took a breath, eyed the toast, and tried to stick to exactly what she'd seen. Her grandfather had claimed to have seen a UFO set down in a lake outside of Longmont, but he had refused to embellish it with made-up details. He had once told her that anybody who wanted to know what he reported could find the original police report and read it.

"An hour plus. You know the descent from Black Squirrel Pass."

"And you really couldn't say what the man was dragging?"

"No."

Slater pondered things for a second, his mustache-covered lip buried in the coffee, his deep brown eyes penetrating down through the tabletop to somewhere.

Coil with a cop-*like* guy? The idea was a constant source of amusement. It wasn't necessarily forever, but nothing yet made her think that would be unbearable. He didn't seem to have the typical government mentality. Also, he was strong and straightforward. Coil had never before been with a man who could be classified in the "straightforward" category. Slater was a trim six-footer with an engaging face, dark eyes over a slender nose. His jaw was strong and his teeth, neat rows arranged by a perfectionist, sparkled on cue when needed. Coil liked the way he moved and talked, all careful and in control, but he could flip over to relaxation mode without much effort.

"You're going to report this?" asked Slater.

"Report what?" inquired Coil. "Dead elk in the woods? I can see the headlines."

"You got a point there," said Slater. "The dragging part, maybe it fits in with our MIA. Maybe not."

"I'll report it. Got to. Who the hell knows? I've gotta go," said Coil. "They'll kill me. We've got two big crews heading out today too. It's practically every horse in the outfit."

She had to interrupt Slater's thoughts in order to kiss him.

"Me too. Hell," he said, looking at his watch. He leaned up for the kiss at first, then stood all the way up and gave her a long, powerful hug. Slater was a long-term possibility.

Slater grabbed his coffee cup and headed out. She stood in the doorway as he climbed in behind the wheel of his government-green pick-up, started it up, and grabbed the radio, trying to raise somebody.

* * * *

"Hear someone's missing?"

It was Popeye Boyles, retired Navy cook turned guide.

"No," Grumley replied. It couldn't be Rocky, Grumley thought. There's no way somebody thinks a hunting guide is already missing. It could take a week before somebody even asks the first question.

"Heard something on the radio this morning." Boyles' hobby was playing amateur cop. He was wedded to a scanning gizmo that picked up every police frequency, or at least the signals that bounced around in the narrow canyons and hollows of Ripplecreek.

"What did you hear?" asked Grumley. Boyles teased. He always had to be asked.

"One of them eco freaks."

"Them?"

"Protesters. Kids. I first heard that Dawn chick all concerned, talking with a sheriff's deputy last night, getting ready to contact Search and Rescue."

Boyles talked like he was explaining a batch of overdone scrambled eggs to the commander of an aircraft carrier.

"The guy's tent was empty last night and when they went to check it, they didn't even open the thing."

"How do you know?" asked Grumley.

"Because one of the deputies asked them on the radio."

"Did the eco protesters locate the lost guy's gear or tent?"

"That's what the cops asked," said Boyles. "And Ellenberg—that's her name, I think—says yes, but they were sure he wasn't in there. There's this long pause. Then the cop—I didn't recognize the voice and I usually do—figures it out and asks straight out did they actually look inside the tent? Now there's another pause and this time she says he couldn't have slept through so much noise—I suppose of them talking outside the tent—but they didn't want to invade his privacy."

"His privacy?" asked Grumley

"Yeah. They're looking for a missing person in a blizzard and they won't even crash his tent to make sure the guy hasn't passed out or conked out or died of fuckin' embarrassment for being part of that stupid protest."

Boyles laughed and Grumley joined in.

The barn was busy with the usual pre-hunt rituals. The next batch of hopefuls was packing up. Grumley had already checked in with a few of them and chatted them up about the usual good locations and the proper way to quarter a carcass. Everyone liked to chew on a bit of Grumley's world. It was part of the package, even on this side, the legal one. He had showered and chugged his way through half a pot of coffee, then fretted around and criticized a few guides, for the hell of it, as they loaded up the packhorses and mules.

"He's a goner unless he was a near professional mountaineer," said Boyles, trying to make conversation. "But from what I gather, he was the kind of guy who would have had a tough time with a sleepover in his own backyard."

"Nasty up there," said Grumley.

News delivered, Boyles drifted off.

"One other thing," said Grumley. Boyles stopped like a dog on a choke chain and turned around. "Find somebody to go tell my hunting buddies that something came up and they're on their own for a few days. However long they want to hang around is fine. Marcovicci knows his way around; he can handle anything."

"Done," said Boyles.

"And tell 'em, too, that Applegate headed off. Might be back, might not. Tell 'em I'll be back to check in a few days. Make something up, okay? Maybe I got busy digging out a back-country camp or something."

* * * *

Grumley plunged his old Ford pick-up down the slope through the bog birch and parked it in the pristine powder. No one had been in or out of Rocky's mobile home for a day or more. The handle turned. It was unlocked, a typical backwoods practice.

The interior of the old Streamliner was cramped, more like a steel cave than a home. It was only five short steps from front to back. In the middle, where the airplane sized bathroom and storage closet faced each other on opposite sides of the floor plan, Grumley's shoulders scraped the walls. There was a bedroom in back, near the door where he had entered, and kitchen up front.

Small wonder, Grumley thought, that Trudy's company and Trudy's closeness held a certain appeal.

The refrigerator, no bigger than the oven next to it, yielded nothing but sour milk and a half loaf of stiff, moldy whole wheat bread.

Everything looked normal. The kitchen was straightforward enough, including the photographs taped to the cupboard doors: Rocky in various poses with hunted game, in various seasons and in various terrains. The game included a mountain lion, a big horn sheep, and a half-dozen elk and deer. There wasn't much Rocky hadn't killed. One of the elk sported a towering rack, near trophy size. Rocky had wedged himself in between the antlers, grinning a wicked grin. He appeared simultaneously ecstatic and angry, as if his main spring was wound one crank too tight.

Grumley took $45 out of a tin box next to a tape deck on a ledge above the bed. Then he checked the closet-sized bathroom for secret compartments. Fuckin' Rocky, he thought. The business now produced more cash in a month than the sporting goods store generated in a year and it was not to be fucked with, by anyone. Rocky had been among the best. Until he got stupid.

Grumley went back to the picture. Rocky wasn't quite as sheepish, perhaps, as his quiet manner once suggested, upon first hire. Christ, that grin. Another poser. Grumley was sick and tired of the fakers and their bullshit. Rocky had been a coward, no question, and a fool for having been sucked into Trudy's world. He had wanted something for nothing. Worse, he'd been a fucking irritation. For a second, staring at that semi-leer between the elk's huge headgear, Grumley wished he could kill him all over again.

* * * *

Suddenly, reporters. A whole little flock. Maria Nash was back, but she was now flanked by a stringer from *The Denver Post* and two—count them, two—television cameras from two Denver stations that had somehow managed to show up at precisely the same moment, as if they had shared notes. One of these TV types was proving particularly obnoxious. Ellenberg wanted to clock him, but it probably wouldn't look good on TV.

"So you didn't find the note until this *morning?*"

"Correct."

"And he had left it on his sleeping bag?"

"Correct."

Ellenberg tried to remember her training in media management. Never reveal anger. Always appear calm, especially with cameras recording every blink.

Ellenberg was tired and emotionally drained. The walk down from camp to the county road through the snow had been grueling. A thin snow fell, but splotches of blue could be seen through the clouds to the east.

"But you knew this individual was missing—what?—more than twelve hours before you looked in his tent?"

"Yes," said Ellenberg. "There didn't seem to be much we could do."

The reporter's over-sized parka included a fur fringe. She wanted to point out how animals were being used to make him appear warm.

Ellenberg counted six television cameras, five still ones, and ten reporters fanned out in a semi-circle in the tromped-down field.

"What do you think the note means?"

This one was from good old Maria Nash. Ellenberg wondered if she would hear the phrase "meat-eating statistics" if Robert P. Calkins III was not there.

"I'm not sure."

Never get trapped in a cycle of speculation. Answer facts and always bring questions back to *your* themes and issues.

"Did you have any standards, were you doing any checking for physical fitness for your . . . your whatever you call it?"

The badger again.

"Protest," said Ellenberg.

"So the answer is no?"

"That is correct."

"And so, you basically would have let anybody join your event?"

"It was a peaceful protest against a particularly invidious form of violence," said Ellenberg, with an ever-so-slight smile. "Not an event. We welcomed all those who wished to help show the world about the level of barbarism being committed every day, right here in Colorado."

"Would you have called it off had you known—which you claimed you didn't—that the snowstorm would be this severe?"

"I think . . .," Ellenberg checked herself, "yes," she said. The other reporters stood around, waiting to see if the badger had another chomp left. He looked at the others, who stared back. The badger tucked away a pen he had never used. The press conference was over.

Ellenberg took a deep, invisible breath and drifted off toward the FATE trailer that had been used as headquarters throughout the protest. A giant banner had been draped along the trailer's side: *FAIR IS FAIR. LET'S ARM THE ANIMALS*. She reached the door of her trailer, turned casually around, feeling a reporter or someone had followed, and fought the impulse to gasp.

The man stopped, inches away. For a second, she remembered one friend's suggestion that she consider having a shadow, a quasi-bodyguard. The man was solidly built and over six feet tall, dressed head to boot in hunter's camouflage. His face was smeared with green-black paint and the look on his face was serious, cast in a snarl.

"Dawn Ellenberg?"

Maybe he was a reporter for *Field And Stream* (*"Fire And Aim,"* as they called it).

"I wanted to tell you . . . "

"What . . . ?"

She couldn't quite tell whether he was angry—or what, exactly.

"Your protest. I mean, I'm a hunter. I have finished hunting. What happened here has . . ."

He stopped to fight some tears, nearly blubbering.

"What is it?" she asked. "Are you okay?"

"I stopped and thought . . . what's the point?"

"It's okay," said Ellenberg.

"No, it's not. I'm giving it up. I want to help."

"Help?"

"Clean up. Whatever."

"There's certainly plenty to do."

"It took guts to do what you did."

"Several hundred others, too," she said.

"I admire you all."

"And you're from—"

"Denver, just outside."

"I think some news folks might be interested in your conversation."

The story would be very effective, with him decked out in camouflage garb.

"I'm not doing this for anything like that."

"Your story might pay certain dividends for us. I'd be grateful. I'll introduce you to the whole PR team."

"I was going to take the bus back to Denver, but I could stay."

"Splendid," said Ellenberg.

"Thank you," said the man. "I'm starting to feel so much better already."

"If there are no reporters who are interested now, it might be tomorrow or so. I'm sure we can find you a spot to camp, and some gear. We've got to get you out of those clothes, though. You're likely to spook a whole bunch of folks around here."

"It's all I had."

"That's okay. Thanks," said Ellenberg, holding out her hand for a shake. "And your name is?"

"Applegate. Dean Applegate."

* * * *

The more they asked questions, the more Coil realized how little she had seen and heard. A shot. A man doing something bizarre and unusual, or so it seemed. A dead elk lying in the rocks.

The ring of officialdom had stopped their search planning long enough to listen to her tale. Sheriff Sandstrom, no doubt, had wanted to designate some low-level deputy to have her sketch her route and key landmarks on a topo map. But then she said it: "It might have been a human body."

Coil blurted it out before she had really thought it through, but it was something she had been digging from the recesses of her mind.

Slater had helped her nail down a minute with Jerry Sandstrom, *Sheriff* Jerry Sandstrom, with the spiky ear hair and backwoods gruffness. He had been sheriff since Nixon was president and was recently given another four-year deal from the voters. Jerry On-The-Spot Sandstrom. He always liked to be there in murder cases before the last wisp of steam rose from the corpse, according to Slater. Sandstrom stood next to Slater's boss, District Ranger Gary Bridgers, who seemed intent but clueless. He took notes and tried to look as if he might have a good idea any second now. A camp jockey flanked Bridgers, one she recognized from the trails, an overly nosy sort who was one of Grumley's crew.

They all stood under the barn-size canopy that jutted off the barn that was the heart of Pete Weaver's Ripplecreek Ranch. Weaver was long gone. He had headed off with the two groups of hunters, but not before Coil had pulled him aside and told him she'd probably be busy with the authorities and why.

"What makes you say *human body*?" asked Sandstrom. "You were how far away?"

"As the crow flies, hard to say," said Coil. "Something about the way the load dragged, the way he . . . whoever . . . was pulling it."

"And you had a good look at it all, even through a friggin' storm?"

"With binos. Good ones."

Now they took her to the hood of a pick-up truck, with its nose out of the hard snow, under the canopy. A topo map was taped to the green metal, and the map already sported a series of red dots and trails, marked in felt-tip. One said "D.E.'s camp." It was the only sure thing.

"Where were you?" asked Sandstrom.

Sandstrom's head shook and bobbed of its own free will, even when he wasn't talking. The rooster-like flap under his jaw amplified the condition. He towered over Coil, so she got an unwelcome look at the quivering pouch.

"Here," said Coil, quickly finding the tight concentric circles that indicated Lizard's Tongue. She showed him Black Squirrel Pass and where she had camped the night before. The officials huddled around Sandstrom and tried to figure out if it was possible for their missing protester to have traveled so far.

"What time was this?" asked Sandstrom.

"Late morning. Maybe noon. I'm not positive."

"You're not?"

"That's about how many hours it would have been, given the distance I covered."

Coil found Slater's face in the huddle of men, listening, and he gave her some encouragement with a faint smile.

"Anything else unusual or out of the ordinary occur?" This was Bridgers, trying to wedge himself into matters. "Anything you saw or heard, anything you found?"

"No," said Coil bluntly. "Well. The elk. Dead one. Good-size bull, too."

"A carcass?" asked Sandstrom.

"Dead, so, yeah, carcass. But a fresh kill."

"You're sure?"

"He was still warm."

"And this was . . . ?"

Sandstrom showed a flash of impatience.

"Right at the spot where I saw the guy, near the base of Lizard's Tongue."

"Good Christ," said Sandstrom. "A dead bull in the wilderness. I'm sure all of the cows are upset, but we've gotta start with our missing boy and keep this investigation—for the time being, you know—concerned with the Homo sapiens. Okay with everybody? Thank you, sweetheart."

Coil squeezed her way out of the circle of Sandstrom's huddle.

"We'll need a good bloodhound to find the trail of the missing protester," Sandstrom said to Slater.

"Maybe that one in Grand Junction isn't busy. The one that followed the bomber home," suggested Slater.

"Call and find out," snapped Sandstrom, as if his authority extended to all government.

"Done," said Slater, who was known fairly well in Glenwood Springs and around. He had mediated a dispute between mountain bikers and hikers on a popular National Forest trail and had settled a long-standing feud between back-country outfitters competing for access to one of the best elk herds—something to do with camp locations in the wilderness area. But Slater's role kept the "accidental" shootings to one. Still, Coil thought Slater might roll his eyes at her any second, as if to say, get a load of this old cop. But Slater played right along. His attitude made Coil smile, inside. The last full-fledged boyfriend she'd had, after the airplane accident, was hung up on every mystical song Van Morrison had ever sung. He was a mental drifter, a searcher, who calculated the price of belonging to every structure or organization as some sort of personal sacrifice.

Not Slater. He was somebody who saw his place, or at least knew how to pretend he did. As a result, the picture of comfort and suggestion of stability was strangely inviting.

4

"Something tells me we're getting close."

This was Applegate, who had pulled up behind Ellenberg as they trudged.

"What makes you think so?"

"A hunch, I don't know. If he wasn't well to begin with, it's hard to imagine he got much farther, even with better conditions."

"True," said Ellenberg.

Someone had found Applegate a fresh set of clothes. He had shaved and cleaned up. He looked more at ease, less severe, out of the camouflage.

Ellenberg and most of the others had spent the evening in the camp's oversized canvas tent, singing along with a trio of acoustic guitars to everything from John Denver to Neil Young to Kurt Cobain, *Nirvana Unplugged*. The mood of the singers had been subdued and earnest. It was not a party, it was a bonding, and everyone was thinking about Ray Stern.

"Sleep okay?" Ellenberg asked Applegate.

"After that great serenade," said Applegate, "of course. Thanks for the loaned tent."

"Not a problem. Thanks for your help, by the way," Ellenberg said.

"My pleasure."

"I hear the interviews went okay."

"They've all got the same five or six questions," said Applegate with a smile. "I thought one of 'em from the *New York Times* was gonna write my life story, though."

"Didn't I see you being tortured by that slick-haired guy from Channel 9?"

"A strange breed, that one. He had it figured that I was set up by you guys to look like a hunter."

She had urged the reporters to all visit the singalong, to show the group's strong common beliefs and sense of community.

"Did you convince him?"

"I remembered I had a picture of myself with a big old elk I killed several years back. Nearly trophy class. The picture was sufficiently faded. Now even *Time* has it, *Time* magazine."

"Fantastic," said Ellenberg. "You dealing with this okay?"

"I've never felt better," said Applegate. "I feel, I don't know, somehow cleansed."

Applegate took a deep breath. Whether it was from plowing through the snow or from thinking things over, Ellenberg couldn't tell.

"My decision seems so small if it means, you know, prompting someone else to think about animals in a different way," he said.

The day had dawned clear and strong, with purpose. It revealed a valley frozen in white, from cornices on the wind-whipped ridges to the west, to the rounder hills off to the east. The scene was defined by what was not white: the south-facing trunks of most trees, the occasional boulder large enough to avoid a complete cover of snow, and wisps of grass or bush that poked through the surface, so slight the snow had quickly blown away. A giant, invisible razor had given the scene its final grooming touches, turning the snow blanket smooth, clean-shaven.

The bloodhound led them up through a stretch of valley where the walls closed in and the woods grew dense. The entire troop—twenty cops, friends, and fellow protesters—had come to a complete stop as the dog poked around. A TV helicopter buzzed them overhead for an aerial shot.

Applegate realized he was breathing harder than normal, perhaps with emotion. With binoculars, Ellenberg could see the bloodhound work a series of concentric circles from the point where he had first pulled up. The handler and Slater stood rock still. It was remarkable that the dog could smell anything in the cold.

The bloodhound suddenly plunged off into a thick stand of trees, stopped, and started pawing at the surface. His handler smiled.

"I hope Ray Stern felt some release," said Ellenberg. "A moment or two."

Applegate buried his face in one mitten-covered hand and put the other on her shoulder.

* * * *

Grumley was anxious to get a grip on his entire operation. He wanted time alone in his office, a small square of space in the center of the barn, between the shop and the saddle room. The office was big enough for a couple of old desks, a sagging red couch, a telephone, a space heater, and a stocked rifle rack that circled the room on three sides. The rack was now home for Applegate's Sako, a beautiful weapon much too nice for the likes of such a pathetic "hunter." The rifle was now another blade of grass in a football field.

He didn't really need Popeye Boyles nipping at his heels, but the guy might sulk if you didn't scratch him behind the ears.

"You look refreshed." It was Boyles, toting a shovel coated with muck.

"Nothing like home cookin'," said Grumley.

"And being the old sailor I am, I know you don't mean food."

Grumley grimaced.

"What's up with the search?" he asked.

"They're up there now, bashing around," said Boyles.

"They?"

"Some bloodhound from Grand Junction, a bunch of cops and rangers, a pack of them protesters, and the dead guy's brother."

"Dead guy?"

Boyles stopped for a second and cocked his head to the radio strapped to his waist. Grumley could hear a soft voice, too, but could not make it out.

"Just somebody sending out for donuts," said Boyles. He then stood there, like he hadn't been asked a question.

"Dead guy?" Grumley repeated.

"Pretty sure dead. A bloodhound can track the trail of a filet mignon hanging out the window of a car door three days later, as long as you have a piece of the original steak. He'll find it."

"Where's the sheriff on all this?"

"Sandstrom on a hike? In the snow? Uphill? Please."

"Well?"

"He's monitoring things from base camp, over at Weaver's place. What's gonna be interesting is if they wind up where that one guide said she saw somethin'."

"One more time, Popeye."

"One of the guides over at Weaver's place said she saw some strange goings-on up near Lizard's Tongue."

For a split second, the announcement didn't seem connected to Grumley's world. How could anybody have seen anything?

"Strange what?"

"She's tellin' the cops about hearing a shot, seeing somebody doin' something. Some of it was pretty darn unclear. She got herself a few minutes with Sandstrom."

Grumley tried to think of the questions a normally curious guy would ask. The key was to fix on a point between overly interested and not nosy enough.

"Herself?"

"Allison something."

Grumley remembered her, an applicant, a city girl with a lot of want-to, trust-me in her eyes. "Coil?"

"That's it."

"Why does she think it's anything?"

"Have to ask her. Oh, something about a dead elk, too."

Grumley suddenly realized how everything could unravel. *Heard* a shot. *Saw* something. She might make enough fuss that they'd go look.

There was no chance of finding the body until spring, however, even if somebody gave enough of a shit to keep complaining that Rocky Carnivitas was missing from the face of the earth. Even then, cops would have a dead guy and a bullet, right? Hunting accident. Applegate was the complicating factor.

Boyles shuffled off, turning up the volume on his police radio.

For two hours, Grumley made routine calls while the working part of his brain sorted through various scenarios of cop investigations. Two clients were due next week, one for a bull elk, the other for a trophy-class mountain goat. Both were repeat clients, a Hollywood B-movie producer and a San Francisco banker. The banker didn't want things to be "too easy" this time. There should be two crews getting both animals ready. They would have to tranquilize the bull and tie it down one or two days before the scheduled hunt date. Rocky's bull would have worked fine, but that was water under the bridge. The mountain goat could be moved after he was sedated.

Then he made a call down to the store. Sales were good, not spectacular. They had run out of camouflage vests because of some screw-up with the distributor, but there was no shortage of ladies' swimwear.

The schedule showed two two-man crews out servicing camps. One camp was due to break the day after tomorrow. Both were five-man groups, one with a supplied cook and one without. According to the chalkboard, two other guides were following back a messenger from a third camp who had come for help quartering and packing-out a kill. Boyles was scheduled for barn clean up. A guy named Gilliam was on "Trudy Duty," the thankless job of watching his wife to prevent any unattended seizures.

Grumley drove back down the valley. Six miles downhill, he turned back to the north and headed up the eight bumpy, unplowed miles to a cabin where he kept horses and had built quarters for the crews that helped run and organize the custom hunts. The hunts were known among the crews as "George G's Custom Carnage." The cabin sat in a dark, craggy canyon that saw sun only a few hours each day in the summer. From early

September to late April, it was constantly in the shadows. The corral was less than ideal, on a steep slope and wooded, but what did horses know about level? Grumley had built a small shelter for the horses to use in stiff storms, and a small barn for saddles and repair.

Four horses worked on a small pile of hay scattered in the snow. Somebody, at least, had been there recently, within the hour. No one was lolling around in a bunk, drinking coffee, or waiting for orders. There were a dozen men who worked on the carnage crew and they all seemed steady and constant, like marble. They were well-compensated. They earned enough in four months to last them a year, if they didn't convert it all into Wild Turkey.

It was a profitable empire. No mistakes were going to destroy it. Grumley found a bit in the shed and led Trooper from the corral. He found a blanket and saddle and fitted them on, tied a huge coil of rope to the saddle, raided the refrigerator for a wedge of cheese and four slices of ham, and bundled up for the ride. From the headquarters of George G's Custom Carnage, Lizard's Tongue was only half the distance of the main trail up Ripplecreek. However, it was twice the grade in spots. He had to go back up, to fix the problems caused by the meddlesome Coil. A bit of effort to straighten it all out made sense and besides, playing with them would be so easy. Even if it wasn't until next spring, he didn't want them flipping over the elk to discover it was bulletless.

* * * *

They didn't yank Ray Stern from his white grave, they first dug out around him in a square nearly double the size that would have been necessary to simply extract the body. The scene looked to Applegate like a slightly faster version of an archaeological dig, in snow.

The consequences of Applegate's attempt to behave like someone he was not gradually emerged from its grave, twenty yards away. The body looked puny, toy-like. Applegate knew he was no tough guy the rest of the year. What had he been trying to prove? There were a few waves of tears and Applegate felt good knowing he was with company that understood his sobs.

The brown blanket had fused itself to the corpse. They unrolled enough to wave Ellenberg over for a peek, and she approached the body cautiously, then buried her face in her hands. She returned to where Applegate and the others stood, some twenty yards from the body.

The television guys didn't miss a moment.

"It's an animal skin," said Ellenberg. "A fake one, anyway. A huge wrap. He made himself a target."

"He didn't want to waste his death," said Applegate.

"It won't be wasted," said Ellenberg. "Believe me, it won't be wasted."

They carried the frozen lump of Ray Stern to the nearest clearing, up and over a small ridge no more than a hundred yards away. One of them carried Ray Stern's frozen torso around the shoulders. Two others carried the legs. The brown blanket flopped along like a shroud.

Within a few minutes, a mountain rescue helicopter hovered overhead and lowered a sled. The group watched as Stern's body was winched slowly up, cameras rolling.

Applegate couldn't watch. He knelt in the snow and bowed his head, knowing his life would never be the same.

* * * *

The landscape was frighteningly white. Everything.

"Oh shit," she muttered.

Coil looked at Slater, and he understood. As they had climbed the hillside on horseback, the snow depth had increased with every hour. Bear was starting to wade slowly. Walking was hard work. The snow-covered landscape altered her bearings and the intense sun was disorienting. The remaining half-mile of slope up to Lizard's Tongue was a vast, bumpy, lumpy snow farm. It was, perhaps, eight city-sized blocks of chunky terrain, and she was looking for a dead elk lying on its side, the equivalent of a couple of flopped-over Harleys.

The helicopter drone had disturbed the peaceful walk for the last fifteen minutes or so and she turned to watch, a mile or so down the canyon, as it elevated up from a position close to the tree tops, then banked hard, flew off, and left them again in that wonderful silence.

And weird sense of displacement.

This didn't even look like the same slope, but here was Lizard's Tongue, there was Black Squirrel Pass, and they were on the trail—or close enough.

Bear worked along on his own internal radar headings. The snowfall had not thrown off his sense of direction. There was a slight indentation in the terrain that seemed to track with the trail. Slater, who knew the intricacies of the Flattops like most people know their way to work, never questioned Bear's judgment. It was helpful having Slater along. The cops were so consumed with the missing protester that the concerns she had registered were treated like an ordinary citizen complaint about a barking dog or partying neighbors. Slater had been told by his people to interview hunters in three specific backcountry camps. He was on his way to fill that assignment. They would split up at Lizard's Tongue, if and when she could find the elk.

Finally, she told Bear to stop. By her sense of mental triangulation, this spot seemed about right, or as good as any.

"The cops have a bloodhound," said Slater. "Maybe he's done now, and we could borrow him."

"I wonder if he'd need the scent of any-old-elk to do his tricks or if it would have to be this particular bull?" said Coil.

"Probably have to be this one," said Slater, "now that you mention it."

The sun mixed with the cold air and snow to make the temperature manageable. If there was a ski lodge right in this spot, and if circumstances were different, they would both be sipping a Heineken, coats off, listening to some overly loud rock and roll on the tinny outdoor speakers and letting their faces soak up the rays. Instead, they had to hunt for an animal that was already dead.

In her mind, Coil outlined a section of snow. If she was a guy, she thought, she'd say it was half a football field long, maybe, but not as wide. But she wasn't a guy, so it was a section of snow, a chunk of land. It was where they needed to start looking. She walked the perimeter of the area, pounding through hip-deep snow, constantly checking Lizard's Tongue against her memory of it in the blizzard. This had to be about right. She was hoping for an antler poking through the surface of the snow, or maybe a major indentation where the snow had not accumulated quite so quickly because of the elk's dissipating heat. The wind had erased the possibility of the latter, the depth of the snow the former.

Slater had two telescoping probes along, the kind that were used to locate avalanche victims. Walking side by side, three feet apart, they started plowing their field. The elk had not been directly at trail side, so they started closer to the middle, probing down with their rods every step, hoping it tapped something a bit more squishy than rock. All the while, Coil wondered if there hadn't been some way she could have marked the elk's location, assembled some sort of flag or something that would have helped them now. The probing was tedious, the trudging difficult. At this pace, two hours might be enough, as long as they found what they were after.

"Your government dollars at work," said Slater. "Whatever it takes."

"At least I can't moan about the lack of responsiveness from the National Forest Service," said Coil.

"In more ways than one, if you get my drift," said Slater. "And drift may not be the best choice of words, given all this snow."

They both grunted a bit as they worked—stepping out of their last spot, sinking into the next, probing down with the sticks, waiting to see how the feel of the bottom registered on their mittened hands. Coil was dubious this would work, but it beat shoveling or waiting for spring. Slater had once found a dead hunter this way. The hunter's tracks led into an area creamed by an avalanche that had plummeted off a wind-blown cornice, a hundred yards up. It was Slater's probe that found the body and others had come around to see how the probe *felt*. Kind of like training. Slater said she'd know if she hit elk. It was *different*.

Step, sink, probe, wait, feel. A half-hour passed, then an hour. They had snacks and a drink, hot Lemon Zinger from a thermos. Then they were back at it. Coil kept wondering how long it was worth exploring. What if they poked this whole section and came up empty? In which direction should they look? Would there be time, or even the inclination? They were more than half finished with this plot when Slater stopped his methodical rhythm of movement.

"We got a bite," he said.

Digging down and around the elk was hard work, but the effort was eased by the fact that she knew she hadn't been whacked out and had remembered enough to find her way back to this spot. The frozen elk emerged like a breach birth, butt first, like a hairy, unwieldy rock. Then Slater worked from the antlers down, and she from the rear up, scooping snow off the carcass by hand, until he had been half exhumed.

"Nice one," said Slater, standing back to admire the specimen. "Healthy size rack, too. But what made you so sure, *makes* you so sure he's not completely shredded underneath?"

"Two things. This guy didn't fall, he decided to get down. He's not crumpled up. Second, no exit wound. Sure it's possible, but not even a nick on this side? Nothing. It didn't look like this guy had been in pain."

"Interesting," said Slater. "I don't think it would have ever occurred to me, but you might be right."

They dug underneath the elk's legs, fitted ropes up and around the front set and tied them as close to the body as they could, walked their horses around, tied one rope to each saddle, and then stepped the horses away. The rope pulled taut, and the elk's feet slowly rose up, pointed oddly to the sky, and flopped over. They scraped through some caked-on snow, studied the elk's head, and double-checked the rump and belly for holes, blood, or trauma of any kind. There was nothing.

"He was a beauty," said Slater.

Coil was on all fours, peering into the elk's face, where the shadow from Slater's head moved and something flashed, a glint off something steel. She had to refocus her eyes on the bright snow to catch sight of it again, then reached down and wiggle free a rectangular metal box not much bigger than her hand

"GPS," said Slater.

"Yep," said Coil.

"Your basic gear for any wildlife biologist."

"For tracking," said Coil.

"And study," said Slater.

"So this is strange or not strange?"

"Somewhat. We get our share of people who want to study the elk migration or diseases or impact on the habitat. It's possible something was authorized that I didn't know about."

"But to have him go down now, at the beginning of the hunting season?"

"Odd, no question," said Slater.

"And why didn't the elk survive?"

"Do we know all the ways they can die?" asked Slater.

The GPS collar, which Slater now flipped around in his hands, at least put a human in the area where Coil said there had been a human. She thought this, but did not utter it out loud. Wasn't that obvious? She stood and stared, mostly down the hill, looking for anything out of place, out of line, out of the ordinary. The snowfield returned a blank stare.

"Whatcha gonna do?" asked Slater.

"Me?" said Coil. "How about the authorities?"

"We'll see if we can trace which scientists might be using the Auditrak 535," he said, reading off the monitor. "But it's the equivalent of asking which hikers wear boots."

Coil looked away, thinking she'd wasted Slater's time and trouble. Or maybe somebody would come climbing back up out of the snow right now and explain it all, the same way dead-looking bodies, no doubt her own among them, had scrambled up out of the Long Island Sound. Only here, the pristine and unforgiving cover of white snow seemed to have swallowed all the possible answers.

* * * *

Grumley squeezed a hunk of horse manure in his bare fist and felt the heat in the lump's core. Two horses, and they hadn't been gone long. He could catch them if he wanted.

The field of snow was churned up, and the elk was flipped over. Fuck. It wasn't hard to imagine his house now filled with cops and the barn, too, as they looked for him. And Trudy might be there answering questions or filling in some blanks for some detective.

What the fuck? How could things have gotten so screwed up?

The bullet in Rocky. Was it *in* Rocky? What would they make of it? What had anyone seen? How much?

Applegate. Christ, Applegate had better stay cool or the whole thing could be unzipped in a flash. Maybe he'd spill his stinking guts and think he'd take all the honorable, puked-up blame himself for killing the protester. And then bumble his way around, mention having run into Grumley, who was agitated about something. More than anything, Applegate's muzzle had better stay put.

* * * *

Trudy Grumley didn't start crying until she saw the body being hoisted up to the helicopter. He looked so small and frail, dangling below this mechanical monster by a thread. The sheriff's people and one of Dawn Ellenberg's people held up between them the oversized brown cloth they said he had been wearing. They had a clip of Ellenberg reading the note the guy had left in his tent, pictures of the dog bounding through the snow to find the body, and pictures of Ray Stern as a kid. Trudy let the tears flow and the tissues piled up around her on the blue comforter. And then there was an interview with the sheriff during which he basically said they would stop at nothing to find the stupid hunter who couldn't tell the difference between an honest-to-goodness whitetail and a two-legged human in a cloth suit.

It was a CNN reporter, an older one who looked like an entire vat of coffee wouldn't put a jolt in his heartbeat, who first used the term "creative suicide." The other stations picked it up within a few hours. It was a neat, simple description that made her ache. She felt the strength of the dead protester's decision, the conviction that went with it. There seemed to be nothing more admirable.

And then they showed an extended interview with Dean Applegate, who had also been in the search party for the dead protester. He was dressed in his camouflage outfit now, sitting in a barn on an out-of-place chair plunked down in the middle of the dirt and muck. The guy seemed too familiar. He talked about how the protest movement had affected him, made him stop and ponder the real need for hunters, the real necessity of "ripping an animal apart" with a high-powered bullet. "The sport is an anachronism," said Applegate in the interview. "Everything else has changed in this world but the way we treat animals. And that's changed for the worse. Now we can scope 'em from a mile away, fire bullets that are really small missiles. I simply came to realize that it isn't fair."

Something about him was old-friend-familiar, or met-once-familiar. High school?

And still no Rocky. The wait was agonizing.

Trudy sat on the corner of her king-size bed, the right hand absently snipping the air with her pruning sheers and the left flipping the satellite dish from one end of the sky to the other, looking for bits of news about the dead protester. It was starting to get repetitive.

Smoke, the gray cat, gave himself a bath on her lap while two black kittens played with a ball of string on the bed behind her. She glanced down the long driveway, watching for cars. The only delay that made any sense was that Rocky got mucked up with the animal people, an event so well-orchestrated that it had drawn coverage by CNN, all the network news operations, and, of course, every television station out of Denver.

Trudy was impressed with Ellenberg's pure sense of spunk. Ellenberg was one of those women willing to lead a rebellion on an entire cultural issue—fighting for all those living things, disrupting all of those hunters, screwing up all those cops.

Trudy scratched Smoke's chin and gently put him down on the bed. The delay was worrisome, the uncertainty worse.

Trudy's world was her house, a massive stone structure at the end of a long, snaking driveway off in the woods, a couple of miles from the Colorado River. George had picked the spot for its seclusion. Eighteen trees had been plucked to make room for the site, and they still had half the timber in firewood stacks off the garage. Six years in the house and nine trees' worth of wood had gone up the chimney.

A moss rock fireplace dominated the living room, a giant wood-burning stove nestled inside. A stone ledge fronted the fireplace and then some, as long as the living room was wide. Three matching leather couches formed a U-shape around a coffee table, which was a varnished slice of tree from the tallest Douglas Fir they had destroyed to make room in the woods for themselves.

The living room was for show. They rarely had guests or parties. Trudy spent half the time in her greenhouse, tucked off the over-sized kitchen. She had gradually covered the greenhouse and kitchen in plants, her mute pals. The collection now coated the living room, hung from the ceiling, and took up all the otherwise unused space in the corners.

It was an easy life that had put roundness, a layer of padding, and real hips onto her bony build. Her frame, gaunt in high school, was now more recognizably that of a woman. The humidity from the plants, especially in the greenhouse, kept her skin soft. Her hair hung down to the middle of her back. Her face was long, with clear brown eyes, and it looked okay, nothing spectacular, with straight teeth and a smallish nose.

The problem, of course, was mobility. Seven years now of seizures. She

had simply come to accept the house as a somewhat comfortable, familiar cell. She could drive, but it was risky. The doctors had trained her to
watch and sense the faint aura in her vision, like a smear of Vaseline on
what was before her, as a warning sign. She could stop the car and wait for
the seizure to pass. The doctors had said her spells didn't seem to be violent, but they could not guarantee that would never be the case. They only
wanted her to drive on the back roads, where she could go slowly. But the
only way to Glenwood Springs and Eagle, the two closest towns, meant 14
miles of interstate in one direction, 22 in the other. Take your pick. She
didn't want to be going 65 and watching for auras. She didn't really want
to be picking her way around the winding roads that hugged the banks of
the Colorado River and worrying about where she would pull over to let
the episode run its course. She didn't want strangers trying to take care of
her, calling ambulances and all of that.

And when they did start, there went the sales clerk job at the clothing
store in Glenwood Springs and, gradually, her sense of independence.
When George was gone for one of his long stretches, either on a hunt or
flying his plane up to some remote spot, one of his crew was given the task
of stopping in once in the morning and once in the afternoon to check on
her, to make sure she hadn't keeled over in a fit, and to do any odd chores
she wanted done. They called it "Trudy Duty." It hadn't taken her long to
get over feeling strange about having what amounted to a personal valet.
Few of them refused a warm plate of her best food—Chinese chicken,
Thai beef salad, pork chops in apricot-ginger marinade. It was one way of
saying thanks to those who helped her out. She could get chauffeured into
town when she wanted and go to the bookstore or eat lunch. Groceries
were delivered once a week off her list. The satellite TV dish was installed.
Trudy was made to feel her illness was being compensated for and accom-
modated. But it was not treated.

George had stalled when it came to her desire to travel to Denver
where, she had read, specialists were beginning to experiment with her
type of seizures. They could peel off a chunk of your skull, attach a bunch

of probes or something, reattach the skull, wait for the next seizure, determine precisely which part of the brain was going haywire when the seizure took place and then, if the part of the brain involved didn't seem crucial to memory or speech or motor control, snip it out.

"Wait until they perfect the procedure," George had said. "We don't have insurance or the $30,000 to put up front. And what's wrong with the way things are?"

That's where Rocky, at least, had offered a refreshingly different point of view. There was something sweet and amiable about Rocky, despite a slightly tousled and unschooled manner. He had drawn "Trudy Duty" three days in a row once, earlier in the summer, and had held her and comforted her through a somewhat fierce seizure that came on while they sat in the car in the dirt parking lot after the annual rodeo in Eagle. The rest of the night Rocky had stayed close, like a first-time dad. Rocky was the only one of the hands who had shown any interest in her situation. The others all wanted to know as little as possible.

"If he doesn't say it, he manages to imply it somehow," said Trudy, "that he doesn't have the money."

"Christ, he's worth ten times that. Or twenty," said Rocky. He had driven her up to an overlook in Glenwood Canyon a few months earlier, for a picnic. George had flown to Texas, meeting new clients. They sat on a blanket, up on the rocky cliff more than 1,000 feet above the river. A bottle of wine and curried chicken sandwiches were slowly devoured. A fleet of rafters bobbed in the sparkling river below.

"He says some months we barely make the mortgage. I mean, it's a great house, but from time to time he'll grumble about business and say something about getting a smaller place."

"He's got the money for your operation," Rocky said. "Trust me on that."

They slept together that afternoon. A few tentative gropes on the picnic blanket served as prelude, and they finished back at her house in the cool sheets of the spare bedroom—neutral territory. She discovered a yearning to be close to him. He was patient and listened to what she knew about plants and herbs. George's whereabouts weren't too much of an issue. He was rarely home mid-day, and Rocky's presence was not something that needed to be concealed.

Now Rocky was way overdue, and she missed him. When it came down to it, she realized Rocky had filled an aching gap and she did not want the gap to reappear. Perhaps someone else cared that Rocky was missing, but she didn't know who that would be. However, amid the crash and crush of the media coverage about the "creative suicide," a missing guide wasn't worth a blip.

5

"I suppose Ripplecreek has made a name for itself," said Slater. "The worst kind. I just saw two local reporters interviewing someone from the network about why this story has attracted such attention. They're getting desperate for new people to interview, I suppose."

Slater refilled two crusty plastic coffee cups perched on the flopped-down glove compartment door of his Forest Service truck. The coffee dribbled from a beat-up steel thermos. They sat in the truck, engine idling, outside Pete Weaver's Ripplecreek Ranch, which had been commandeered by Sandstrom as a kind of temporary base camp and police headquarters, a place to hold news conferences and issue a few orders.

Two days had passed since she and Slater had split up their investigation, a half-mile down the canyon from Lizard's Tongue. Slater had found hunters near a few of the camps, but none had any useful information, or just didn't want to involve themselves.

"It's perfect for Sandstrom. He laps up the national press while the case drags on," said Slater. "The guy is sixty-three. He's not going anywhere, but pretends every case is his next ticket to international fame."

"Maybe he's hoping for one of those movie deals about his side of the story," said Coil. "Be a good retirement bonus. These days, it doesn't take much. But it would look better, in the key scene, if it was *him* holding up the deer suit," said Coil. That's what the media started calling it: *deer suit*. As if it came with a coat and tie, Coil thought.

Coil cracked her window for a breath of something fresh and ran the palm side of her knuckles over the straight, bristly hairs on the back of Slater's neck.

"Ever have long hair?"

"In high school. Over the ears. I was extremely rebellious. We had military dads, with all their rules and bullshit. My dad had a real, live barber's chair, for crying out loud. Now I get antsy if it's not trimmed once a week, and my job comes with its own set of rules for grooming. Something I promised myself I'd avoid. What gives?"

"Indoctrination. That's the city life, too. It wears you down. Conform or else," said Coil.

"Really? I thought the city was where all the weird folks could hide, do their own thing. I thought non-conformity was the point and why people liked living in the city, to watch it all go down."

"Conformity at the corporate level, I suppose," said Coil. "Wear certain suits, read certain books, hang out in just the right places, say just the right things."

"Well, you fit in here, too," said Slater. "Half the folks in the mountains out here are runners, anyway."

"I didn't run from anything."

"No?"

"I just needed trees and sky. And I knew I'd never fly in an airplane again."

"So you needed a new home. I'm no philosopher, but isn't that all of us? Either happy with our homes or looking for something better?"

Slater was a relative of a friend of Pete Weaver. Coil had forgotten the exact connection, but it was that tie that put them together. He was on the trail with an entire Boy Scout troop from Glenwood Springs one cool fall day before the hunting season. Coil, the guide, only had to lead the gang up to an aspen grove below a nearby ridge for a cookout.

She admired how Slater managed to bounce easily among what the kids coughed up, from problem to complaint to fussiness. He often turned a sour moment into a funny one. Slater was the stern but somewhat goofy shepherd of the olive-green flock. He showed them environmental damage from mountain bikes, talked about a proposed gravel pit application outside the wilderness area and showed them all how to make the best s'mores going by barely melting the chocolate before loading it into the graham cracker and marshmallow sandwich for the final heating. He danced artfully among small teams of scouts in the afternoon as they did various merit badge projects and he showed no sign of fatigue at dusk as they returned. In order to determine if Slater might be eligible for some gentle pursuit, she had separated a few key pieces of information about Troop Leader Slater's marital status from one of the near-Eagle Scouts. And then Slater, easily the best looking man she'd ever approached on her own, seemed genuinely flattered when she suggested that she was going to be visiting friends in Glenwood Springs the following week. It wasn't true, but it sounded good. She had asked if they could meet for a drink. The drink led to a dinner date and the third date was a day-long horseback ride. That day ended in her bedroom and lasted until breakfast.

"And you?" Coil asked.

"And me what?"

"Conformist?"

"That's what being a cop, of any variety, is all about," said Slater. "Rules, order, everybody in line, make sure chaos is controlled and renegades are reined in. Speaking of which, I've got to interview every hunter out of Weaver's camps."

"Six or seven are coming out today, I think, and seven more tomorrow," said Coil. "Today's won't be out until early afternoon, though, at best."

"Doesn't matter. They want all the bases covered. In case they saw or heard something, you know. The government thinks of everything. And thinks it's everything too. You can't have too many bases covered, even if the bases are way the hell out in left field or foul territory."

"Oh, a baseball metaphor."

"It's true," said Slater. "If there's anything that makes me madder than wasted taxpayer dollars, it's *stupid* use of taxpayer dollars." He was not amused.

"Which is there more of?"

"I don't know. Some days it's just do everything because, in government, everything can be done. Eventually."

"Any mention of elk biologists working up in Ripplecreek?"

"I'm checking," said Slater. "There's a permitting process, or supposed to be. But there are five ranger districts so they could have come out of any one of them."

"You going to tell Sandstrom?"

"About?"

"About the dead elk?"

"Why would I?"

"Don't you think it's still a bit strange?"

"Sure."

"And confirms that I wasn't seeing things?"

"What would I tell him?"

"I don't know. Maybe it's all connected, somehow. If you're part of the briefings, mention it, that's all. Remind Sandstrom and the others about what I saw. Maybe somebody else knows something now. Put two and two together."

"Okay," said Slater.

"With enthusiasm?"

Slater bounced his head around, thinking.

"I can't believe you don't believe me," said Coil.

"Well, I do. But I also think there's a reasonable explanation for what you heard. You know, somewhere in all the other stuff, with the protester. The elk is strange, no question."

"I've got this little thing about seeing pieces of the world being picked up and put back together. Call it a quirk."

Coil lightly kissed the first two fingers on her left hand, pressed them to Slater's cheek, and opened the car door.

"I'd call it a challenge," said Slater.

"Works for me," she said.

* * * *

"Wasn't there an Apple something or other who was one of your hunting friends? He was on the news."

"Dean Applegate?"

"That's the one," she said.

Trudy plopped her watering can down on the cement floor of the greenhouse and started refilling it with a hose.

"Why do you ask?"

"He was up there where they found that protester, the dead one," said Trudy.

"He left with the others," said Grumley, thinking that Trudy must be mistaken.

"Tall, lanky guy? Kind of a military haircut. Always looks a bit shell-shocked when he talks? Said his hunting days are over. He's giving interviews."

"Interviews?" asked Grumley. "What do you mean, exactly?"

"He and Ellenberg are buddies, by the looks of things."

What the fuck.

Trudy flitted from one plant to the next, poking the soil, shoving in inch-long vitamin sticks, pulling off yellow leaves, and generally looking content. He wanted to tell her to fucking stand still for a minute.

"They even had a live hook-up with the *Today Show* this morning," she said. "I almost woke you up. It's not often one of your friends gets on national TV, right there in your own house, beamed in."

The telephone rang. George leaned back in his chair to reach the wall-mounted phone. He mumbled briefly, then covered the mouthpiece with his hand.

"It's your company-sponsored chauffeur, who didn't realize I'd be back. Need anything I can't handle?"

Trudy wanted to ask which of the helpers it was, or make up an errand.

"Are you going to be around?"

"Just the morning."

"Tell him to call back at noon and we'll probably do groceries, okay?"

"Call back at noon," George said into the phone.

"Which hired gun today?" Trudy asked.

"Does it matter?"

"Some of them," said Trudy, "are plain better than others."

Trudy was at the sink, Grumley thought, making up work.

The doorbell sounded and Grumley cursed. "Never any peace," he said.

Grumley retreated from the kitchen, secretly glad to remove himself from Trudy's fussy world, and shoved a brown calico out of his way that was trying to make friends with his boots. Grumley picked up the cat by the scruff and let him dangle freely as he opened the door.

Sheriff Sandstrom stood there, needling a toothpick around in his gums.

"Home playing with your favorite pussy?" he asked.

"Yeah, some fun," said Grumley, flicking the cat aside. It landed with a thud and an accusatory meow.

"Ooh, that one wants to bite back," said Sandstrom. "Not my type."

"Not generally rated in the top ten," said Grumley. "Come on in."

"To what do we owe the pleasure of your driving all the way out to east bum fuck today?" asked Grumley, leading him to the pot of coffee.

"I wish it was gardening tips I needed. Then I'd know the trip wasn't wasted," said Sandstrom. He stood looking down into the greenhouse, his back to the kitchen. "My word," he said. "Enough jungle for Tarzan and all the apes."

"Trudy," said Grumley with a sigh. "She knows her fertilizer."

"She around?"

"Somewhere," said Grumley.

Sandstrom plopped himself down at the kitchen table and wrapped his thick-knuckled paw around a big blue cup.

"Probably got the biggest pot farm in the west right here, and I'm having a cup of coffee like I don't care."

"If that's true, then I gotta talk about getting my share of the action," said Grumley, head racing to think what real questions would be coming.

"Talking about my babies?" asked Trudy, striding confidently into the kitchen. The rubber boots had been replaced by white tennis shoes. The white T-shirt had been covered by a blue-checked shirt, open to the navel. Grumley wanted to say "Shoo," but had to admit his wife had a certain damn look. He tried to squelch the pride.

"Just commenting on the quantity," said Sandstrom, extending a hand to shake without getting up. "They are in beautiful shape."

"Thanks," said Trudy.

Grumley thought he'd be sitting right across from Sandstrom in the café-style booth. Trudy now occupied the seat. He didn't want to sit next to either of them but felt awkward standing.

Grumley pulled over a stool and plunked it down next to the table.

"My wife," Sandstrom continued, "couldn't grow mold on old food. That's quite a talent you've got."

"Thanks again," said Trudy.

"But I'm not here for how to get my thumb green," said Sandstrom.

"The murder," said Trudy, quickly somber.

"We don't know *murder*," said Sandstrom.

"*Accident?*" asked Trudy sharply.

"Stranger things," said Sandstrom. "Unless one of the animal protesters had the guts to pull the trigger on his own buddy, the one wrapped in the deer suit. That would be murder."

Sandstrom took a sip of coffee, it seemed, as a way of letting the concept settle over the room.

"See what I mean? It's not hard to imagine. A zealot will do about anything. But that's not why I'm here, to spout loose theories on what makes city people go wiggy in the head. George, your name's on a list and we gotta check off a few questions. Where were you the day this fella decided to make himself a true fool, not that I'm taking sides?"

"Hunting," said Grumley. "By myself."

"Where abouts?"

"Down the east from our camp, away from the protest, for obvious reasons."

"Not with your buddies?"

"No. They wanted to lay low completely, ride out the protest, and then get back to serious hunting."

"So you were by yourself?"

"Like I said."

"Why weren't you with your buddies?"

"Too much business to tend to," said Grumley. "This year, I was only going to join 'em for the opening weekend. Besides, short trip this year. These days, everybody's so damn busy."

Grumley tried to keep plausibility within bounds, and be wary of trip-wires. But he couldn't wait too long to answer. He'd already established a rhythm. He tried to remember what he was saying.

"Didn't see no small brown humanoid traipsing around?"

"Uh, no."

"But you got no way of proving where you were?"

"Uh, no."

"See any others up and around there? Anything strange? Hear anything?"

"Nothing that comes to mind," said Grumley.

"Well, this visit has been good for high-quality caffeine and bad for solid information," said Sandstrom.

"I'm sorry we can't help," said Trudy.

Sandstrom stood up. Grumley followed him to the door and then outside.

"If things settle down and you need some thrills . . . ?" said Grumley, trailing off.

"Thanks," said Sandstrom. "The elusive big kahuna will have to wait another year, fatten up for Sheriff Ahab. You always have a way of finding the big ones."

"Not likely if it snows like this all winter," said Grumley. "No forage."

Sandstrom plopped himself behind the wheel and snapped the ignition. "I know he's out there," he said. The car purred with a low, pleasing warmth. "And I know who to call. What's your slogan? Best Dag-Gum Guides In The Valley?"

"Very amusing," said Grumley with a smile, hesitating, not knowing whether to push his luck. Had he already slipped? Had Sandstrom already spotted something he'd said? Was something out of whack? Had anybody noticed that Rocky Carnivitas hadn't been around?

"Maybe one of your people actually saw or heard something. Do me a favor and ask around. Oh," Sandstrom slapped the steering wheel. "almost forgot. I'll need a list of where to reach all your hunting buddies. Could you give me that? Addresses and phones too? Have it called-in or dropped off down in Glenwood Springs, say, by afternoon?"

"Sure," said Grumley. "So, say, uh . . . this must really be something. All the media, all the questions."

"There's more cameras here than at Kodak HQ," said Sandstrom. "But I'm telling 'em who has got the fuckin' information and when they're going to receive their daily dose."

"Anything else going on?" Grumley asked, trying to appear casually curious.

Sandstrom gave him a funny look. "Jesus, ain't this enough?"

"Course it is. I just making conver—"

"You seem a little worried about something."

"Not me," said Grumley. "Just wondering. One of my guys said he heard somebody who said he saw something way the hell up there. Didn't know if it was related, or might have been."

"Oh, the little guide that could. A little screwy in her mind, I think, with her directions. Women. Maps. You know. She heard a shot, she thinks. Hey, you go to see a waterfall, there's going to be a splashing noise. It's hunting season. Well, you get my point. She didn't have much worth taking to the bank."

"Who was it? Anybody I'd know?" Grumley tried for a casual tone.

"Now that seems like confidential police information."

Grumley stared.

"Allison Something. Kind of a small gal."

Popeye had been right.

"Yeah," said Grumley. "Seen her around. Where was she?"

"When?"

"When she saw what she saw."

"Coming off Black Squirrel Pass."

"Gee, Jerry, sounds like you know your mountain terrain."

"Fat chance," said Sandstrom. "Onward and sideways."

Sandstrom backed out as Grumley stood there, trying hard to look indifferent.

* * * *

It was a glorified motel with a few hotel-like amenities such as room service. Nice enough. The lodge sat off the interstate in downtown Glenwood Springs. From his motel room, where FATE had set up a "PR camp" to exploit the media frenzy over Ray Stern's dramatic exit from Planet Earth and milk the story of one odd hunter's miraculous conversion, Dean Applegate could see the ever-wafting steam billow up from the city's public steam bath, a block away. Day or night, it didn't matter. The steam was endless. He badly wanted a dip to soak off the last days of worry and fatigue. It bugged him that the camera crews, reporters, and even Ellenberg once, he noticed, sported a bitter, slightly sulfuric perfume that had become telltale proof of a thorough soak.

Applegate had become used to the cameras and the lights and waiting for crews to set up. He even knew how to loop the microphone cord behind his shirt buttons so it didn't show. The repetitious questions were getting old, so he had started to embellish his tales a bit, as a means of entertainment. Maybe in his old hunting days he hadn't felled the most stunning elk, but he could say he had helped his buddies stalk them.

Maybe he hadn't filled his freezer with venison every season, but he could talk about the thrill of the hunt and what he used to believe was an energizing, manly, and fair sport. His description of the conversion never wavered, how the realization of Ray Stern's protest stopped him in his tracks. But his hunting yarns were sometimes spun with a tougher or more interesting weave.

The camera crews were legion. All the news stories. The morning shows. The magazine shows. The networks and the independents: how could anybody really tell the difference? Same questions, same faces, same line of thinking. Between interviews, the phone rang, and he listened to various agents from New York and Los Angeles wanting the right to pitch a movie deal based on his story. One working title was *I Will Kill No More*. They whispered great sums that made sleep a dicey prospect. He thought about a debt-free existence and Caribbean vacations.

Even Ellenberg's close scrutiny showed respect. She was not nearly as cool or militant off stage, it turned out. He had even seen her drink a few glasses of Chardonnay and get rather giggly. Applegate had fantasies about the ex-hunter making an item with the Queen of Animals. Ellenberg was cool. Her laugh was throaty and full. She tucked her long chestnut hair up and over her ear like a high school kid who realized, for the first time, that boys watched every move girls made. She had skinny hips and a somewhat hippie-dippy look. He wanted to buy her champagne and tickle her toes, just to hear her laugh. This was something he had never done for any woman.

More than anything, Applegate felt a new, warm cocoon of family. There was almost a religious bond inside the group, a touch of zeal mixed with a few common beliefs about how the world should work. He would not let them down. Suddenly Grumley and the others seemed out of touch. Hunting was uncivilized, unnecessary, and cruel. What was the point? How could mankind consider itself decent and refined when it spent so much energy and showed so much interest in slaughtering lesser beasts? The hunting culture could claim they were following centuries' worth of instinct. Individual hunters could say they did it for the meat. And the state-sponsored so-called experts could say hunting was vital to managing the wildlife populations. But it all came down to a rifle and an innocent animal being shot and killed to tease and excite a man's base instincts.

Applegate watched the surging steam and yearned for a dip. He was exhausted. He poured off three fingers of bourbon in a plastic cup from the bathroom and fetched some ice from the machine near the lobby. He sat on his bed, sipping away as he watched the late news on CNN, and thought about his stupid, but brilliant, mistake.

His last.

* * * *

"What's in the woods?"

"A chance to get naked," said Coil.

"I don't like getting naked when it's below a temperature that can freeze certain tips of one's anatomy."

"I love it when you're reasonable," said Coil, climbing out and making a point of showing him she had the keys. "Freeze here or come with me," she said.

Coil led the way, using a flashlight to follow the tracks of others through the crusty snow. The night was noiseless, as if the temperature could convince the wind to lay low. They trudged a couple of hundred yards down through a densely wooded slope to a small clearing that opened to a canopy of stars. Coil slipped a five-dollar bill through a slot cut in a metal box that had been nailed to a tree. The money paid for upkeep and the ever-present pile of wood, dried and split. A fire burned casually, kicking a soft glow across the hot springs. A soft giggle bounced across the water, high and clear. Two heads bobbed in the center of the pool.

"Come on," said Coil, peeling off her parka and hanging it on a branch. She took the wine bottle from Slater and nestled it in some rocks next to the pool, untied her shoes and pulled down her jeans.

"In two minutes you'll be so warm and relaxed you'll never want to leave," she said.

"Strangers," said Slater.

"Come on, Mr. Boy Scout. You've seen one weenie, you've seen them all. Besides, those two could care less about *you*."

"Oh, thanks," said Slater.

"And if you'd noticed," she whispered, "it's two women and they're not hugging because it's been a while since they've seen each other."

Slater took a tentative look over Coil's shoulder.

"Don't stare," she said.

"You are quite observant," said Slater.

"Thanks. Now, let's go."

Coil was down to her underwear. She peeled them off and stuffed all her clothes in a plastic bag. "If you leave them out to the elements, the steam from the pool gets them soaked and then they freeze. Put yours on top of mine before you get in. That is, if you decide to join me."

Coil waded in, ignoring the hot shock on her toes. The bottom was rocky. Finally, at hip level, she pushed off the bottom and floated off. Slater was down to his American flag boxer shorts and then slipped those off. She admired the view of his taut, slightly hairy stomach and the fire's golden glow on his skin.

She found the bottle in the rocks and they drifted to a corner of the pool.

"So in their minds there is only one case?" asked Coil. Slater had been permitted inside a day-ending inter-governmental briefing, closed to the press.

"Sandstrom's got a laser beam on Ray Stern. He's got a large army of crackerjack specialists buzzing in a swarm, looking for something, but they've got zip-oh. They need a break, somebody with a morsel of useful information." The autopsy, Slater explained, left few clues. The bullet had come to rest against the victim's spine, the seventh vertebrae. The dense material of the deer suit had slowed the missile down, but it couldn't have been a rifle that was overwhelmingly powerful. There were traces of THC in Stern's system, enough that he had probably smoked dope in the 24 hours prior to his death. Two other marijuana cigarettes had been found in his tent. The doctor who performed the autopsy reported, accurately, that leukemia patients often were prescribed marijuana for its therapeutic and pain-relief benefits. Sandstrom told the press that Stern's brother confirmed he was one of 18 patients in the state who had been permitted medicinal use of dope and had joined a class-action lawsuit against the FDA, which was trying to declassify marijuana as a beneficial drug.

"So Stern got high," said Coil. "Doesn't change what he did."

"Enough people will think it means he wasn't in control of his actions," said Slater. "Taints it a bit, diminishes the impact of, say, a totally sober decision. But I haven't told you the best part."

Slater pulled himself up off the water and sat on a rock for a second, his body steaming, his concern for being naked beginning to fade.

"Okay, the best part," said Coil.

"Stern's lunch," said Slater. "He had a Tupperware container with him—but it was empty. Remnants indicate it was cheese and crackers, probably cheddar and some kind of salty thing, most likely Ritz."

"So he ate it."

"No. That's the point. He didn't. He had an empty stomach."

"How do they know it wasn't an old, empty Tupperware?"

"The cheese crumbs."

"Cheese *crumbs?*"

"You know, cheese bits. They were fresh."

"So whoever shot him ate his lunch?"

"It was no bear or raccoon resealing a snug-fit plastic lip."

"Yuck," said Coil. "Ooo, so you're looking for a stupid, really bad hunter who might steal your lunch, too. Any fingerprints on the plastic?"

"No. He probably kept his gloves on. Stern's water bottle was emptied, too. The guy needed food and water."

Slater sipped some wine and passed the bottle over.

"So, is Sandstrom going to see this through? I mean, does he know enough, care enough, to get it done?"

"He'll need some luck."

"Until you get lucky, you gotta plug away. That's what my dad used to say. An accountant's mind at work, mind you. So, where is the Sheriff's Department going to be plugging?"

"I don't think they publicly reveal all aspects of an investigation. Especially to key witnesses."

"To you—or to the feds?"

"Like two snarling cats. Teamwork is unheard of. My boss, Bridgers, isn't even told when and where the task force meets. It's pathetic."

"So you don't even know the strategy?"

"Do what I'm told, which isn't much now that every hunter in the state has been quizzed."

"What if I heard the shot that killed Ray Stern—way up higher, but I heard it. Reports said Stern wasn't too big. Maybe he got shot and then the killer needed to move him. Dragged him for a ways, got tired, plunked him in the middle of nowhere, but off the trail."

"Long ways from where you were. And how's that fit with your elk?"

"I wanted to know why nobody thinks these things are related, that's all."

"Long way to carry anybody. Think how weird you'd feel moving a corpse around."

In the drink of Long Island Sound, she had bopped around with a few others who hadn't been so lucky. Slater was right.

"One question, okay?"

"Shoot."

"Do you believe me?"

"What's to believe?"

"I was wondering if, more or less, you thought I saw what I saw. And heard."

"Of course," said Slater.

The two women were climbing out. Steam flew from their skin. The vapors were quickly zapped by the cold night. Slater slipped back into the water, and Coil watched Slater as he watched them.

She eased her hand down Slater's chest, over his stomach, and let her hand linger where the hair on his belly floated mindlessly and soft. She found him limp.

He reached over with his free hand to stroke her breast.

"Relax," she said.

He was harder now, or nearly there. He passed the bottle and she took a second to take a long drink. Slater moaned softly and closed his eyes. She cradled him in her hand and he stroked her cheek with his palm. Her fist kept splashing in the water where his hips broke the surface, yielding a sound like a frustrated fish working its way upstream. He counted down "three . . . two . . . one . . ." and his whole body quaked. He sunk back into the water and let out a long sigh. He shuddered and rolled to his side. Coil took the bottle before it spilled over and took a sip, letting the wine tingle on her tongue.

Slater was right. It was hard to logically connect the death of Ray Stern with what she'd seen and heard. But that was logic and logic, she knew, didn't always hang together. She could not stop thinking about the man and his awkward, nearly angry, work—dragging something like he was taking out the trash and none too happy about the chore.

6

"Who else is left?"

"It's a freelancer. Some guy says he needs to stay in his room at The Hotel Colorado. He's working on a book or something, parts are gonna run in *Rolling Stone*. His theme is the dilapidated state of the American protest movement. Says he wants to use our organization as a success story and he wants to talk with you."

Applegate sighed. He felt spent. A candle-size glow of self-esteem continued to burn steadily deep in his guts, however, and it wouldn't hurt to feed the flame.

"No problem," he said.

Ellenberg hitched a leg up on his bed. He was relaxing with a Bloody Mary in one hand and the television remote control in the other. *Wheel Of Fortune* seemed pleasantly numb right now.

"We'll go over later and jump in the hot springs. The manager called over. Turns out he's one of us. Said he saw you on CNN this afternoon and wanted to offer us a few minutes of peace and quiet."

They had commandeered a section of the hot springs' pool deck that afternoon for a live-via-satellite debate with the editor of a prominent elk journal, *Bugle*. Applegate had taken the editor on with all the emotion and passion he could muster. The words came quickly and easily. He was polite. He listened and didn't step on the other guy. He waited his turn and then objected—strongly. He challenged every claim and talked in warm and clear tones about the senseless destruction of natural beauty. With fervor, he made up a story about having seen a hunter drop an extra elk, for the pure joy of it, while packing out the carcass of another. The second elk was left to rot, its antlers cut off and hidden in a spot where the hunter would return later and retrieve them.

He focused on the issues and he remained composed. That was one of the tips from Ellenberg; to appear reserved and relaxed. Ellenberg said it was important to *"out-friendly"* the hunters.

"You were great today, Dean," said Ellenberg, casually putting a hand on his leg.

"When does the freelancer need me?"

"Twenty minutes or so. Stop by my room when you're done, and we'll see about dinner and the soak."

The prospect of the date alone sent Applegate out the door of The Roaring Fork Inn with an extra lift in his step. The hotel was a few blocks away. In the fading light of day, a steady flow of cars plodded along, most headed up the interstate from Aspen and Carbondale. A day of strong sunshine had turned the streets and sidewalks into sandy, sloppy muck. He passed a gas station where cars waited for the pump. He passed BJ's Velvet Freez, which shared space with a one-hour photo shop, and a spiffy new café that advertised espresso drinks. An Amtrak train was coming to a stop in the station, which sat across the Colorado River.

He had a flash that the pick-up truck at the end of the block looked a lot like George's. He was about to quickly cut across the street and duck out of sight, when the voice came up behind him, so distinctive and clear. The voice said the door was open and to go ahead and climb inside.

"Hey, whatcha doing? How's it going?" he asked, trying to sound casual as he climbed in.

Grumley started driving, pulling a U-turn. He honked his way across the lane of oncoming traffic, then made a nuisance of himself to edge ahead, going the other way.

"George, I—"

"Shut up."

"I've gotta be there for an interview, back in the hotel."

"With *Rolling Stone* . . ."

"Yeah—how did you . . .?"

The truck screamed west on the interstate less than a mile, pulled off at the only other Glenwood Springs exit, and Grumley turned up behind a convenience store in a muddy lot that was empty and dark. Applegate flipped the door open and stumbled from the truck, considering which way to run.

Grumley climbed down too and came around the front of the truck, slowly. Grumley's fist landed deep into Applegate's jaw, and Applegate spun helplessly to the ground. He came to rest with his shoulder in a pool of brown water, and sharp pebbles embedded in his cheek. Applegate's jaw burned. Surely he had lost a tooth or two.

"You're interviewing days are fucking *over*," said Grumley. "I save your miserable butt up there in a blizzard, help you figure out how to clear things up, and your thanks is to go saddle up with the animal huggers."

"You don't know how I felt shooting that guy," said Applegate, noticing Grumley's foul breath.

"Shit," said Grumley.

"Nobody knows; nobody will ever know," said Applegate. Was Grumley going to hit him again?

"Christ," said Grumley. "Cops all over the fuckin' place. You don't really know who saw what or what they can figure out."

"They'll get nothing outta me."

"The good fuckin' idea was to lay low, and instead you plaster your face on every TV screen from here to Timbuktu."

Applegate touched a spot on his left jaw where the pain was sharp. Maybe the physical punishment was over.

"We got a guide said she saw you."

"Huh?" mumbled Applegate. The statement did not connect. The idea had never even so much as bothered him, the idea of a witness. "No way."

"Bullshit. You think you could see everything?"

"What'd he see?" asked Applegate.

"She."

"*She?*"

"The guide. A she," said Grumley.

"What the hell is she saying?"

"Beats the shit out of me. She's talking to the cops. Sheriff was out at my house asking all sorts of nosy-ass questions. Sheriff's got something, count on it. But you've made it a lot harder for yourself to slip around unnoticed and find the fuck out what it is. What a joke," Grumley said with a scowl. "Mister tough guy hunter one week, mister softie the next."

"The cops haven't even touched me, come to me. They can't. I didn't see nothing," said Applegate. "Nothing."

"And when they ask to see your gun?"

"They won't."

"They might."

"And your alibi?"

"There's lots of hunters out by themselves."

"And what if she got a good look at you, your equipment. Something. Anything. You got your hands full and you're out there with your face all over TV."

"What can we do?"

"You serious?"

"What?"

"*We*. You can't do anything except disappear."

"How?"

"Tell them you need a break. Get back in the truck."

Applegate studied the open door, pondered his options, and stood there.

"Back in the fuckin' truck," said Grumley, grabbing him by the arm, practically winging him inside.

"My stuff, my friends."

"*Fuck* your fucking friends," Grumley screamed, bouncing the truck crazily through the potholes in the parking lot, then flooring it as they hit the ramp to the interstate. Grumley didn't say anything, and Applegate didn't know how or when to start. It was one short run to the other Glenwood exit and there was no time to think.

Grumley headed the truck up on the overpass above the interstate and then turned to the left, cutting in front of a lumbering dump truck and then fast up a busy side street toward the train station, where a silver Amtrak idled.

Grumley reached in his coat and pulled out a ticket.

"Go," he said.

"My things, my stuff."

"Have your animal friends pack it up for you and send it down."

"You want me to lay low, okay. But I ain't going to Denver now."

He was thinking of his promised soak with Ellenberg.

"You're getting on the train. You're staying on the train," said Grumley. "You're getting off in Denver. You're going home. You're going back to tinkering with computers or whatever it is the fuck you do. You're gonna dig yourself a hole in the fuckin' back yard and stick your head down in there for about a year and mind your own fuckin' business. You don't get on the train here, now, maybe your rifle gets dropped off at the sheriff's by one of my guides who happened to fuckin' find it about 200 yards from where poor Mr. Stern was dropped. It'd make things a lot simpler for all of us. I'm already in it, helping you cover all this up. We can get this over with real quick, and I'll risk taking my bumps. I know where to find the sheriff. Now there'd be some good pee-*are* for you and your nut case friends. Go."

Applegate studied the ticket being propped in front of his face and took it. He got out and headed onto the platform, pissed off and unsteady. What the hell was happening? How could Grumley do anything? He showed his ticket to a man in a train uniform, one of the last people hanging around outside, who said his car would be three cars up but he better climb on now. The train started moving. Applegate hopped on and headed up the stairs inside to the second level. He walked through three cars of private sleepers and sank down in a row of empty seats in the car with the general masses.

"Hey," said a young cowboy who looked, with his tough-boy jaw and his red bandanna, like a rodeo escapee. "Don't I know you from somewhere?"

Applegate sprang out of his seat and told the kid to save it, he'd be right back. The next car up had a snack bar, and Applegate ordered a bottle of Budweiser. The stoic bartender poured it into a plastic cup. Applegate found a seat that swiveled so he could face away from all the others and look out, into the dark. The interior lights on the train created a reflection on the window, and all he could see were car and truck headlights moving along the highway on the opposite side of the canyon.

The train found a steady clip as it climbed. Applegate chugged the beer, then got up and found the stairs below to another passenger compartment. The travelers were settling in, trying to get comfortable for a snooze. He opened the sliding door between cars and stood on the swiveling, steel platform. The floor bounced and wiggled, and the windows were up and snug. Looking down into the lower level on the next car, a sleeper, he could see a couple uncorking a bottle of wine inside their cubbyhole. A family was unpacking blankets, snuggling in. A cool breeze was coming from somewhere. The canyon widened. A conductor passed through and asked to see his ticket.

"I'm up in general admission," said Applegate. "Taking a tour."

"No problem, but keep touring," he said.

The train slowed. Applegate prayed it down to a complete stop. There was no way he could just leave. He rolled the window down and peered out. It was a long drop, but he hitched a leg over, then two, and lowered himself until he was hanging from the window ledge by his fingers. He let go before he started to think too much. The landing was rough, with rocks and wood ties. He rolled over his shoulder at an odd angle, trying to absorb the impact. A sharp horn blast brought him to his feet, and he scurried back to where he had dropped as light flooded the empty set of tracks. Another train was coming from the opposite direction.

Applegate counted four engines and then boxcar after boxcar headed toward Glenwood Springs. He froze, worried about tripping. The pace of the click-clack sounds slowed, ever so slightly at first, then with purpose, and the freight came to a stop.

He jogged toward the rear of the freight, looking for an open door, stepping as gently as he could because it was impossible to see the footing. The night air whipped through the canyon. His light jacket was not offering much protection. His jaw throbbed, his fingers stiffened. The boxcars were all sealed tight. He was approaching the front of the Amtrak train and already wished he had headed the other way. He crouched lower and wondered if any of the crew might have climbed down while they waited. The next two cars on the freight were loaded with pick-up trucks, factory fresh. Applegate found a grip on the platform, above his head, and had to jump to hoist himself up. The jump seemed to force the freight forward. It lurched and Applegate could hear the rippling b-b-b-BANG! as the slack came out of the couplers down the line. He rolled over and stood up.

He could see the people back inside the brightly lit Amtrak, a few yards away, cozy and comfortable. They all started to move. No. It was the freight—or was it? The back end of the Amtrak disappeared and, in the glow of its red taillights, he could see that they were stopped. He couldn't think of one good reason why they would lock the doors on the new trucks. Sure enough, they hadn't. He slipped in behind the wheel, tilted the seat back, and hoped the damn thing had reason to stop right around Glenwood Springs.

* * * *

The voice on the other end of the phone was tentative, small.

"Allison Coil?"

"Yes."

"I know this may sound crazy. There's only a few other people I know to call."

Coil stood in the middle of Pete Weaver's barn, using the phone in the saddle shop. She had been out in the corral, brushing down a mule, when she'd been called.

"My name is Trudy Grumley."

"George's wife?"

"Forgive me for interrupting. This won't take a minute. I've already talked to most of the guides who work for my husband. And they haven't been able to help. Well, help much. So I thought I'd check with a few others."

The woman was so hesitant, so word-by-word careful that Allison instantly wanted to somehow reassure her.

"I know this sounds—"

"Please," said Coil. "How can I help?"

"I was wondering if you might have seen a friend of mine?"

The word *friend* was surrounded on both sides by a moment of silence.

"Who?"

The pause was agonizing. Coil thought she heard the woman swallow and briefly thought they'd been disconnected.

"It's so hard to know who knows who," said Trudy.

The world around Coil seemed to have come to a halt. The voice, in its utter meekness, commanded her total attention.

"You want to know if I've seen somebody?"

Another pause.

"I know it shouldn't be that big a deal. It seemed all right to ask the others who work with my husband. Now, I feel like . . ."

Coil felt like talking, to the fill the space in time. "Where are you calling from?"

Waiting for an answer, Coil was worried she had insulted her.

"From home."

If she remembered correctly, Grumley had tucked his home up at the end of a long driveway near the mouth of the canyon, closer down by the Colorado River. Weaver had pointed out the driveway, but she had never been up. She was having a hard time getting a mental fix on Trudy; it didn't match with George's gruff, all-man exterior.

"Who's missing?"

"*Missing* isn't for sure."

"Overdue."

"I don't know if you know him, even. Rocky."

"Rocky Carnivitas?"

"Yes."

"Sure. Everyone knows him."

Trudy was waiting, now, for the answer.

"No, I haven't seen him."

Coil had nearly finished her work for the day. There was a saddle repair that could wait; minor surgery. And Slater was off on one of his backcountry treks. It could be a day or three, depending on what he encountered or how long he felt like being gone. She was never sure how he decided to stay out or return home.

"Oh well," said Trudy. "Thanks, I'm sorry—"

"I did see something, but . . ."

"I know."

"How?"

Coil suddenly wasn't sure if this was good or bad—the whole call.

"The blotter. You must have filled out a police report."

She had, as much an exercise in accuracy as anything, and because Sandstrom had insisted on some record.

"The paper picked it up, ran a few paragraphs, probably straight out of your report, stuck in their weekly police blotter." The voice had gained a bit of courage. "That's one reason I called you. Rocky isn't usually so, you know, late. And I was wondering if they even figured out what it was that you saw."

"No, they haven't. How long is he overdue?"

"A few days. He wasn't exactly due back, you know, at any set time."

Now it was Coil's turn to build in a pause.

"Is your husband worried?"

Rocky, after all, was George's worker. He was a legendary guide, skilled hunter, and notorious loner.

She remembered Rocky on the trail the first time. She was heading up on a sort of training mission with her boss, Pete Weaver, and a crew from Minnesota that oozed "golly gee" all about them. They were true young bucks on their first hunt. Weaver had them wide-eyed. Rocky was heading down on his own with supplies and a three or four-horse string.

Weaver stopped. He and Rocky chatted, and Weaver introduced her from 30 or 40 yards away, bringing up the rear. But then Weaver signaled her to climb down and come up to see how not to pack a saddlebag. Rocky sat smiling as Weaver, known throughout the valley as an overly fastidious know-it-all, unpacked one of the bags on Rocky's string and showed her how the weight was all wrong: bad knots on the manty rope; no quick-release knots on the basket hitches that connected the string; slipping D-rings. The loads weren't balanced. A case of Mountain Dew here, boxes with canned food there; a bow case thrown here, a duffel bag tossed there. The trail was littered with stuff. Weaver was busy showing her what he meant about the science of a well-packed horse. Rocky was watching, amused.

Coil thought, then and there, that Weaver's outfit had been a bad choice all around. Rocky worked for Grumley's Double X Ranch and she should have held out for a slot, even though they said they were all full up. Weaver had taken her "on spec." Too many city folks, he'd said, had come up on a whim and couldn't stick it out through all the barn duties, wrangler business, and odd guide jobs. But Weaver's treatment of Rocky at the time—it wasn't until later that she saw beyond Weaver's cool exterior—had sent her sympathies to this hapless kid and his badly packed train.

Rocky eventually got re-started and the next time she met him was in a bar over in Eagle. Off his horse, Rocky was smaller than she'd remembered. He had deep-set brown eyes surrounded by a weathered face that had the ability to flash an off-center but slight grin. There was just a bare glimpse of mangled teeth. They finally got around to a dance by the jukebox, and Coil tried to come up with one really solid reason why she should not encourage him.

When she moved to the mountains, she had promised herself to not be so picky. But she found it puzzling how the personal electricity turned cool, like a switch, after hours of talk and several rounds of bourbon and beer. She felt sobered-up and disinterested. She always felt as if she was peering around the next corner, trying to look into the next room in her life, and all she saw was his likely hairy back and no emotional connection. It was easier to change your handwriting than your attitudes.

Rocky pressed himself on her as they stood by the hood of her second-hand Blazer, and she let him grope for a minute and gave him a good kiss or three and then wriggled out, said something about another date sometime, and left him in the dirt parking lot with a bulge in his pants and nothing but hope on the brain.

"If he's worried, I wouldn't know," said Trudy. "I've probably taken up enough of your—"

"Could I stop by?"

"I suppose."

"Is anybody looking for him?" Coil asked.

"Not that I can tell, no."

"Where does he live?"

"Well," said Trudy. "That is one thing I need help with. And, if you won't mention it, I happen to have a key. Can you stop by and pick it up?"

* * * *

Trudy hung up, shaking.

She hadn't been able to say good-bye and then realized she had expected Allison Coil to know where she lived, or to find out. They hadn't discussed directions. Perhaps everyone in the whole valley knew. Maybe this was all stupid, unnecessary. Maybe she had gone too far, stirring up questions. Maybe Rocky would slide through the door any second, but Trudy knew better.

Trudy busied herself by straightening the always-neat house. She plucked a few not-quite-yellow leaves, fed the cats, topped off their water trough, and paced in the darkened living room. She badly wanted to hop in her car and go find him, to show the world she knew what she was doing and that she could handle it—or handle anything. But being out and about, by herself, was a scary prospect. What if she had a seizure? How could she explain it if she wound up stuck where she wasn't supposed to be? Then she had remembered the key to Rocky's trailer. He had given it to her "in case" she ever needed a quick hiding place that was not too far, halfway back up the canyon. She dug it out of her dresser drawer and clutched it in her hand.

The trees down the road caught a glow and a pair of headlights worked their way up the drive. Trudy stepped back to the kitchen, so there would be appropriate waiting time after the doorbell sounded. She stood with her arms folded, telling herself to make the visit quick. It was possible George could return, really screwing things up.

* * * *

"Trudy?" The door opened a crack. "Allison Coil."

"Come on in," she said, stepping away. "Thanks for doing this."

"Really, not a problem."

Trudy Grumley had extraordinarily long hair, thick and flowing. She was trim and pleasant looking, earthy. Coil noted her tentative movements and hesitant way of moving around her own home. She and Trudy were identical in height, neither of them very tall, but Trudy carried more femininity. She was rounder, more voluptuous, and soft-featured.

"I probably sounded like a weirdo—on the phone."

"Hardly, please."

Trudy led her into an over-sized living room as a swarm of cats came to check out the visitor. For a second it seemed this would be where they would sit and chat, but the cats led the way, or so it seemed. She followed them and Trudy to the kitchen and, then, off back, into the greenhouse. A small round table and two chairs waited for them.

"I'm more comfortable here," said Trudy, but didn't sit down. "Tea?"

"Sure."

"I think we can spare a few minutes. I really—forgive me—don't want George to see I've got a visitor. He's a little funny like that."

"He and I have met. I applied at his ranch, ended up with Weaver."

Coil had wondered if they might have a glass of wine, or something stronger. A drink was routine after a day around the barn, but not, she told herself, required. Nothing about Trudy, although she appeared calm, suggested this would be a time to linger.

Trudy already had hot water on and poured it into two cups, then returned with them to let the tea steep. Coil smelled orange and herbs.

"So you read the police blotter? A regular thing?"

"Sometimes. It's a glimpse at the state of mischief."

Breathing the humid air reminded Coil of the hotel spas in the $175-per-night hotels from her old traveling days. Trudy's in-person graciousness stood in stark contrast to the disjointed telephone conversation and her demeanor quickly swamped out any sense of caution. Trudy looked, in a word, so tame. She was a picture of the word meek, with long, slow blinks of her eyes and too-easy smile. She was a true flower child, frozen in time.

"Nobody has seen Rocky's place?" On the way over, Coil had thought of a few questions, in case Trudy's caution persisted.

"Not that I know of," said Trudy. "I don't get out."

Coil listened, with increasing respect, as Trudy described her personal health and general situation. Trudy looked into the steaming tea more than anywhere else, but she spoke now with clarity and purpose.

"And George hasn't gone to look?" Coil asked when she was done.

"We're husband and wife, I suppose," said Trudy, "but not that close. Anymore. Rocky was one of several who came around to help me out with groceries, errands, whatever. Fix this, carry that. But George doesn't know that we're good friends, and I don't want him to. George has his secrets, believe me. This one's mine."

Given everything else, she certainly seemed justified.

"Where does he live?"

"In a trailer, he told me, about half way back up the canyon. You'd never see it from the road unless you were looking, but it's right there before the road forks. I'm going on memory, having seen it only from the road. I've never been there."

"I'll ask around."

"It shouldn't be too hard to find, I wouldn't think."

"You haven't even asked your husband?"

Trudy took a breath and sighed slowly.

"I can understand why it would seem a bit awkward—to help."

"No, look, I'll stop asking questions. I do want to help. Rocky—we were friends for a while, although I haven't seen him around much. We went out a couple of times. I liked him; he's a helluva hunter. You know, he could be absolutely anywhere."

"Sure."

"But you have reason to believe—"

"He hasn't stayed gone for so long. And, well . . ."

Another one of those telephone pauses.

"George's airplane."

"What about it?"

Word in the valley was George would fly certain clients up over the Flat Tops to Meeker, give 'em an aerial buzz of some of the herds, whet their appetite.

"I have a friend at the airport, the Eagle-Vail airport, in general aviation. He calls whenever George lands back here. It's a favor. It puts me on alert that he's in the area. It seems to change my whole view of the world, even my rate of seizures, so it's helpful to know. Anyway, I called today. Sometimes Rocky would go with him, on a long hunt. But George's plane hasn't budged in weeks."

"Another plane?"

"Why? And Rocky would have told me he was going off for days and days. He would have, believe me."

"I do."

Of all the things she could trust in the last few days, this was without question. The earnest expression, and the gentle heart that went with it, left little doubt.

"Do you have the key?"

As Trudy stood up, the side door to the garage, off the kitchen, opened and slammed with authority. Trudy didn't so much as flinch—and handed her the key.

"George," she said under her breath, not turning around. "No mention of this."

"None," said Coil back, taking the key.

As George stood there in the kitchen, a dumbstruck look on his face, Trudy turned and offered a smile.

"Hello," she said, as if the world had suddenly started to spin on an endlessly cheery axis, "we have company."

* * * *

Coil drove home up the dark canyon, knowing she would wait for morning. What did one more night mean or matter? She wasn't about to return to Trudy's, or even call, as long as George hovered around. George had been spooked, no question. Coil had said hello and then good-bye—"Just leaving."

Coil drove slowly down the stretch where she figured Trudy had indicated Rocky lived and she found an opening in the thicket. Her headlights, poking in a bit, found a silvery trailer, dead and dark. It could wait until morning, until she had daylight for bearings and nerve.

She slept fitfully in her A-Frame, painfully aware of Trudy's predicament, too clear that it might bear no connection to anything. There was no sign of Slater. She might have to go into Rocky's place alone, without a semi-official wing of authority to protect her, to tell her it was all right. Open the door, see Rocky wasn't there, tell Trudy. Open the door, find him drunk, tell Trudy. Open the door, find him dead, tell Trudy. Open the door, find something, tell Trudy. Why did this seem so daunting? It wasn't as if she was breaking in. It was a passed-along key, surely a sign of trust.

In the morning, feeling a bit woozy, she awoke thinking she'd steal a half-hour from her personal routines and a half-hour from her boss before showing for work. She was, by far, the most punctual guide in the bunch. Old city habits. Coil drove down to Rocky's trailer in a bit of a mental fog, letting her promise to Trudy pull her along. At the entrance, she noticed that one other set of car or truck tracks headed into the clearing, but the tracks looked old and windblown.

She parked next to the trailer, where the previous vehicle had stopped, and climbed out. The feeling of quiet and cold was pervasive. A layer of snow clung to the trailer's roof. Certainly, with somebody here and the heat running, it would have melted.

Coil knocked. And waited. Hoping nobody was watching, she slipped in the key, gave the door a push, and called out, "Rocky?" The key wasn't necessary; the door opened before the lock turned.

The trailer was empty, or at least lifeless.

She checked to make sure. It was empty. There were no notes, messages, or signs of struggle.

She checked a few pictures up on the cupboards: Rocky with some of his kills, all decent-sized animals. Coil stepped to Rocky's kitchen table, picked up a three-year-old biker magazine and flipped through it, wondering about the world of a lonesome, 35-ish guide in the mountains, and about his personal hopes and dreams. Was he working for anything, toward anything?

The catalog underneath the magazine was cheap and crudely made. At first, it didn't even register—the cover photo of a man kneeling in a field, holding up a palm-size gizmo a little bigger than a cell phone. It wasn't really even a catalog, but more of a brochure.

Unprecedented accuracy, said the caption under an inside photo of two men hunched over a mountain lion, attaching a radio collar. *AUDI-TRACK. Features: auxiliary sensor data, long term data storage in animal unit, operates under canopy.* Coil flipped the page over, and a clear picture stared at her. It was the identical GPS gear she had found next to the bulletless elk. *Download by radio. Built in VHF Transmitter. Spreadsheet to determine battery life. Adjustable neck. Durable.* On and on.

Coil stuffed the brochure, addressed to Rocky Carnivitas at some P.O. box in Glenwood Springs, in her back pocket.

She explored the trailer a bit more purposefully, meticulously, and found a matching GPS collar in a closet off the bedroom.

This one sat next to an unplugged battery charger.

Rocky the wildlife biologist? Coil had a simple answer for her own rhetorical question: *I don't think so.*

* * * *

Coil called Trudy from Weaver's barn and had a quick conversation with her to convey that Rocky's trailer was empty, and that she would keep looking. Trudy thanked her profusely and didn't even ask if Coil could return the key.

Throughout a day of packing up a new hunting party and delivering another group's kill to a nearby taxidermist, Coil ran through the odds of Rocky not being involved, somehow, with the dead elk. The answer was obvious.

After the taxidermist, she drove up to Grumley's barn and sat in her Blazer next to the corral for a minute, to let the moment settle. She had to have her questions ready—and what if there was a ready explanation about Rocky? The spot where she was parked was where she had stopped on her very first visit to the canyon, responding to a small ad in the Glenwood Springs paper: *Guides needed. Horse exp. required. Will train other skills.* Grumley had done the interviewing and, clearly, didn't trust her city looks, soft exterior, and background. She had sat in the car too long, working herself up and questioning if she could complete the long strange trip from ad exec to mountain woman, via plane crash. She hadn't interviewed well, in part, because she had left a mental door ajar where self-doubt could creep in. She couldn't let that happen again.

Remembering the packed gun rack, Coil started by knocking on the doorjamb at the office inside the barn and asked, first, for George.

"Not around," said an older, whiskered man in brown chaps, getting ready to ride. She recognized him from the talk with Sheriff Sandstrom, held underneath Weaver's barn eaves.

"I'm actually looking for Rocky," said Coil.

"Why didn't you say so?"

Coil didn't answer.

"Haven't seen him, now that you mention it. But it's not too unusual." He pronounced it *unuzle* and seemed to relish the mangled word.

"Up with the camps?"

"No doubt."

"Seen him since the big dump?"

"Can't rightly say. But—no, *probly* not. My name's Boyles. Yours?"

"Allison Coil." She noticed a walkie-talkie on his belt. "I work down at Weaver's."

"I'll ask the boss when he comes back. *Ack-shoo-lee*, we have a chalk board right over here."

Boyles led the way to a board mounted between a couple of stalls. "Says Rocky . . . well, it says nothing about Rocky. Looks like someone erased his last destination. Now sometimes, that boy will get a little deep in his cups, need a few days to come out of it. His trailer is—"

"No answer. I've been by."

"That doesn't mean—?"

"No sign of him," said Coil. "At all. Would anybody else know?"

"What?"

"If he's been around."

"Not likely. I'm here the most: chief cook and bottle washer. Believe me, he'll turn up."

She couldn't persist too long and hadn't planned to.

"Thanks," said Coil. "It's really no big deal. I know somebody who wants to talk to him."

"Whatever" said Boyles. "No doubt the storm slowed him up a bit. But in about any tough situation, I'd put my money on the old Rockster. No question."

Coil thanked him and left, wondering about the gnawing in her guts, maybe the same one Trudy felt.

* * * *

Grumley showed Boyles where to park and Boyles punched off the headlights. The moon lit a broad field, the corner of a corral jutting into it on the left, an A-Frame nestled against a stand of trees straight across. One window revealed a soft glow from inside the house.

"Coil's place," said Boyles. "City girls."

"What do you mean?"

"The old leave-one-light-on-bit. You know, when nobody's home. A city thing."

"You can tell she's not home?"

"I'd bet dollars to donuts. Do we want her home?"

"Not exactly," said Grumley.

"What are we doin'?"

It never took Boyles long to get the drift.

"Pokin' around. And, if nothing else, delivering a message."

"No time for U.S. mail?"

"Not exactly. She needs something to think about."

"One inquiring little bitch," said Boyles. "*Probly* thought I was going to get all alarmed, like she was the only one to notice Rocky ain't been around."

The sight of Trudy talking with the Allison Coil pest had been enough. But then to hear Boyles tell about her asking around, probably on Trudy's behalf: that called for a shot across the city girl's cute little bow.

They crossed the snowbound field quickly, skirting the edge by the creek bed, so they could come up behind the house through the trees.

Boyles knocked innocently. He'd make up something on the spot if she or anyone else answered. A second knock. Grumley hung back.

Still nothing.

Boyles tried the handle as Grumley came up on the porch.

"Locked," said Boyles.

"Give it a shoulder."

The door showed some give.

"Give it the old linebacker tackle."

"I played wing."

"Whatever."

Boyles took a step back and lowered his shoulder.

"Sure you want this much damage?" asked Boyles.

"Better ideas?"

"Kitchen window, south side. Sometimes they'll get a little careless."

Boyles put his heel in a cup formed by Grumley's gloved hands. The window slid up an inch or two, and he shimmied it the rest of the way. Boyles eased up and disappeared.

Grumley heard a thump, coupled with the sound of something breaking, then waited at the front door, which opened in a minute.

"Goddamn flower pot on the windowsill."

"Like we care," said Grumley. Potting soil covered the counter around the sink. "Don't worry about it."

Grumley placed Boyles at the door, to watch. "This won't take long."

First he emptied the closet, throwing everything out in a heap. Then he emptied the dresser, all five drawers, from underwear through sweaters, on the floor. Toss the bed, leave all the cupboards open. He was not quite sure what he was looking for—something he'd overlooked from where Rocky went down in the snow, something he couldn't get a grip on. Clothes and junk were tossed everywhere, leaving nothing in its original place. Then he went upstairs. But there was not much to do, only turn over the twin beds and mess things up.

"Lights on the road, slowing," said Boyles.

Grumley found himself balling sheets and blanket into a big knotted mess.

"Turning, on the driveway," said Boyles.

"Shit."

"The mess in the sink," said Boyles. "I don't think it'll stand out."

"Fuck it," said Grumley, skipping down the stairs. "Fuck it."

The headlights were snaking their way in across the field, bumping up and down.

"Come on," said Grumley. They both jumped off the porch and ducked off to the side as the headlights swept the front of the cabin.

"Christ," muttered Grumley, after they jogged across a few yards of open clearing between the A-Frame and a stand of trees.

Boyles crouched down as another light clicked on inside.

"Message delivered?" asked Boyles.

"Shit," said Grumley. "I was just getting started."

7

T he sheriff's office, one block off the main drag in Glenwood Springs, was cool and clinical. The receptionist, Officer McNabb according to her name tag, pointed Coil toward a deputy who waited a slow minute to stop reading a newspaper and then finally grabbed a clipboard. He was plump, bored, and had seen it all. Coil ran through the details of the burglary at her cabin, what she'd found, the hours she had been gone, and so on.

"Anything missing?" asked the deputy. His name tag said Gerard.

"Nothing so far. Even a stash of cash, a couple hundred dollars, was overlooked."

"Sometimes you don't realize what's missing for a while."

"I know." Coil had been hit in Denver once and had not realized for weeks that a camera was gone, along with the obvious TV and VCR.

Coil wanted to remain calm about the explanation. But the moment when she realized a stranger or strangers had been stomping around in her private place, tearing it up came back to her. It wasn't a big deal compared to a swim in the icy Long Island Sound with airplane parts and dead bodies as your companions. But it had rattled her.

"The geranium was smashed, the one by the kitchen sink. The door wasn't broken, so that's how they must have got in."

"They?" Deputy Gerard, shifting back in his chair, studied her.

"I think 'they.' There were two sets of footprints in the snow this morning that led off."

"But they didn't get anything."

Hadn't this been covered?

"I don't have much."

"No idea what they were after?"

"No. None."

How could they think she had anything?

A radio crackled somewhere. Gerard cocked his head to listen.

"Big cheese is pulling in."

Gerard stood and suddenly managed a more formal air.

"Anything new on Ray Stern?" asked Coil.

"Zip. Of course, that's not official. Of course, I didn't say anything."

The front door opened and Sandstrom clomped in, trailing a couple of deputies. One was guffawing at some bad joke but when he spotted a woman in the vicinity, he squared up. Together the three created a huddle of leather jackets, olive green uniforms, guns, thick black belts, and angry boots that had lost of bit of their shine to the mushy streets.

"It's the guide," said Sandstrom. "Allison something."

"Coil," she said.

"What's new?" he asked.

"I was burgled. Your staff has a report."

"Ransacked," said Gerard. "Nothing stolen. Technically—"

"Unusual," said Sandstrom.

"There is something else. Someone missing," said Coil.

"Who?"

"A guide named Rocky Carnivitas. Works for George Grumley. Hasn't been seen since before the snowstorm. You need to know."

"Need?"

"It's part of it."

"And you're sure he's missing?"

"Nobody has seen him. He's not here, et cetera."

"And he's a what?"

"A hunting guide, you know."

"Who could be out on a long trip, correct?"

"Possible. Unlikely."

One of the deputies shifted a toothpick back and forth in his mouth, one side to the other, and offered a squinting grimace.

It was tempting to tell Sandstrom about the GPS collar and the brochure in Rocky's trailer, to add some juice to her information. But how would she explain it, or what it really meant?

"You weren't that far off, you know, from where the bloodhound found Ray Stern," said Sandstrom.

"A half-mile up hill. That's a long way."

"Not that far, really, if you *really* think about it," said Sandstrom.

"A whole different terrain; if you'd go up there, you'd see."

"You saw the guy trying to hide Stern. And it's possible with the storm you weren't exactly where you thought you were. Correct?"

"Wrong." Sandstrom's stubbornness was maddening. "I could show you the precise spot Bear was—"

"Bear?"

"My horse." One of the deputies smiled. "—was standing. It was a ways up from where they found Stern."

"A ways?" asked Sandstrom. "No chance of a mix-up? Have you thought of that?"

There was no chance, was there?

The chant started low, but clear.

"What the—?" said Sandstrom.

The chanters were stepping off a school bus, instantly moving in formation.

"Two, four, six, eight, don't forget to investigate. Three, five, seven, nine, maybe murder isn't a crime."

"What the—?" Sandstrom said again.

There were about twenty of them in a neat parade on the sidewalk. They all sported bright yellow sweatshirts with big blue letters across the front: FATE

Sandstrom's reaction to plunge outside couldn't have been more perfect from what Coil could see of Dawn Ellenberg's elated response. It was Ellenberg who wielded a mini megaphone and shouted the loudest. After one refrain of their chorus, the group was pointing its placards squarely at the gaggle of cops across the thirty yards or so of parking lot that separated them. *Ray's Killer: There's a Home On The Range; Cops Are A Hunter's Best Friend;* and *Cops And Hunters, Birds Of A Feather.* The half dozen television cameras wasted no time panning over to focus on Sandstrom and his bunch standing there idly watching the proceedings.

"Good Christ," said Sandstrom through a half smirk, stepping back inside after seeing all the cameras. "Somebody hand me my rabbit gun. This is like the arcade games in the carnival, and I'm slightly out of practice."

"Looks like we're down to the hard-core protesters," said the toothpick chomper.

Coil stood behind the knot of cops, out of view, she hoped, from the cameras.

"She has one shrill set of pipes," said Sandstrom. "I'd rather listen to twenty girls with a fresh manicure scrape their nails on a blackboard."

"Isn't that Dean Applegate?" asked Gerard. "Right behind Ellenberg."

"Who?" asked Coil.

"The hunter with a sudden case of conscience," said Gerard. "Claims Ellenberg and company made him think twice about killing animals."

Coil studied the lanky string bean behind Ellenberg. He hardly looked like prime hunter material. There was something tentative about the way he walked. And chanted.

"The reformed hunter," said Sandstrom. "I believe you're right. By the way, did anyone talk to him?" asked Sandstrom of his crew.

The deputies looked at each other and then at Sandstrom.

"You guys play mumbly peg or whatever it is you do to decide who gets the privilege," said Sandstrom. "But do it. Don't make a big scene here. Wait 'til he's back at whatever place they're staying or whatever hole he crawled out from."

"Gee, chief, don't you think this would be one you'd enjoy? Making him sweat?" asked Gerard.

Sandstrom considered the suggestion.

"I believe you're right. Now that you mention it, I believe you're right." A gleeful, boy-like look spread across his face. "Now, we could stand here all day like we've never seen a stupid parade before," said Sandstrom, "or we could go inside and get back to work. Right now, we're sort of helping Dr. Doolittle's wife prove her point. Men?"

Sandstrom back-pedaled into the station and waded around to a back office. His posse followed smartly.

Coil stood for a few minutes outside, watching the protesters from a closer vantage point. One camera crew was breaking down. The other was doing an interview with Ellenberg. Applegate had the megaphone now. The chants were starting to lose their zing. The moment was over; the protestors had sent their message.

Coil pulled up closer to listen to the interview with Ellenberg.

"...It's just clear this is not a priority for the sheriff. Painfully clear, painfully obvious—and tragic for Ray Stern."

"What exactly do you think the sheriff should be doing?"

"Well, I'm no detective," said Ellenberg. "But the first thing I'd do is find out who was in the valley that day and do an interview with every one of them, one by one. Seems pretty basic. But even Dean Applegate here, he hasn't been quizzed. It's obvious they just want to kiss it off but there's a hunter up there, somewhere, who can't tell the difference between a 145-pound man dressed in a deerskin and a legitimate—if you can even use that word—elk target. Someone pulled the trigger and it's the sheriff's job to figure out who it was."

The reporter turned to his cameraman and some invisible signal indicated they were done.

Ellenberg turned around as if she expected another reporter to be waiting.

"Hello," said Coil.

"And you're with . . .?" asked Ellenberg.

"Nobody," said Coil. "Just me."

"Here to sign up?" asked Ellenberg. "Looks like you might be another convert like our friend Mr. Applegate. Are you a hunt*ress*?"

"A what?"

"A hunter."

"No, I haven't actually ever killed an elk or a deer. You know, pulled the trigger. My name is Allison Coil and—"

"Why all the hunting attire, then?"

"I work for an outfitter, a hunting outfitter. I'm a guide. I help the hunters. I know what you think about hunters and hunting, obviously, but that's not why I wanted to ask you . . ."

"What?"

The protestors, several dozen in all, had slowly gathered around their leader. Dean Applegate had moved in close and was standing behind Ellenberg. They were more than comrades.

"I heard you were up near where they found Ray Stern's body."

"That's right," said Ellenberg.

"Excuse me."

The voice came from a man coming up behind Coil. It was Deputy Gerard.

"Dean Applegate?" the deputy inquired. "We'd like to ask you a few questions in private if you don't mind."

"Mind?" asked Ellenberg. "Now? Right now?"

"Excuse me," said Gerard. "I'm talking to Mr. Applegate here."

Ellenberg and Applegate exchanged glances. If Coil knew anything about reading a face, she sensed a touch of fear beneath Applegate's wan, forced half-smile. Applegate shuffled off with the deputy.

"Tell them everything," said Ellenberg, grabbing Applegate's FATE sweatshirt near the T. "Ask *them* why they haven't done more until now to figure out who killed Ray Stern."

"I guess you got their attention," said Coil to Ellenberg.

"We'll see," she said. "I'm not too impressed with your police authority talent up here."

"There are some good people on the force," said Coil. "Maybe they're just stretched a little thin."

Ellenberg's crew still mingled closely around her, protecting the FATE queen bee.

"Hard to see the effort," said Ellenberg.

"But you were up there?" asked Coil. "How close were you?"

"Close?" asked Ellenberg. "I identified his body, right where some chicken hunter left him. Can you imagine? Making a mistake like that, making a huge mistake like that, and then just *leaving*?"

"No, I really can't," said Coil. "I have to agree with you on that."

"It's clear you don't agree with us on much else."

"How do you figure?" asked Coil, wondering if this could turn confrontational.

"Your whole hunting guide garb here," said Ellenberg. "And you already said you help the hunters with their slaughter."

Coil could see the bait dangling and tried not to nibble or swallow.

"I was just wondering if you could show me on a map, maybe, where you were, where they found Ray Stern?"

"Why?" asked Ellenberg. "What's it to you? What difference does it make?"

"I was up there, the day he was shot. I saw somebody dragging something, probably a body."

Ellenberg focused her gaze and cocked her head ever so slightly. If Ellenberg had learned the move by watching spaghetti westerns with Clint Eastwood, thought Coil, she was a poor mimic.

"Have you told the police?" asked Ellenberg.

"Yes," said Coil. "Everything. The thing is that somebody else is missing, too. Another guide. He works for a different outfit than mine, but nobody has seen him. His friends are worried sick. They think he might have been up there too, at the top of Ripplecreek Canyon."

Something in Ellenberg seemed to relax.

"What did you see?"

"A man dragging something. I was looking through a snowstorm. It was all fuzzy, like a TV with bad reception. The cops think I saw the man who shot Ray. I think what I saw was something else."

Coil scanned Ellenberg's crew: a few older women, a few earnest young men, some scruffy and some clean-cut. One reminded her of Vic, the young stud she'd met at the camp on the day all of this started unraveling. He looked enough like Vic to be his brother. She glanced around the ring of Ellenberg supporters: FATE, FATE, FATE, FATE, FATE on their sweatshirts. As if Coil needed a reminder about the difference between one airplane seat and the next.

"I'm not much help," said Ellenberg. "I couldn't tell you with any degree of accuracy exactly where we were. Maybe the cops have GPS coordinates from the spot where Ray was murdered."

Shot, thought Coil. *Accidentally.*

"I don't know," said Coil. "They think I'm the one that's confused."

"Sorry," said Ellenberg. "But how exactly do you sit there and watch these beautiful animals being killed and carved up?"

Actually, I don't sit there, I show them exactly how to gut and quarter.

"Probably not a good idea to get into it," said Coil. "I think we can just agree to disagree on that one."

"No, seriously," said Ellenberg. "These majestic, beautiful creatures. Slaughtered. And you think it's okay? You seem like a woman with a bit of a world view, if I'm not mistaken. It's just a hunch but you seem smarter than the average local up here."

Coil again checked the FATE throng. They were waiting for an answer.

"I'm from the city, originally, it's true," said Coil. "I respect what you're doing and I respect your point of view. It's just not mine. The fact of life today is that you can't let the elk and deer population explode unchecked. There are just too many. And hunting is older than the wheel. It's just the way it is. You can't go back and undo the fact that human beings have the ability and the desire to hunt. It's an animal instinct."

Ellenberg shook her head slowly.

"You think people—societies, whatever—have no control over their future?"

"I think reality is reality," said Coil. "That's all."

Some people die accidentally. Some people die because they are hunted and killed in war. They all end up in the same situation. Hunting is part of human nature.

Coil took a tentative step back. She knew this was headed nowhere but ugly.

"I do wish you well in pressing the police to figure out who killed Ray Stern," said Coil. "All hunters are trained to identify what they are shooting before they pull the trigger."

Coil hoped the common ground would signal truce.

"But you enable the slaughter of deer and elk," said Ellenberg. "That's what you do. You helped put this moron in the situation where he *could* pull the trigger."

"Sorry," said Coil.

"You are?" asked Ellenberg.

"No, I didn't mean sorry, *sorry*. I meant sorry, that's not the way I see it."

"Then there's blood on your hands, too. Animal blood."

The FATE bunch stirred and Coil could feel their stares.

If looks could kill, she thought.

* * * *

"You did what with your rifle?"

"I know it sounds crazy. And I shouldn't have littered. But first I whacked the barrel on a rock. I mean, it's not useable or anything, wherever it is."

Sheriff Jerry Sandstrom attended to his notebook, and Applegate waited, thinking about the best way to look relaxed and unconcerned. He considered the notion that there would probably be a whole battery of folks interviewing him if Grumley had told Sandstrom. On the other hand, they might be going low-key, to see if they could set a trap. Either way, Applegate felt his eyes were too blurry and wondered if that was noticeable. He wondered, too, if there was any way Sandstrom could tell that a muscle high up on his cheekbone had begun to twitch.

"Do you know which cliff?"

"Can't remember. It was a spot where the thing went a long ways down."

"And what type of thing was it?"

"A Winchester."

"What model?"

"A .270 I think. I don't think the hunting was in my blood, which is where it belongs if you can bring yourself to shoot—"

"No lectures, please," said Sandstrom.

Applegate sipped coffee from a Styrofoam cup, studied the creases in Sandstrom's pant legs, and tried to keep his story straight. Ellenberg had offered to accompany him, but he decided it would look too protective, too paranoid.

"So you guys got word of Ray Stern's death? When, exactly?"

"The first day back down."

"And then you hike your rifle back up to some spot somewhere. Isn't that going to a lot of work?"

"It seemed appropriate," said Applegate. "That's all."

"You didn't tell any of your old college buddies what you were doing?"

"No. It wasn't something I thought would go over too well."

"Where, approximately, did you decide to heave it?"

Applegate shifted uncomfortably. What if they actually had the gun right now, and this was all a ruse? He had no choice but to keep the storyline up.

"There's a trail that leads up the next drainage, east of Ripplecreek."

"An hour's hike, two?"

They weren't really going to look.

"Two or three. Somewhere in there."

"And where were you on the day Ray Stern was shot?"

"I took a walk."

"A walk as in hunt, or a walk as in hike?"

"I think I had my rifle along, but it was a joke. We hadn't seen any-thing bigger than a marmot, bless their fuzzy little bodies, the whole two weeks. The others wanted to lie low, except Grumley."

He realized this was a subject he shouldn't have raised. It brought up all the sticky issues about time and place. Sandstrom didn't ask a question, so Applegate thought he would fill in the blank. "He didn't miss a chance to hunt. The rest of us were on our own," said Applegate.

"So, a hike. And you went—where?"

"Down the valley, if I remember right, even though I was kind of interested to see the protest and how it was going to work. I guess I had some sympathies, perhaps, even then."

Enough, enough, Applegate told himself, although now it would be difficult to appear curt and cool after putting on a chatty side. And he was having difficulty imagining what Grumley might have told them. In a sep-arate line of analysis, he wondered if Grumley had fed the cops enough stuff, perhaps anonymously, to put them all on his tail.

"Draw me a line where you hiked—here," said Sandstrom, unfold-ing a topographic map.

"It's been so long."

"The best you can," said Sandstrom.

Applegate studied the map. He spotted the ridge where they had camped and he doodled a line from there in the opposite direction from where Ray Stern had taken his last steps.

"And where you chucked your rifle, approximately."

Applegate drew a line to a place where the contour lines were jammed closely together and it looked like it might be steep enough to toss some-thing off.

"So you were up by Lizard's Tongue on your hike, the day you didn't expect to find anything?"

"In that area."

"But you didn't see anything else. Tracks? Nothing?"

"If I did, I'd tell you," said Applegate.

"And you returned to the camp at the end of the day?"

"No, I hiked out all the way when it started to snow."

In fact, Applegate had headed down as instructed by Grumley, but he was too afraid to start a fire or try to survive a night in the wilderness, alone. So he had stumbled down the trail, somehow managing to stick to it, and snuck into one of the barns, where he had shivered and sobbed until dawn. At light, he walked to his car and went for a long enough drive to warm up. He found a café out by the interstate and he ordered food but couldn't eat.

"It's not every day a hunter changes his mind like that, about what he's been doing." As Sandstrom said it, he turned an imaginary key in his right temple.

"Now you want the lecture?"

Applegate smiled; Sandstrom didn't.

"It's heart and mind in this case," said Applegate. "And the protest, for me, was that. His death, Mr. Stern's, made me think. But almost like there was no need for thought. It felt like I was living in the wrong camp—and perhaps I was. Never had that feeling? That gun of yours, it's a symbol of what's gone—"

"Please," said Sandstrom. "Really. And you'll be in Glenwood how long, if we need anything else?"

"Don't know," said Applegate. "I think that's up to FATE."

* * * *

They seemed to be hovering. The frosty Flattops stood motionless below. The same wind that was trying to push them back to Eagle was blowing giant puffs of white fizz off the ridge that climbed up the west bank of Ripplecreek. Grumley trimmed the nose down a notch as the Mooney bored into the teeth of a snarling, high pressure howl at 12,000 feet. He guessed the headwind at 80 or 90. Above, the sky was crackling blue.

Grumley dropped down with the sinking elevation, all the while asking lame questions about Dabney Yount's supposed exploits in other corners of the world. Yount paid cash up front, carried four customized Weatherbys, and oozed money. He hadn't made any amateur comments yet, hadn't shown an ounce of concern about the airplane's slow progress, and didn't seem worried about the schedule.

But Yount also didn't mind being served. He watched as Grumley loaded their gear from the plane into an old Ford pick-up. He then let Grumley assemble a plate of food for lunch: gourmet bits of smoked sausage and sharp Gouda cheese with rye crackers, grapes, and homemade soup from an oversized thermos. Grumley cracked caps off two bottles of German beer. They ate standing up on the dirt strip next to the Mooney, which provided a break from the persistent wind.

The truck bounced over rutted dirt roads, which zigged and zagged at right angles back toward a cluster of hills to the north. Grumley followed directions scratched on the back of a used envelope. The envelope had been left behind the pick-up's visor. The roads were unmarked but the distances between them served as a gauge and what landmarks there were— a mailbox, a telephone pole, a type of fence—were used for double-checking purposes. The roads started climbing, and their structured grid collapsed on the steeper terrain. The snow covering the road amounted to wind-blown patches, at first, and then obliterated the hard-packed soil altogether.

They reached a north-south shelf that offered a panorama to the west, a hundred or so miles down an immobile ocean of forest and rangeland. The snow had piled high on the road in spots and Grumley dodged them where he could and gunned through the hubcap-high drifts where he couldn't. The road petered out. They stopped behind a pick-up truck with a camper shell. Three horses stood silently nearby, two saddled and ready, the third with saddlebags, all hitched to the side mirrors on the front of the truck.

Yount turned down the offer of hot coffee in the camper and watched as Grumley organized the loading of the packhorse with their personal effects and weapons. Grumley and Yount dressed in heartier winter gear in the camper. Yount climbed up on Dozer, a large chestnut and white appaloosa. Grumley took Flapjack, a smaller but surefooted quarter horse.

Two hours later, most of it spent climbing, the horses kicking through a foot and a half of snow, they arrived at a four-man canvas tent. A campfire burned outside. The tent sat in a clearing ringed on three sides by a tightly packed grove of blue spruce.

One of the guides heard them coming and stepped outside. Grumley introduced Yount, who seemed impatient, looking at the sky. The rifles were taken down, unpacked, checked, and loaded. After hearing the herd was less than a mile away, up and over the ridge behind them and likely to be nestled down in some scrub and heavy cover, Yount chose his .340 and packed some 250-grain bullets. Grumley had a Savage 99. The other three of Yount's rifles would stay.

A guide produced a walkie-talkie, muttered something softly into it, and waited for the response back. Ten seconds of silence preceded the whispered response. Grumley led Yount on foot, heading for a jagged knoll on top of the ridge. Yount tried to hide the fact that he was finally having to work. The slope required them to jam their toes into the grade for balance. Grumley set a steady pace, knowing it was harder to stop and start repeatedly than it was to keep plugging.

He could not take his mind off Applegate and Allison Coil. Applegate must have stepped onto the train on one side and off on the other. Grumley would have to track him down, again. This time would be the last. Trudy had called him in from the garage, where he had been welding a busted hinge on an incinerator. Trudy said they had teased a report on the evening news about some protest at the sheriff's office, and she was pretty sure she had seen another picture of his "pal." Sure enough, the first report showed Applegate and the bitch, Ellenberg, stomping around the cop's parking lot, demanding action. The one thing he couldn't do was reach through the television and grab Applegate by the neck and use the microphone cord coming off the reporter's camera as a fucking noose.

"Last bit of full-blown daylight."

It was Yount.

"We're fine," said Grumley.

From the stone outcrop, they spotted the guide crouched low behind a boulder halfway down the not-so-steep slope on the other side. The guide saw them, too, and used both his arms to signal them to stay low. They did, hunching over as they walked down. The wind was in their faces, which helped.

"Three hundred yards," whispered the guide, using his thumb to point up and over the boulder. "Some beauties. Watch your step. A coupla stragglers have ventured over this way in the last hour or so."

Grumley led the way out, heading parallel with the ridge top, out of instinct, to maintain the higher ground for as long as possible. The ridge was dotted with massive Douglas firs and lodgepoles, which seemed to ring an old burn. A red-tailed hawk circled silently in the dusk. Grumley spotted several sets of elk track a good three feet between the double-register steps, as they wound through a stand of aspen. He saw one pile of the distinctive, elongated scat, too. And it was fresh. Yount spotted an elk first and offered a soft cluck with his mouth as he stopped and squatted slowly, then cocked his head to the left to point in the direction. A long-necked cow was picking her way around the base of a lodgepole, chewing some bluebunch wheatgrass that poked up through the snow.

Yount shook his head *no*. Too small.

The elk munched, oblivious. Grumley signaled to stay put and still. The cow drifted off, tugged by some unconscious force of nature. Grumley led the way in behind it, using the trees and the steady breeze in his face as cover. The snow crunched a bit too much for his liking. The overnight freeze had created a crust on the snow that would make it difficult to sneak up on anything. Any attempt at forward progress could spook the cow and, as a result, the whole herd. Wherever it was. The good news was the snow depth, only a foot or so. The elk weren't having any trouble finding food to keep them satisfied. But the hunters' best bet was to stay put. Grumley figured twenty minutes of shooting light remained. Perhaps the herd would drift back in their line of fire.

Yount pointed in the direction he wanted to go. He was ten yards back, hanging low.

Grumley pointed, in order, to his boot, the snow, and his ear. *Too noisy*, he tried to charade.

Yount shook his head 'no' and pointed ahead. Grumley put up his hand like a cop stopping traffic. But Yount started walking, bent at the waist. He headed straight for the close cover of the pines and skirted them, staring ahead. Every step came with a crunch, soft and audible, like a cannon shot to elk radar. Trying to avoid a pattern, Yount took three steps and waited, then two steps and waited, then four. He crouched in the distance, at the base of a tree.

Grumley took aim at the back of Yount's head, lining up the crosshairs on the spot where the top of his fleece collar touched his neon green cap. With his scope, made for spotting the spine of an elk at 300 yards, the back of Yount's head filled his field of vision. *Pop, pop, pop* said Grumley, to himself. Why did some of 'em always think they knew better? He wanted Yount to turn around so maybe he could catch him in the face.

Yount stepped up and around the tree, out of sight. Grumley raised the rifle and propped the butt of it in the snow so he could lean on the barrel. He waited and listened, thinking he could hear Yount's steps, but it was just his imagination. A black-backed woodpecker swooped through two nearby lodgepoles, landed on a third, and chiseled for beetle grubs. The tops of the lodgepoles swayed steadily, but the wind at ground level seemed to be easing. Grumley waited fifteen minutes, figuring Yount had taken responsibility for his own hunt.

The bull appeared, rock still in the space between two trees. A gift. Grumley automatically took in the length of its antler beam, a cinch fifty-incher. It was probably not fifty-five, but a good fifty.

On cue, the bull dipped its head down to feed, and he could see the antler tips were as high as the top his shoulder. The rack was deeply curved with long brow points and nicely shaped sword points. The bull, giving Grumley a broadside view, looked up. Its ears jutted back. Grumley tried to keep his thoughts from moving. The bull took a step to its left and turned slightly, the ears going slack. Grumley lowered the sight on its shoulder. Eight yards, maybe a hair less. The spine would shatter easily. His brain and finger were considering the shot when he heard another *crack*, not far away, the report surprising him. He had almost forgotten Yount. The bull wanted to bolt, too, managing to bound off its hind legs. Grumley followed the target as it reared and answered the shot in the distance with one of his own before the first had stopped rattling its way through the woods. The beast pulled its rear legs in and sat down uncomfortably, like its bed was too prickly, or it was stiff from a hard work out. It collapsed over and away, its front quarter rolling over a bit higher, showing less control than any nap-bound animal. Grumley lowered the rifle and jogged toward his kill.

The elk was a gasp or two from its last. No finishing shot was required.

Grumley's shot had torn its spine.

Grumley stood ten yards off, wary until he saw that nothing on the animal twitched or had a mind of its own; nothing subconscious that would try to overcome such serious devastation to its own foundation. The hind legs scratched and pawed, digging for traction out of instinct. Grumley kept the rifle pointed at its neck, hoping he wouldn't have to risk ruining anything else. It would take the whole crew to help quarter and pack out so much food. The horses and the help weren't far, but the gutting job would have to be done by campfire light.

He heard Yount before he saw him, the boots *clomp clomping*. He came running like a three-year-old who had discovered candy.

"Holy—" he said, half out of breath, taking in Grumley's kill. "I thought mine was—*Jesus*, look at this mother."

"Father," Grumley corrected. "You got one?"

"A cow, nothing to write home about."

Yount was breathing hard, whether from excitement or exercise Grumley couldn't tell. Some hunters were like that with adrenaline, the idea of killing something.

"One shot," said Yount, inspecting the blood-caked hole in the bull's backbone.

"Yours?" asked Grumley. "Where'd you hit her?"

"Rear quarters," said Yount. "She got about five paces and called it quits."

"I'll trade you," said Grumley.

Yount looked at him like he had spoken in another language.

"This baby is trophy class."

"Cow meat is sweeter. You tell your story, I'll tell mine. Switch the bodies."

"Quite the guide service."

"Hey," said Grumley. "You drop something better tomorrow, we'll switch back. You don't, you hang the rack."

"Best damn outfit this side of the Mississippi."

"We like repeat business," said Grumley. "Let's go raise some boys to excavate all this meat and hang it up to cool. Unless you'd rather—"

"It's getting awfully dark," said Yount. "Not sure I could handle a sharp knife in these conditions. And I'm a mite thirsty from all the aggravation that goes along with this hunting business."

"Feeling tuckered?"

"Christ," said Yount. "The only way to have made it any quicker would have been to chain these suckers to a tree."

* * * *

Coil was stepping out of the shower, replaying the "conversation" with Ellenberg over and over in her mind, when she heard the horse snort. Coil grabbed a towel, yanked open the bathroom door and shouted "Just a minute." Underwear, socks, jeans, and sweater were tossed on as quickly as possible, the jeans battling damp skin. She opened the door barefooted.

"Just waking up?"

Bobby Alvin, one of Grumley's hunting grunts.

"Making up for the hot water we all miss during season."

"No need to get dressed on my account."

Bobby Alvin was a three-night fling, many months ago. He had seemed at first like the cool, low-key, earthy sort whose every move and thought was born and bred in the back-country soil. He had short hair and square but rugged good looks, with deep-set eyes. Her downfall. Alvin had seemed like a guy whose attitudes were as natural, normal, and relaxed as a cow grazing in a pasture. He was a big one, barrel chest over knobby, gnarled legs that flopped beyond the end of the bed. But Alvin's world didn't stretch much beyond horses and hunting, and she realized she had been mistaken when he couldn't communicate, and didn't seem to care, about anything outside his shallow puddle. It was Coil's relationship with Alvin that made her realize her own interest in the rest of the world was not so easily squelched. The sex had been forgettable, coarse and abrupt. When The Boy Scout—Slater—showed up on her radar, Alvin hadn't put up much of a fight.

"Coffee?" she offered, already heading to the pot to fill the tank with water.

"Got any bourbon?" asked Alvin, plunking himself down at the table. He sat sideways in a chair, then tilted it back so he was leaning against the wall.

"Most likely," she said, opening a kitchen cabinet to check the supply. She found a bottle of Wild Turkey. He poured himself an unhealthy portion.

"So what's all this about?" he asked.

"I was wondering if you could tell me who camped last week with that guy Dean Applegate."

She was careful to put the focus on Applegate, not Alvin's boss, Grumley.

"The quiet one."

He knocked back his first drink and reached for the bottle.

"How's that?"

"I helped pack Grumley and his buddies up and down three years running and I never could get a fix on that one."

She let it dangle, having already decided she wouldn't appear too interested in anything he said. She wanted to poke around, get a clearer picture of the airplane before take-off, but didn't want to sound like the FBI.

"Now I hear he's all over, talking like a raving madman. Go figure. I couldn't get ten words out of him. Not like the others."

"The others," said Coil. "The others were—"

"Pretty cool. Flatlanders, don't get me wrong, but they knew it. Applegate always had to have his camouflage."

"Do you know them?"

"By name?"

"Yeah."

"*Nick*names—two of 'em. 'Fishy' Marcovicci and 'Locks.' Oh, and another guy named Frank. And Grumley and Applegate. Why don't you ask George?"

This was the hard part, not knowing how secretive to appear, not knowing how much she could trust Alvin. This was the part where she had hoped he would play stupid.

"He's a busy guy . . ."

"It has to do with Rocky, right? I heard you were poking around. I've had questions myself. I mean, it's been a long time now. Too long."

"The cops are petering out," said Coil, "and don't seem to care."

"And that's because—"

"They're too busy with the guy in the deer suit," she said.

"And what do you think these three have to do with anything? They're puppies, let me tell you, who could barely manage to survive for a day by themselves in a stocked hunting camp with a full-time maid."

"I'm curious if they know anything."

Alvin buried his nose in his drink and crossed his eyes to watch the fluid go down.

"You don't think the cops already got to 'em? Hell, they found me. One of the guys from one of our camps got pinned down on his way out, just because he was driving out from Grumley's barn. He tried to explain that they had been hunting eight miles north of Ripplecreek."

"You're probably right," said Coil.

"It's possible Rocky got caught, strayed from his camp, and couldn't find his way back. Froze or something."

"I suppose," said Coil, trying to sound convincing.

"What you need is all the guns in the valley that day, test all the ones that could have handled the bullet that zipped into Mr. Deer Suit, get one stupid murder or accidental shooting or whatever it was off their minds, and then get the cops to help find Rocky."

Coil, who had been pacing, fiddling, sat down across from Alvin. And the phone rang.

"Allison?" It was Trudy.

"Yes. Hi."

They had been talking on the phone daily, but this was the first time Trudy had initiated the call.

"Do you have a second?" Trudy asked.

Alvin took a drink, looked tense, but wasn't going anywhere.

"I just need a second," said Trudy. "My airport friend called. I told you George took the plane out. He's coming back late this afternoon. Very quick trip. An overnight, which is unusual. And the jet that brought in one of his customers—well, the pilot is there now, and they're prepping it. I guess it's some new-fangled corporate jet. The airport people are all in a tizzy. A Gulf Something."

"Stream," said Coil.

"Expensive," said Trudy.

"Very," said Coil.

Alvin looked at her and smiled.

"I thought I'd let you know."

"Interesting. Thanks," said Coil.

"Did you get your house back together?" asked Trudy.

"For the most part. It looks okay. Look, I've gotta go now, but I'll stop by real soon. Thanks."

Alvin's grin was gone; he was now stone-faced.

"Was Rocky fighting with anybody that you knew about?" asked Coil.

"Cops asked that one eight ways from Sunday. No."

"You think he was up there working?"

"Sure."

"He wasn't doing anything—"

"Peculiar?" asked Alvin.

"Yeah."

"Rocky Carnivitas? Maybe he smoked a joint now and then, maybe he drank too much in the shit-kicking joints, I don't know. You think you're concerned, go ask Trudy Grumley."

"Why her?" Coil played innocent.

"The Grumley crew, that was one of things we had to do, rotate in on 'Trudy Duty.' Woman's got a problem with her brain, it freezes up, I guess. I've never been there, thank God, when it's happened. Anyway, we've got to babysit her, take her places. She can't drive."

Alvin stopped as if that completed a loop of logic.

"And Rocky?"

"Was her favorite. He started picking up shifts, seemed like, to be with her. An A-1 hunting guide spending his days shuttling her around? I think she took a fancy. I bumped into them one day in the grocery store. Sick woman and her helper? I don't think so."

"But—"

"No, I don't think anyone would take the chance of playing footsie with the boss's wife. Most likely, they were friends. Anyway, that was Rocky. He could get real sympathetic."

"George didn't notice?"

"Who's to say? Go talk to her, but bring your machete."

"Huh?"

"Her house is a fucking jungle. Plants growing out of every nook and granny. I mean cranny." He started to laugh.

"Oh, and cats, too. Every shape and size, climbing on everything. Mind if I use the bathroom?" he asked.

"Can you get me the names of the other three hunters?"

"Yes," said Alvin. "Of course. If you want to get your hands all dirty."

He wobbled a bit as he walked and stood a moment before opening the bathroom door. She started thinking of how to scoot him out. She wondered if Slater had the sources to find out which cop might have talked to Fishy, Frank, and Locks. Lockwood.

Alvin came up behind her and put a hand on each shoulder, rubbing the muscles. His hands felt like steel clamps, stiff and indifferent. Built to grip, not to touch. She squirmed, leaning forward.

"Aw, the big brush-off."

He worked his way around to her chest, or was headed there. She stood up and turned around.

He held up his hands like an innocent and feigned surprise.

She leaned against the table, eyeing him and getting a whiff of the bourbon, either from him or the bottle, which he retrieved, drank from, and then passed to her like an invitation. She shook her head, unsure of how stubborn to appear, thinking it might be best to talk him out of his mood.

He took a step forward, standing almost between her legs, and cupped her face in his hands.

"It's been a long time," he said.

"Bobby."

"Who's gonna know?"

"It's not going to happen."

"Going to? Going." He pronounced the full word. "The girl from the city. Going. It *is* happening."

She gripped the table as he went for her arm.

"The girl from the big city. That's how they talk. Going. Is that how they tease, too?"

"I thought we could talk."

He reached around, grinding his pelvis against hers as he did, and grabbed for the bottle. He knocked back a swig. "One little go 'round," he said. "Like the rodeo. A go 'round."

"No," said Coil, thinking that to strike him might be like whipping a spooked horse.

She felt him hook a finger in the top button of her Wranglers.

"Don't do this," she said.

"Animals do it and they don't even know why," he said. "You're not going to deny a guy who's a bit down on his luck. One little peek at that cute butt." He cracked a slick half-smile, working to provide a glimpse of warmth. "How does such a petite thing like you learn how to ride them big ol' horses, anyway? Okay, let's pretend I'm the horse. Saddle me up, strap me on."

She turned her head slightly as he moved in for a kiss. He landed his desperate, dull mouth on her cheek. She kept her arms propped and jammed back against the table behind her and, she hoped, looked unconcerned. He rocked his pelvis, wanting her to feel his excitement.

He had already worked his way around to the back of her neck, giving her a nuzzle. She resented his size and position and demands. The top button of her jeans popped loose. She put a hand on his, where it was searching for the next notch of hope, and gently pulled it away.

"Please," she whispered in his ear. "I'm sorry if you thought this might be a re-start." She gave him a soft kiss on his cheek. "Don't. Please."

He stood up, slow as a bear after hibernation, and looked her in the eye.

"Jesus," he said. "Sorry. I thought maybe, thought we . . ."

"I know," said Coil.

"If you ever . . ."

"I know," she said.

"Yeah," he said. She watched as Alvin re-buttoned her jeans. "I don't know what . . ."

In the world of events, she thought, a romp with Alvin wouldn't have hurt. But it might have given him hope. And there was the complication. Pieces of the heart, once frozen over, should never be de-iced.

8

C oil parked beyond the perimeter fence of the airport and picked up her binoculars. There was no problem picking out the Gulfstream, a showroom-clean and bright white jet parked amid the smaller props. Four men were sorting gear and moving equipment around. George's Mooney was wingtip-to-wingtip with the Gulfstream, which could have been its still-nursing mother. Trudy had given her the Mooney's tail number, and Coil jotted down the Gulfstream's.

A small truck was parked nearby and, even without its sign, Coil would have recognized it: Ted's Taxidermy. The enclosed rear of the truck was refrigerated. It was not possible to pick out George until right near the end of the 15-minute or so exchange of stuff. The last item moved was an elk or a deer. A sizable set of antlers poked out of the canvas wrap that held the skin. Elk. Then two men shook hands and one headed to the steps that led up to the Gulfstream; the other one, who went back to his pick-up, had to be George.

"Where's Rocky?" she said out loud to herself. "Where's Rocky, George? Do you know?"

The staircase automatically folded up into the Gulfstream and the clutter of men and equipment vanished from the jet's skirts. Coil rolled down her window to listen to the engine's whistle, then watched as the machine lumbered out to the runway. Without stopping, and without an ounce of extra noise, the jet reached take-off speed with no visible signs of struggle and shot up into the clouds. Ninety-nine point nine nine nine nine percent of the time, she thought, aircraft function like they should.

Coil stayed in her car until George and the Ted's Taxidermy truck drove past. There was one road in and out of the airport and she slumped down as they approached. She could see that George's truck was full of other guys. The taxidermist followed George, and she slowly turned her Blazer around after they left. There was no need to follow. Ted's destination wasn't a question.

* * * *

Slater's desk was one of four in a jumble that supported an apparently free-floating swamp of newspapers, newsletters, memos and junk that indicated not a trace of organization.

The rangers' district office was upstairs in a renovated old warehouse, overlooking the train station. The floor was the original bare wooden planks, and the soft clomping of staffers and secretaries echoed and creaked, at the slightest movement, below the exposed-beam ceiling. Slater's desk and the three others were each propped over braided area rugs, as if this defined an office.

"Thought you were working," said Slater, hardly surprised at seeing her.

"Thought you were up-country," said Coil. "Stopped by on a whim."

"Just got back, changed at home, and came here to do, uh, paperwork." He glanced at the menacing pile on his desk.

"Right," said Coil. "Hard to believe."

"And you?"

"Called in sick. Outright lied."

"So we can go back to your place?"

"And . . ." It dawned on her. "Yours is closer."

"Yours is more comfortable."

Slater lived in a trailer park south of town. She'd seen it twice. It was a doublewide, neatly kept. He was saving money for something. But it was a trailer, in a trailer park, with trailer people. She wasn't that sound a sleeper.

"What are you up to, if you're not, in fact, ill?"

"Trying to figure out a few things."

"Still," Slater said, more a statement than a question.

"Nobody's seen Rocky Carnivitas for a real long time." She walked him through a few details he'd missed the last few days, particularly the identity of Rocky and a few bits about Trudy: just the rough picture. She did not want it to sound like a crusade. "So the missing Rocky is number one. I found parts of a matching GPS collar in Rocky's trailer—"

"Oh?"

"Trudy asked me to take a look and gave me a key. No Rocky. But I found a unit identical to the one we found up top, with the dead elk."

"I meant to tell you," said Slater. "A team from CSU got a federal grant to study harem size or something, a five-year grant. Your taxpayer dollars at work. I should have told you sooner. They were supposed to notify us which herd they were going to track. But they've been working it all through the Meeker District office."

"So this is coincidence?"

"I'm just saying there are biologists all around."

"And why the dead elk?"

"Shock? Overdose? I don't know."

"We should have taken a piece of the dead elk," said Coil, "and sent it to the lab for tests."

"To find out what?"

"How it died, maybe. Wouldn't you want to know if these biologists screwed up?"

"I should have taken a sample," said Slater.

"I'll get you one," said Coil. "I'll be up there soon, I'm sure."

Slater stood up, found a chair, and brought it over. "What else?" he asked earnestly.

"I don't know. What was Rocky doing with GPS gear?"

"I don't know," said Slater. "We'll ask him."

"If he shows up."

"Rocky? He will. It's not like these people are on a schedule. You should know."

"I have a bad feeling. Plus, it pisses me off that Sandstrom thinks I don't know where I was."

"He said that?"

She told Slater about her place being ransacked, then her reporting it to the cops and running into Sandstrom.

"I know where the heck I was," said Coil. "To the inch."

"Of course, of course," said Slater.

"Can't you do something?" asked Coil, knowing he couldn't. She didn't even want to go into the business at the airport. What business was it anyway? Just hunting and hunters, fancy style.

"Declare stupid cops are banned from these parts? Or go find Rocky myself? Sure, I'll get right on it."

"What if Rocky and his buddies use GPS to track game?"

"Then they'd be bad boys, and we'd step right in, no question. But you need more than parts in his trailer, and you'd still need Rocky, to ask him about some stuff."

"You don't seem that concerned."

"Lots of speculation."

"About everything, including who shot JFK."

Slater threw her an eyebrow-popped glance. "At least there you had a body," he said.

"I know, I know. But you didn't hear the shot. I did. You didn't see this guy dragging a load. I did. It wasn't down the hill where they found the deer suit guy. It was right there in front of me, down a ways, but in front of me."

"Yes," said Slater. "But it took you awhile to come off the pass. By then, you know, he—"

"Who?"

"He, whoever, could have covered lots of ground. Even in shock, from having killed this guy, he would have had some adrenaline pumping. He might have considered turning himself in, admitting to the accidental death. Then the adrenaline runs out, he's tired of carrying the body, and he decides to hide it in the woods. And decides there's no way they can figure out who killed the guy. And so far, he's right—100 percent right."

"And the dead elk?"

"A fluke. A separate deal, but a fluke. Give Rocky a chance to turn up."

He's had a zillion, thought Coil, and hasn't taken one.

Coil stood up, trying not to show her exasperation, trying not to challenge Slater's logic.

It was logic to a point, but it didn't connect with what she felt.

"I'm going home. Maybe I need a rest," she fibbed. "I'll be there later, if you want to swing by. Up to you."

She smiled.

"I'll see," said Slater. "I'm a little pooped myself."

She looked around and gave him a quick kiss.

"Any federal rules about that?" she asked.

"If there are," he said, "I'm going to court."

* * * *

Ted's Taxidermy took up all of a low-ceiling barn that faced the Colorado River halfway between the interstate and the main road up Ripplecreek. The truck served as signage, always placed in the same strategic spot, down near the road, for maximum impact.

Ted Slowik was tall, thin, graying and forever with a pipe in his teeth, whether or not the Sangria-smelling tobacco was lit. He had a couple of helpers and had grown to know all the outfitters in the area. He was the best taxidermist in the area, the most meticulous. He really didn't need to advertise. From head mounts to full body mounts, Slowik prided himself on high quality work.

Coil parked and walked into the barn, which was constantly heated by a pumping wood stove. Two German Shepherds looked up from their naps and a black rabbit, Midnight, hopped over to greet her. Nobody new.

The dogs went back to sleep; Midnight was quickly distracted by a stray wood chip. Coil picked up the bunny, found her pile of browning lettuce near her cage and fed her by hand.

"Another one?" asked Slowik, who was spreading a skin out on his workbench.

"Nope. Just stopped by. I wasn't sure if I'd given you the name and address for that doe I brought over yesterday."

"The head mount? Sure you did. It's SOP for us. Let me check."

He pulled a file from a shelf above the bench. "Here it is. Trabowski, Oak Park, Illinois. Got it."

"Wow, that's a beauty," said Coil, admiring the bull and its enormous antlers.

"Biggest rack so far this season. Weighs 40 pounds alone, bank on that."

"Whose?"

"Who else?"

"Again?"

"Well, Grumley's client, anyway."

"But George always brings 'em in. Who was the client?" It was an innocent question.

"Jeez, you should have seen this guy's jet. Huge. Brand new. Engines that burn more fuel in a minute than you and I use in a month. George introduced me, but damned if I remember the name. Not without looking it up." Back to the files. "Dabney Yount. Houston, TX. Thought I smelled oil money out there at the airport."

Coil traced the antler rack with her hand, felt its sharp points and the smooth woody sensation. It was hard to believe blood flowed through the antlers like sap in a tree.

"Grumley's crews are lucky."

"Or good," said Slowik. "And rich. They bring in more full body mounts than any other outfitter, that's for sure. That one'll take some time."

"Quite the gash," said Coil, eyeing the ripped skin near the spine.

"That's the easy part," said Slowik, putting a match to his pipe, making it puff. "Try finding some insides for this guy that bring him back to life."

"I've thought about that," said Coil. "If you had elk lungs, elk heart, and elk innards, I'll bet you'd know where all the parts go. You better than anybody else."

"Maybe. All except the on-off switch," said Slowik. "That's the one funny one. I'm just never sure where to put it."

* * * *

Applegate tried to stop fixating on what the cops were thinking and doing: whether they would burst through the door any day with the bloodhound sniffing a path to his heels. And if that happened this second, if they could get through the door unannounced, the dog's nose would be working overtime as it took in the lush, slightly acrid aroma of sex, just minutes old. Or perhaps they didn't need the dog. Maybe there would be some other incriminating scrap of evidence, a piece of fabric from one of his mittens they found at the scene. Or a cast of a boot print taken, somehow, from within a snowfall. Was that possible? And they would ask to see his outdoor equipment and some scientist would be standing by, right there, to confirm the match. The dog would wag its tail.

Applegate had days of unbridled fear, registered as a constant chatter that chewed on his other thoughts, the ones up front, the ones he was supposed to be concentrating on. He wanted to whack down that voice, the one in the background, but the ideas it spoke were hard to ignore.

Ellenberg shifted on her side. Her naked breast grazed his chest, and she sighed. In his book, which was a thin one, it had been a gangling, awkward half-hour of tumbling. But it had also been satisfying.

Ellenberg had come to his room with a bottle of red wine. They sat on the bed cross-legged, facing each other. She poured and told him it was time to pack up and leave Glenwood Springs. And then one toast ended with a kiss, more like a tap on the lips, nothing deep, and that was that. She was a kindred spirit. He admired her spunk, and the kiss made him think it was possible to wriggle free from his old snakeskin and put on a new layer.

She pushed him over on his back. They hugged and explored each other's mouth, her long brown hair creating a private pup tent. She smelled of Ivory soap behind her ears. With the wine, the kisses carried a perpetual tingle. She did not object to a hand on her slender rear, and then he had slipped a hand up underneath her red-checked, flannel shirt. She buried a wet tongue in his ear, jammed her pelvis down on his and offered a throaty growl of approval before she stood by the side of the bed and stripped casually, displaying a bit of pride in her lean body, boyish hips and cone-shaped, high-set breasts.

Standing naked, she unlaced his shoes and pulled down his pants and underwear in one swoop, stopping to give his erection a red-wine smack of its own. She helped him off with his shirt and made him feel that being able to make love with him was the grand prize in a long-odds contest. She straddled his knees and licked him. Then he kneeled on the floor and tried his unskilled best to return the favor for a few minutes between her spread legs. She spun around on top of him and lowered herself down. She pumped slowly, her hair tickling his face to the rhythm. He tried to hold back for a minute, but couldn't, and he bucked her wildly from below as she grabbed his chest, looking for a handhold, and endured the ride.

"Eye yie yie," she said when he was done. Her hair had stuck to her warm cheeks. "Now that we've got the ice broken . . .," she said and let the thought dangle.

She rolled off and snuggled down alongside him, a hand returning to cup his crotch and give it a pat. Was this a deal, he wondered, that Ellenberg would want to take public? Perhaps she did a lot of the guys. Perhaps this had been a thank-you screw, a kind of sympathy fuck to put a cap on the protest.

"Dean?" She thought he was dozing. Actually, he was picturing the bloodhound leading troops to their motel. "You know it's not over," she said. "Your work with us, I mean."

"It's not?" he asked, somewhat surprised.

"We don't worry a whole lot about titles, but everyone would like to see you come on board and keep doing what you do, plus a lot more. You won't believe some of the projects we have in mind. The spring bear hunt, the new aquarium in Denver, and we're getting some information about some nasty experiments with rats at the university."

"Rats?"

"There's so much to do. Besides, you can't crawl back in a hole. Not now."

"What would I do, exactly."

"We tend to let the roles evolve. It's more natural than making up a job title and job description, and then wedging people into them. You start hanging around, we'll find stuff for you to do. Don't worry."

"Manager of stuff."

"Now there's a spiffy title."

She rolled back over on top of him, apparently for a hug. Her skin was gluey and warm. He ran his hands down her back as she buried her nose in his neck. Relax, he told himself, and try to enjoy it.

* * * *

"She's very curious. Enough for a whole cat house."

"Yeah?"

"Nosy. Lots of questions. Wondering about Rocky."

Grumley shifted in the squeaky swivel chair behind his desk. Alvin seemed nervous, perhaps half unsure why he was telling any of this. Boyles sat on the couch, running his fingernails over the tip of a pocket knife. Whether it was to clean them, or for fun, was not clear.

"Wondering what?"

"When he's going to turn up, stuff like that. She thinks the cops need to talk to your other buddies, the ones besides Applegate."

"And why not him?"

"I suppose she figures they've already grilled him, I don't know."

"You told her who was who?"

"I told her it was none of her damn business, that she oughta let the fuckin' cops do their thing."

Jesus, Coil was a pain. First with his own damn wife, right there in his own house, then questioning Boyles. And now this.

"Thought you'd like to know whenever your name is being mentioned behind your back," said Alvin, "especially in connection with—"

"With what? I've talked to the cops and I don't care if you're working for the fucking cops or you are a fucking cop yourself, it doesn't have much to do with me."

Alvin studied his mucky boots. Boyles stopped fiddling with the knife.

"Miss Coil has some theories, too, I suppose, about the death of the jerk in the elk suit?" asked Grumley.

"No," said Alvin.

"But I do," said Boyles.

"Care to fill us in?" asked Grumley.

"It was an animal hugger that pulled the trigger—had to be. No real hunter would've mistaken a 120-pound man wrapped in a brown cape for the real McCoy. So they staged the whole thing and tried to hang it on the hunters. They even had a plan for destroying the gun. It's a fucking ruse."

"I like it," said Alvin.

"Best one I've heard," said Grumley.

"Cops said they talked to all the protester types, too, but let's be serious, okay?" said Boyles. "What would the chances be—that on that day they would have run up against a hunter with the IQ of a brick. They had to do it themselves, trust me on that one."

"So they killed a human being to prove a point about killing animals. Makes sense to me," said Grumley. "Coil comes snooping around again, holler, okay?"

"Will do," he said.

Alvin muttered something about mucking a stall and headed off.

"Some people can't leave well enough alone," said Grumley.

"Sure seems that way," said Boyles, standing up and sliding his knife into a sheath on his belt. "What's next?"

"I don't know," said Grumley. "I got a business to run. I need these headaches?"

Boyles knew better than to answer.

"So what is little Miss Allison doing?"

"What's the difference if she knows who you were hunting with? What's she gonna do?" asked Boyles

"Try to get the authorities curious."

"So what do we do?"

"Keep close tabs on her—and Trudy."

"And what are we looking for?" asked Boyles.

"See if she's fucking around or trying to fuck us."

9

A firm mid-winter breeze bore down as Coil walked to her lawyer's office. The wind seemed to gain strength from the empty, cold caverns of a city on a weekend.

The office was near the top of Denver's tallest building. The reception area featured a staggering view of the mountains from Mount Evans clear north to the Wyoming border. Pollution? The wind today made it someone else's problem.

"Allison."

Even on a Saturday, Paul Reitano was all business in his button-down collar and silk tie.

"You guys have moved up in the world. Literally."

They shook hands.

"Corporate merger. We picked up a few accounting firms, clean ones not tainted by the Enron meltdown. Well, *charged.*" He smiled. "But not tainted. It makes for pleasant surroundings, anyway."

He was sixty-ish and soft-spoken. He came across like a kindly professor who could scorn a set of bad grades with a look of deep dismay, one that carried weight. He had piercing blue eyes, puffy bits of unkempt white hair, and the weathered skin of a lifelong skier.

Reitano led her down halls lined with contemporary art to his small office.

"Thanks for making the trip down. They've had a test-run trial in New York. It was a real trial, but it's used as a means for determining who pays what amount. It's like dividing the check at a restaurant: determining who ate more, drank more, and therefore who gets to pay more. The two major parties were the airline, of course, and the airplane manufacturer. The airline tried to find something mechanical that went wrong. And they failed."

She listened as if it had just happened, as if she was still dripping and crouching awkwardly on a rock near the water in the harbor. The water continued to chop and churn. There were bits of stuff everywhere—jackets and magazines, suitcases and those under-sized airline pillows. And there were people, some struggling and flopping around in the water, not seeming real at all, more like actors in a bad movie. Shock coated their pain, bewilderment covered their agony. Some were making it to shore. Some didn't move at all. And one or two peered down into the black water, floating lifelessly.

Reitano talked about de-icing and how long an airplane is airworthy, once it has been hosed down, until the glycol solution loses its battle with the elements. He mentioned that they could have opted for a second kind of solution that was an anti-icing agent as opposed to a de-icing one. He talked about how the pilot asked the co-pilot to check the wings thirty minutes after they had been through the de-icing station and the co-pilot, according to the tapes they pulled from the wreckage, came back with the all-clear. Only de-icing solution on an airplane wing has an "effective window" of 25 minutes, no more.

She remembered someone in uniform coming down the aisle, peering out the windows a few rows back. Everybody watched him study the wing. The "everybody" included a few people who were in their last few minutes of life, the co-pilot among them. He could have seen something, even made it up. Why not squirt your windshield one more time when it's being splattered with rain and snow and crud? Why not put the jet through for another swab of pink goo, to hit it again before takeoff? It had been 24 minutes, said Reitano, when the jet was given clearance to head for Denver. But what good was thinking of Denver when you might not make it off the runway?

"Your injuries were major. But, in the end, you recovered your life. The settlement they are offering is $900,000. I could go into the strange ways an actuarial table can change, how emotional distress factors in . . .?"

"That's an offer?"

"No trial. Terms to remain confidential. There's a group of passenger survivors, and the families of others who think the suit has gone far enough," said Reitano, "who don't want to take it another step. They are the ones involved in the mock trials. It looks like the airline and its insurance companies will be asked to compensate victims moderately, as these things go. But there's another group of passengers, survivors and the others, who want the government to pay their share, too."

"The government?"

"It's a delicate balance: regulating the industry and running it. If the airline doesn't follow the recommended safety standards set by the glycol manufacturer, the government wants to be able to say that it's none of their business, that it's a cut and dried decision on the part of the airline and its pilots. Twenty-four minutes? That must be okay. They think their air traffic controllers should have no monitoring function, no oversight. It's not that hard a thing to track the time and the weather. But the tapes recovered from the airline conversation with the tower show there wasn't a lick of concern from the tower about how long your jet had been parked and waiting. To put it another way, the government thinks that if they post 65 on the highway and you go 66, it might not be their fault if the asphalt is poor quality, some bad road popped your tire, and you wound up in the ditch."

Reitano paused and spun gently in his chair.

"We want to keep pressing this lawsuit. There are only eight of us left. It's a bit of a risk, not taking what they are offering at this, uh, juncture."

"Nine *hundred* thousand?"

"Less my fees and taxes."

Coil couldn't imagine what it would be like to be responsible for, or think responsibly about, a pot of money that size. Or maybe larger. Was it possible to grasp this as having any connection to swimming in the sound when she should have been flying?

"But is it greedy to seek more?"

"It's not greedy. It's a risk. Lawyers in my end of the business have a saying we borrowed from investment bankers: *Pigs get fed, hogs get slaughtered*. You're looking to get fed, trust me, no more."

"But wasn't the government doing its best, or trying to?"

Reitano leaned up on his desk, coupled his hands together so the middle knuckles interlocked neatly.

"On that basis, so were the pilots. So was the glycol manufacturer. But the government is another thing we can challenge."

"How much more could we . . . win?" It was a difficult word to use.

"Hard to say. And there's more to it than financial value. It's a matter of proving a point, cleaning it up for others. Someone once said that the government is both a dangerous servant and a fearful master. The government is us. It's all of us. Watching and monitoring. Providing checks—and balances. It's little people pointing out problems, and being rewarded for their suffering. Suing your government doesn't mean you hate *them*. It means you respect your fellow citizens, that you want to make the world a better place."

"More than $900,000? That's hard to grasp."

His demeanor was too steady to be troubling, his reasoning too solid. She pictured the de-icer *trying* to work beyond its limits, as if it had a brain to know how important it was to keep the wings from freezing.

"I'll take your lead on this," she told him.

"The principle is with us, on our side. Remember, it's not the individual people we're going after. It's the system, the way they do things."

"Do I have to decide now?"

"No. We have a few weeks to notify the airline if we'll settle at this stage. You want to think about it, I understand."

"I like the idea of having it over wtih, that's all. Tying up all the loose ends."

"The money is tempting," said Reitano. "Don't think I don't realize that."

The whole conversation, its premise, seemed so far removed from her world on Flat Tops. Or maybe it was the steel and glass setting that gave the discussion an unreal quality. How could you make such a decision? On what basis? What was $900,000 *worth*?

After staring off for a moment, Coil stood up. Reitano also began to get up but politely sat back down as Coil did.

"I've got a favor to ask."

"Shoot," he said.

"Different matter," said Coil. "Isn't there some sort of state system that keeps track of debts? Posts them?"

"The UCC. Uniform Commercial Code. It's a registry in the Secretary of State's office. Invaluable."

"Can you show me how to access it? And, if you're online, I was wondering if I might spend on hour or so on the Internet? There's a big spender in Texas. I want to see how much cattle comes with his big hat."

Reitano smiled. "We have a spare office," he said. "Right this way."

* * * *

Coil flopped on her unmade hotel bed, a half-acre of cushion. She had barely messed one corner of it and wished Slater could come help her tangle the sheets.

"Why in the world would they talk with me?" she asked. She tucked the telephone between her tired head and the pillow.

"Because you want to know. If you think not being a cop is a disadvantage, you're wrong."

"They don't have to talk to me."

"Of course not. But when people talk to cops, their lips might be flapping but they don't always say very much. Or they make it up. Like Applegate."

"What did he have to say?"

"Sandstrom gave an update at a summit meeting today. Applegate said he gave the rifle the old heave-ho off a cliff, after hiking back up through three feet of snow. I don't think so. If any of those guys can give us an idea of what Applegate was up to, it would shed some serious light."

"Sounds like you're dubious."

"Ask any of 'em if they know where Applegate's rifle might be, and find out if they saw Applegate anywhere the day those two poor fellows went down."

"Gee, I feel like a deputy, but don't you have to come down here and officially deputize me?"

She would spring for the best bottle of champagne the hotel could muster and maybe tell him about the $900,000, seed money for their lives together.

"I would if I could," said Slater. "That official ceremony will have to wait."

"I still feel nervous—and alone."

"Nobody's forcing you to do anything."

"Could be we're barking up the wrong tree," she said, "or even poking around in the wrong forest."

Coil studied the list in her hand. Bobby Alvin had called back the names: Bobby Marcovicci, Frank Cassell, and Darrell Lockwood.

She wanted Stern's killer caught as much as anyone did. But she imagined having a conversation with Sandstrom and Stern's killer to exonerate herself from Sandstrom's claim that she didn't know where she had been when she heard the shot. If this was how he absorbed and analyzed information that might be related to the whole snarl of events up on Ripplecreek, whether or not her information was related, it pissed her off.

"Then come on back," said Slater. "Sandstrom claims it's a full-court press. Somebody's going to feel the pressure and crack. Count on it."

* * * *

Bobby Marcovicci lived in an old Victorian that overlooked a small lake on Denver's west side. Some Canadian geese were pecking at the yellow-green grass on the park that rimmed the lake as Coil pulled up. She had picked up the phone to call Marcovicci as soon as she finished talking to Slater, giving herself no chance to brood.

Marcovicci was the closest, so he got the first call. She walked up the sidewalk to his front porch with Slater's minutes-old advice, which she hadn't taken, rattling in her head. She needed to understand, she needed to ask the questions.

Was this hard—asking questions? No. Maybe a touch awkward? Definitely. Was she out of her element? For sure, yes.

Her head kept up the mantra.

$900,000. Nine hundred thousand. Nine hundred. Thousand.

The talk with Reitano made her feel like everything else might be useless. Or everything else might be all that mattered. If not for the accident that led to the $900,000 settlement offer, then she would still be marketing toothpaste in New York City, and she would never have basked in the solace of the Flat Tops, would never have been up there at Lizard Head that day.

The door opened before she could ring the bell.

"That was quick," said the short stub of a man who opened the door.

"Nice view of the lake and mountains," said Coil.

"Denver would be Kansas City, I figure, without the mountains. So y'all may as well look at 'em. Come on in. You said you live in Ripplecreek?"

She followed his chubby, molded-butter walk inside to a living room that dripped leather and absorbed light. Lots of ginger teak and black trim.

He was all blobby roundness. The puffy, reddish orbs of his nostrils looked like miniature versions of his cheeks, which were surely stuffed with tissue. He offered her coffee, which she declined, and then water, which she accepted.

"I was up on top of Ripplecreek Valley, coming down, the day that protester was shot."

"I notice the cops can't figure it out."

"Everybody notices the cops can't figure it out. Can't or aren't. Haven't so far, anyway. Your friend Dean Applegate—"

"Haven't talked to him since his switcheroo. None of us except Grumley really ever understood that dude."

"Us?"

"Lockwood and Cassell and me. When Applegate took off that last day, to go hunting, we kicked back and relaxed, played poker and listened to the wind howl. With the protesters, it seemed the best thing to do was to lay low, stay out of trouble. Who needed the hassle? Next thing we know, Applegate is on television or some newspaper every time you turn around, talking about hunters being the animals. Now there's a twist, coming from a guy who painted camouflage on his face like icing on a wedding cake." Marcovicci patted his cheeks with both hands. "Excuse me, but what a weirdo."

"But Grumley liked him?"

"They got along. Applegate might have had the stamina, but not a lick of technique."

"You're a big hunter, too?" asked Coil.

"Come here, I'll show you something."

Marcovicci led her around through the kitchen and down a back stairs.

"I overhauled the basement three years ago, dug out the old cement floor and built myself the room I've always wanted."

Marcovicci snapped on a light.

The room was a rainbow of browns—walls of tan paneling, animal heads mounted in various shades of brown, picture frames dark and woody, a long brown couch, an old mahogany desk, and a line of dark bookshelves filled with magazines and books that didn't require a filing system to separate the subject matter. There was only one topic: hunting.

One whole shelf of *Field And Stream.* Another of *Sports Field.* There were books on tracking, camping, rifles, and ammunition. And dozens of personal hunting pictures mounted on the walls, one in a frame that was made of wooden, hand-carved pistols.

"My little palace," said Marcovicci.

"You don't seem like the hard-boiled hunter."

"Just something I love: the sport of it, the search, the science. And, of course, bringing home a winter's worth of venison or elk steaks or whatever it might be. Hunters aren't monsters, they are mostly decent people following centuries-old urges. Think hunters do more damage to the countryside than skiers? What about all the ripped-up forests? What about hikers and mountain bikes, with all the trash and all the permanent trails? They turn hiking paths into bald highways. Applegate and his band of merry protesters, they haven't a clue. Applegate, at least, should know better. It's all so silly."

Coil sat down in the chair behind the desk and admired the shrine.

"It's always seemed to me, when I'm up there, spending time with hunters, that there's an awful lot of wilderness, a ton of animals, and that most people who like to hunt also provide a service—thinning herds, being careful with the meat, the whole bit."

"Bingo," said Marcovicci.

"What about Applegate's rifle?"

"Maybe he sold it."

"He didn't. Says he didn't."

"Oh, really? You talked to him?"

"Cops did. Glenwood Springs is a small town," said Coil, anticipating the question. "Said he walked it back up into the mountains and tossed it off a cliff."

"Bullshit," said Marcovicci. "Look, let's cut to the heart of the matter here."

"We need to know where Applegate was, where Grumley was, and where Applegate's rifle might be found, if anybody knows."

"You used the old "we" thing."

"Sorry. *I.*" She smiled.

"Why you?"

"I've been asking myself the same question. I heard a shot up top by Black Squirrel Pass—"

"Nothing unusual."

"And saw a man dragging something. Or somebody. By the time I got down and around to this spot, they were both gone. All this in the first hour or so of the storm. I'd love to turn this all over to the cops, but they don't believe what little I know and I don't have any real trouble to point to."

"No victims."

"Exactly. Have you talked to Applegate?"

"Haven't yet," he said.

"You plan to?"

"It makes sense. At some point. And what if I know something? Why would I tell you?"

"Because I asked." Was that enough?

It didn't take a cop or a detective to read his nervous body, or a book to interpret its language. Something was up.

"I come up with the rifle, you can figure it out if that rifle's in trouble?" he asked.

"I'd get it to the proper authorities."

"You talked to Grumley or the others?"

"No," she said firmly.

"But you know Grumley?"

"Small valley."

"But you haven't talked to him?"

"Like I said."

"Is he the issue?"

"Doubtful," she said.

"Whatever, look. I don't have to be connected to any of this? Identified as a source?"

"About the rifle, I wouldn't think so. Cops need a witness about Applegate's movements—"

"He wasn't up near Lizard's Tongue, or anywhere up by Black Squirrel."

"When did you last see his rifle?"

"A good question that I'm not going to answer."

"You know where to reach me?"

"Write it down, why don't you."

She scratched out her name and the main number at Pete Weaver's.

"Couple of days, do you think?" she asked.

"Yeah, whatever it takes."

They shook hands at the door. His grip was warm and blubbery.

"You really saw something?" he asked.

"Yes," she said, "and it wasn't pretty."

"And you think this will do something, even though there's no way Applegate was up there, in the same vicinity?"

"I don't know," she said. "I'm following my nose. Seeing if the pieces will come back together."

* * * *

It was a long way from the straight lines, white carpet, and contemporary furniture in his suburban townhouse.

The ceiling rafters at headquarters were exposed, and the office was wide open, democratic, and filled with men and women who believed in the earth. Within minutes of starting work, Dean Applegate realized he would need a few scruffy edges if he was going to blend in with the scene. But when Applegate stopped clipping his near-military buzz, a close friend of Ellenberg pointed out that his story would hold more credibility if he kept the old cut. He happily returned to the old routines—haircut every other week, polishing his shoes, flossing his teeth. He felt more than a little out of place.

Unshaved armpits were popular with the women. They even wore dresses that advertised this preference. They were a political commune. Teams rotated providing lunch, which was a time for airing complaints or shooting the shit. There was a camp of workers who looked for the publicity angle of every wisp of an issue. There was another, smaller group who sought to wage this war on a more intellectual level. The publicity hounds were always looking to mount some event dramatic enough that news directors and reporters couldn't resist. Applegate had never realized how the news could be so easily controlled. Anything "visual" did the trick. Applegate was often asked for an opinion on this strategy or that issue, but it was more to make conversation than anything else. Ellenberg made the final decisions.

Some in the FATE fold seemed to trust him completely, about his conversion. A few others seemed less certain. Every national interview he conducted routinely attracted thousands of dollars in contributions, so they couldn't ignore him. But he wasn't one of them. It was all heart for them, especially for the young women. The cement in their foundations was still setting. There was lots of talk about cross-country skiing and vegetarian cooking. It was all subject to change, thought Applegate, or the whims of the right guy.

He helped install new computer programs to track donations and pump out newsletters. He installed some of his own software in the organization's computers: better word processing systems, a more sophisticated spreadsheet for accounting, an income tax program, and a more powerful modem. He took over design and construction of their website on the Internet and made it more interactive. He bounced from project to project, discussion to discussion.

The hardest day, his third back in the city, was when Ellenberg came back from a photo studio with a long cardboard tube tucked under her arm. After lunch, she gathered the staff around, gingerly removed the tube's contents, and, with help, unspooled a life-size photograph of Ray Stern. In the picture, Ray was smiling. Not posed, but a candid shot, as if he'd been caught off guard. The backdrop was solid grass, and he was leaning back on his arms, content. Black and chocolate puppies crawled all over his stomach and legs. Labradors, Applegate guessed. One had scampered up on Ray Stern's chest and was busy licking his cheek.

The staff gasped as she held it up.

"His brother gave me the slide," Ellenberg announced. "Thought we'd hang it on the wall, where you get off the elevator by the front, there. Any objections?"

"Of course not," said one idealistic, herb-tea type. Nobody else spoke.

"Dean," said Ellenberg, "could you help frame it and get it hung up?"

There was a black cloud in his head. Some days it floated off to the edge of the horizon, and he didn't even notice it. From time to time it rushed back, blown by a curiously quick wind.

"Naturally," he said.

10

C oil was unsure of the idea from the moment it occurred to her—but how would Trudy Grumley say no? Politely, if at all.

The horses, Bear, and Stingray, a gray Arabian, were hitched to the outside of the trailer, saddled and ready. It had been only fifteen minutes since she left the horses along the riverside and drove the rest of the way up to Trudy's. Coil didn't mentioned anything to Trudy about the idea until she stopped her truck next to the trailer, which was parked in a wide spot on the road.

"Yours?" asked Trudy.

"Ours, at least for a couple hours," said Coil. "Game?"

"I haven't ridden since high school."

"Then you know there's nothing to it. I've already told Bear to be especially gentle. He's a rock, anyway, and hard to fluster. There's a trail that leads up along the banks of the river. It's a bit chilly, especially with the wind, but I brought an extra coat that Weaver loaned me."

She held it up: full-length, brown, and leather.

"I'm—"

"Nervous? Don't be."

"This is so . . . I don't know. Either I'm at home or in the car, with somebody else driving."

"But you're game."

"Sort of."

"Okay then."

Coil helped Trudy up on the saddle and she smiled. "Whew," she said, "the view."

"What's for lunch?" asked Coil, loading Trudy's Tupperware into Bear's saddlebags.

"Tuna and pickle sandwiches with sprouts on sourdough, yogurt-covered raisins, fresh mango slices, cranberry-almond muffins, and whole-wheat Fig Newtons."

"Fig Newtons?"

"Like 'em?"

"God's gift to guides. A staple."

"I hope it doesn't remind you of work, in that case."

"Not a chance."

Coil led them down a gentle path to the river's edge, and they both waited for a few minutes while the horses dipped their snouts in a calm eddy. The river bubbled cold and white and blue, rippling around snow-capped stones.

"Warm enough?" asked Coil.

"Like a summer day," said Trudy, the cool wind flipping her long hair off her shoulder.

They walked along the river, downstream, and Coil watched as Trudy turned her head to the sun, eyes closed, and basked in the fresh air. It was Coil who had called, said they needed to talk, but there was no hurry, no reason to press things. It was all too unsettling.

The path dipped down, along with the river, far enough below the road that, for a half-mile or so, it seemed they were alone in the wilderness, explorers. The lone signs of civilization were a distant set of power lines and the fact that their trail was so trampled. Then, around a bend, they watched a fly fisherman working a pool, aiming his hook at one particular spot over and over, his concentration—or relaxation—so intense that he didn't notice them coming up alongside him. When he finally did, at the same moment a plump trout exploded up from beneath the surface and snagged the bait in what looked like documentary style. For them, thought Coil. The fisherman smiled.

"Woolly booger?" asked Coil.

"Works every time," said the fisherman.

"Beautiful," said Trudy.

The fisherman held up his catch for them to study, and the sun glinted off the multi-colored fish skin for just a flash. Gently, the fisherman held the prize underwater and let him go.

Trudy clucked Bear along, clearly getting used to this, and Coil took a moment to stretch and look around, back upstream and to the west, checking the skies. A man sat on the guardrails high above them. Coil could barely make out the top of a brown pick-up behind him. For a second, Coil thought the man was simply shielding his eyes from the sun. Then the light reflected off some small binoculars. Or camera? He was not wearing a coat; he hadn't been outside long. For a second, Coil stared back. They were clearly his focus. And then she looked ahead to Trudy, who had gone on around a corner and out of sight. It was probably nothing, and Coil trotted to catch up.

They walked the horses for an hour, mostly in silence. Finally they found a spot where a good-sized boulder shielded the wind and nature had built a dry, grassy embankment a few feet above the water's surface. They weren't too far below the road. They could hear the occasional car or truck overhead, but it was an easy trade-off for the windbreak. Coil tied the horses to a scrub oak a few yards further downstream, huddled down with Trudy next to the warm rock, and cracked each of them a split of wine.

"Screw-top. Sorry," said Coil.

"Like I'm complaining," said Trudy with a broad smile.

"Chilean Merlot," said Coil. "Here's to mountain rivers."

They clinked glasses and took a sip. Coil heard Trudy let out a small sigh.

Trudy picked at her food casually, unhurriedly, as Coil started with the Gulf Stream and ended with pulling the state records that list public debts, which documented the money Trudy's husband George had borrowed, at the outset anyway, to buy his plane and to launch his sporting goods store.

"His plane alone was worth $350,000 new," said Coil. "He probably needed to or wanted to stay liquid."

"Liquid?"

"Cash-wise liquid. So he borrowed it, or most of it, and the debt gets registered with the state."

"I didn't know," said Trudy.

"When my friend, this lawyer I know, saw what I was doing, he took me over to another computer in his office that has a hard line straight into the computer database for the courts. All the records and filings are there."

"I saw a show once, or maybe it was a news report, about these databases," said Trudy.

"Type in his name, boom. Seems your husband isn't a huge fan of the federal government and its pesky little IRS."

"I can vouch for that," said Trudy.

"Three years ago, he was audited," said Coil.

"I remember an auditor who came to the house to look at the books. She looked like your typical suburban housewife mom. Hardly what you'd expect."

"A dispute surfaced. It was minor at first, but, according to the transcript of the trial, your husband came this close to being thrown in jail for contempt of court. Once we had your husband's name and the case number, it was easy pulling the records of what happened. Anyway, he didn't show up for the first day of the trial. Then he insisted that he be allowed to claim the house, your house, as a deduction for his business operation."

"It's a house, like any other."

"Claimed he entertained clients there, and what was the difference between home and going out to a restaurant?"

"Never saw anybody," said Trudy. "Or very few clients."

"A few facts spilled over the falls in the trial. My friend, the lawyer, called again this morning. He was helping me put some things together. Your husband's net worth?"

"Please," said Trudy, closing her eyes.

"We figure it's about five million. This was five years ago. It's been awhile. Interest on that alone would add up considerably."

Trudy seemed to slump at the news. She put her sandwich down.

"Your husband has been successful for quite some time. But that much profit from the store alone? It's hard to figure. And outfitting? He only has a dozen camps under his special use permit with the National Forest Service. And it's not like he doesn't have expenses."

"He could pay for my operation in a blink."

"Yes. He could pay for your operation in cash and let you stay the entire time, before and after, in the finest hotel in Denver."

"Incomprehensible," said Trudy.

Five million, thought Coil, was no more difficult to imagine than $900,000.

"I know a guy whose brother was the nephew of the guy who invented the grocery cart," said Coil. "The grocery cart. It was some big deal when he did it. Everybody started buying more, in the stores, because they could carry everything at once and really load up. It changed the design of grocery stores. The guy inherited a fair chunk. He says it's like discovering a secret room in your house that's chock full of money, stuffed to the living gills. You go in there and take out ten, fifteen grand and go spend it, just a handful. The day you go back for more, though, the empty space has filled up where you took money, and the pile of cash has taken over a small closet to boot. Must be nice."

"There must be some explanation, something," said Trudy. "Maybe he's lost it since?"

Coil let Trudy answer her own question, let her struggle with it.

"He was so kind, built that beautiful house, knew what he wanted to do. Always did," said Trudy. "You must think I'm a fool."

"Hardly," said Coil.

"What now?" asked Trudy.

"I don't know," said Coil.

"It all points in one direction. The radio monitors and all, especially what you said about Slowik, about how often George comes through with kills."

"Big ones, too."

"What about Rocky?"

"That's what I'd like to know."

"It can't be good,"

"Don't say that," said Coil. "You can't think that."

"I can feel it, sense it."

"But we don't know. Not for sure."

Bear snorted at the same time that they heard the scrub oak rustling up above the horses, and Coil looked up. The side of a four-door black pick-up pulled up tight with the roadside. The diesel engine idled noisily, and Popeye Boyles stood next to the cab, smoking a stubby cigar, one hand on the rearview mirror.

Grumley came around from behind Bear, striding hard, and then was beside them.

"Trudy," he said. "You know this is dangerous."

"No, wait," said Coil.

"You wait," said Grumley. "She's not well."

Grumley had Trudy by the arm, pulling her up.

"Give her the coat back," said Grumley.

"No, really," said Coil. "I'll get her back—"

"You'll do nothing. Got it? *Nothing.*"

Grumley was directly in her face when he said it, and Coil could smell old sweat and a layer of rank grime.

"George, really," said Trudy.

But George had her by the arm, kept dragging her off. Coil snuck a glance at Boyles, who had the door to the pick-up swung wide open. From where Coil stood, she couldn't see where Grumley was yanking her up the slope. Wherever it was, Trudy was getting scratched by the bushes and scrubby trees.

They loaded Trudy in the back seat, and Boyles rode shotgun up front. The truck peeled out. Trudy stared straight ahead.

* * * *

The bank of gray clouds overhead was so thick that it was as if the Federal Reserve had stuffed the sun in its darkest vault. The humidity dampened Coil's cheeks, her face her only exposed skin. It felt like her cheeks were slicing through the sopping layers of a tissue box that had been left out in the rain.

Worse than that, no views.

She thought constantly of Trudy, what Grumley might have said, what Trudy would've said in reply, and how ugly their day must have been after Trudy had been snatched away the day before. She wondered how much Trudy might or might not say. She wondered what she might ask about. Her hunch was: not much.

Bear stopped in a boulder field on the southern flank of the butte, a spot where they usually lingered to drink in the vistas. The packhorse ambled to a stop beside them. Bear relieved himself, as if on command. She climbed down and stepped a few paces off the trail to do the same. As she stood up, buttoning up, she heard a distant snort. Horse. Ahead or behind, she couldn't tell. She stood next to Bear and stroked his snout. Was it a false echo on the radar?

"Weird," she said. "I could have sworn—"

They picked their way through the boulders and headed over to the western face of the butte where the trail plunged down through a section of krummholz, belly-high to the horses. Her chaps strummed snow from the stubby branches as they rode along, until the smothering thickets opened up and gave way to a clutch of aspen. She took a deep breath, consciously filling her lungs to capacity with the damp air, and praised the fact that the world wasn't all urban jungle. A Northern Flicker tapped the bark on an old lodgepole pine and then darted down low, swooping at ground level, powered only by the intermittent flaps of its wings.

The trail maintained its heading back to the north, gradually descending for a mile or so, until they hit the bottom of the drainage, and then more steeply back uphill toward a high, lake-dotted plateau thick with aspen, a thriving undergrowth, and every critter known to Colorado. Coil spotted the camp, as the sun briefly threatened to define itself in the haze, and she caught a wisp of shadow, her own, before it evaporated.

"Hello!" she called from thirty yards out. "Anybody home?"

"Hello!" came the call back from one of the canvas tents where a chimney puffed gray smoke in the drab sky.

Coil hitched the horses. A man and a woman, both draped in over-sized parkas, approached with smiles.

"Nice day, huh?" asked Coil.

"If you like the inside of a walk-in freezer at night," said the man.

They all shook hands. Bill and Cindy Pearls. Scottsbluff, Nebraska. Outfitted as if enough catalog camping gear would take care of everything, including sneaking up on a big fat mule deer. They huddled in the tent, the neatest and most immaculate indoor space Coil had ever seen this far from indoor plumbing. Somebody, she guessed, wasn't doing much hunting. One of the other guides had set them up four days ago, but it looked like they had been airlifted in straight from a Martha Stewart hunting camp.

"One day, the first day, we got close to a couple of deer, two small bucks. You couldn't have paid me to pull the trigger," said Bill, laughing. "I love to eat meat and think venison is God's gift to taste buds. Next to elk medallions, that is. But no way could I have been responsible for destroying one of those beautiful, beautiful creatures."

Bill had the tough-guy features of an ex-Marine or a football fullback: moose-like chest, zero neck, and shoulders designed to absorb punishment in a variety of forms.

"It was so cute," said Cindy. "Thousands of dollars for all of this, months of preparation, even shooting practice, and he didn't care."

"But I'm getting some reading done," he said, pointing to a stack of paperbacks. "And when it's been clear, we've gone for hikes to look for the deer or the elk, whatever."

"The other two?" asked Coil.

"They went back out this morning to finish dressing a deer they dropped at dusk last night," said Bill.

"Close enough we could hear the shot," said Cindy, as if that made it more exciting.

They unloaded Coil's packhorse and then Coil followed Cindy on foot to where the others were supposed to be, less than half a mile from camp.

"They weren't quite sure about this part," said Cindy. "But they said they wanted to get it strung up for the night."

The carcass was on the ground in a small clearing, next to a frozen lake guarded by old pine trees that had been charred and stripped of life by a spot fire not too many years ago.

"Professional help at last," said the woman as they approached. It appeared her job was to keep her hands tucked in her pockets and serve as head cheerleader. The man stood up, his hunting clothes in splotches of goo and red.

"I think you'd need to do this once or twice," he said, "in order to avoid making a nasty mess. The video made it look easy."

Cindy introduced them around. Steve and Martha Ellis. She shook hands. He waved at first, then removed his goopy glove to shake, too.

"You had him hung up pretty soon after you shot him?"

"Within an hour," he said. "Tried to get most of the viscera out of the cavity before night fell and propped it open with a branch, but we didn't get all the upper guts, the heart and lungs. We wanted to skin him, too, and get the hide salted, but it was too damn dark."

Steve was compact and stout with a square head, black mustache, and rounded red cheeks. Martha was a couple of inches taller, and she looked lither, but only by a matter of degrees.

Coil helped them skin and then quarter the animal as Cindy and Martha chatted away, saying things like "yuck" at appropriate times, such as when Steve sawed through the eyeballs to save the skull and antlers.

Coil stayed for a late lunch back at the camp. Cindy whipped up some tuna salad that was one part fish and two parts mayonnaise. More goo. Somedays, it just followed her. Trudy's tuna was vastly superior, with a gourmet's touch.

Bear and the packhorse munched some oats as she loaded them up. Because of the quartered deer, she'd have to return to the barn rather than make a stop at another camp up over Black Squirrel Pass. She'd been half hoping to go back that way again and look from the same spot where she had seen the man dragging something, to see if it would help her recall anything useful. She'd also wanted to bring down a good chunk of the dead elk for tests.

"Somebody will come pack you out, day after tomorrow," she said, climbing up on Bear. The four of them stood around, kicking the snow.

"So if we happen to get another deer down today or tomorrow, and you know I've already filled my tag, and you know old tough guy Bill here didn't do the shooting . . .?"

"Well what?" asked Coil.

"You think that's okay?"

"Two licenses, two guns, two hunters, two deer. No biggie."

"Just checking," said Steve.

It wasn't hard to imagine their mini-mansions in the suburbs, with the hand-waxed automobiles, plush carpeting, and fixed routines. Another Friday night, another pan of lasagna or whatever it said on the schedule. She wondered what it must be like to go through life on a static ride, safe and beyond trouble, outside fate's scrutiny, with a steady stream of income, untormented by $900,000 windfalls and decisions over whether or not to sue your own government. She once knew that world herself, she thought. But she couldn't recall, really, how it had felt, probably because she hadn't, then, seen the need to feel it or define it. Minutes ago she had sanctioned the death of another deer. The pilot didn't want to die. Ray Stern did—and why care, then, about his killer? And by muddling in it all, wasn't she in a position to pull up the roots on another stable existence or two? Was it better to let it be? Better for whom?

Bear seemed content with the idea of following his own tracks back to the barn. His steps contained a shade more purpose, but it didn't seem likely they'd make it back before dark.

"Whoa," said Coil, and Bear looked around like he was wondering what she had forgotten this time.

A set of horse tracks headed off the trail and up the ridge on a diagonal line. Not tracks, really, but snow kicked up and disturbed. Distinctively horse. They were only a quarter mile from the camp. She slipped off Bear and walked ahead, down the slushy trail bed. Her packhorse, of course, had followed Bear's line closely. Not much choice. The tracks were clear. She studied the other set, a wider arc on the shoe itself. Perhaps a much bigger horse or mule. The gait was long, too. Back at Bear's side, she peered up the slope, and then behind her, then climbed up in the saddle and looked down the hill. The woods were empty.

Three hours to dusk, and five hours to the barn. Night temperatures headed for the low teens. The footing around the front of the butte, through the boulder field, wasn't ideal in daylight. They would go until an hour before dusk and then stop. "You're going to be mad at me when you see me break out the tent," she told Bear. "It's for the best, though."

The thick woods gobbled up what light the heavy clouds did not. A cool breeze cut across her face and started loosening the treetops from a frozen slumber. The weather might be starting to pack its bags, having already stayed beyond its invitation.

Two hours later, Coil spotted a small, flat clearing down off the trail about twenty yards away. Probably a forest floor coated with pine needles in mid-July, now it held a foot of snow. A ring of towering lodgepole pines guarded the space.

She took the packs off the packhorse and the saddle off Bear. She tied the deer quarters together and hoisted them up on a rope, ten feet off the ground. She set up the pup tent in a patch of snow, after digging out a square so she could stake it in frozen soil, using a hammer. Her hands shook as she tried to hold the stakes steady. She tossed her sleeping bag inside with a small roll of extra clothes. She'd fashion a pillow out of some combination of clothes. Next, she scouted for firewood, retrieving dead limbs from what she could reach. She'd made a fifty-yard sweep in four directions before there was a pile that matched the tent's height and width. A hatchet turned one branch into wood shavings. She made four more piles of successively larger twigs, sticks, and smaller limbs. A dry exterior was the key, dry enough that so she could fool the fire into thinking that it wasn't winter, that all the fuel was prime material.

Next she needed green limbs that could serve as a platform for the fire. Two perfect branches, both slender and clean, would have been reachable if she'd been able to stand on top of the snow. To get to the third perfect branch, she had to hook her left elbow around the opposite limb, stand with one foot on another, and whack away with the hatchet. "You'll survive," she said. "I'm a bee. This is my stinger." Ten more chops, and she was through. Then she made six pieces out of the one back closer to her tent. She lined the six up side by side, wedged together by the snow. She built a teepee of the smallest twigs in the middle of her platform.

The first match blew out. The flames from the second leaped into her vented stack of miniature lumber like they recognized good fuel by smell. A soft crackle went up within a minute. She fed the wood down the fire's gullet. Every taste became another, larger bite. And then nothing, as if someone had covered the fire with an invisible glass hood. The flames shriveled up and then out. Screw it. She went to Bear's saddlebags for a packet of liquid napalm, a plastic tube like those frozen ice pops. She always brought a few spares along. Bear probably knew she was cheating. She dribbled the goo on the wood and lit another match to the glob.

"Hey, okay, big deal," she said to Bear. "Turn me in."

The fire sputtered for a second and then burst into business.

Dinner would be some beef jerky, an apple, slices of yellow cheddar, and water. The fire was roaring, and the earth around it started to soften. She went to check on the horses and give them the last of the oats. She sat by the fire, warming her hands and toes. The orange furnace was the only thing to watch. The flickering light danced to an irregular but busy beat.

The horses whinnied sharply, and she stood up abruptly, out of instinct, except the ground rushed up from the side and whacked her shoulder and head, and she heard herself yelp with surprise and then grunt as she smacked the earth.

Her feet didn't move, and she looked up, groggy from the tackle but trying to kick and move and find out what was happening. She tasted the residue of seawater, its stinging bitterness and its slightly more slimy texture filling her mouth.

How come she couldn't move?

Now she felt his body on her legs and him flipping her over before she could resist, shoving her head down in the snow, all his weight and strength pounding down on her so she didn't want to breathe out, in case that lungful was all that was keeping her rib cage from collapsing. Her cheek on the snow started to freeze. The hand on her butt felt enormous.

One arm was tucked tightly underneath. But he was pinching her bicep now and dragging it around to join the other one. He had come a long way if this was going to be rape. The idea flashed and was gone. He was sitting on her butt, tying her hands.

She risked a breath, inhaled snow, and spit it back out.

"What the—" brought a whack across the back of her head.

"You're fucking around where you don't belong."

The voice was gritty and old, or made to seem that way.

Anger filled her mouth with panic and determination.

"You don't—"

Another whack.

She wriggled and kept struggling, and he groped for control on top of her, crunching her hands. His mouth was now in her ear. He felt two feet taller than her: something about the way he had swatted her down.

"My arm—"

He was fiddling with her ankles, which snapped together, and she could feel the rope.

She was yanked backwards, the fire a bouncing blur and her shoulder crying for relief. She sunk down into the snow and clawed with her arms to search for a handhold. Nothing. Already she was thinking about her knife, and she tried to unclip it from its sheath with her good arm and hand. She glanced up at the man dragging her, and she kept flopping around. The knife came out. He stopped. Her body sank into the snow. Rope flew, and her ankles went up with a jerk. She tucked the knife down along her wrist, then wrapped her hand inside her jacket. Ten feet off the ground? The world spun, and she made him out, a hulking shape, as he tied the rope to a tree.

In the distance, upside down, the fire burned. She spun slowly as she dangled and waited.

The sound of him going, the weird voice, rattled in her ear.

Was he gone? Her left shoulder throbbed and burned. It felt loose and wobbly.

He was nowhere. Just gone. Her hand gripped the knife like a strength test. She did a sit-up, trying to hold herself in that position with her crunched arm, and slice the rope with the good one. The pain was searing. She dangled back down and tried to pass the knife from one hand to the other. She loosened her grip and had started to tell herself how important it would be to not lose the knife when it vanished, sucked down by gravity, and landed somewhere in the snowy void, far below.

* * * *

"Trouble," said Grumley.

The voice grated in Applegate's ear, and he held the phone away for a second, realized Ellenberg might hear it, and pressed it back, tightly.

"What?" said Applegate, eyeing the clock.

"Who is it?" asked Ellenberg.

"It's okay," said Applegate. They had spent the evening at his place, the one he'd soon sell, before maybe moving into Ellenberg's LoDo loft.

It was 12:15. A.M.

"What the fuck?" said Grumley. "You listening? You got trouble."

"Kind?"

"First with fucking me, but you know that. I keep tabs, asshole. But that ain't nothing. This Allison Coil number. She's getting so close to you, she's about to smell what a true asshole is."

It had been such a great evening. The spaghetti hadn't turned out that badly and they had plowed through a bottle and a half of red wine before making love next to the gas-fired fireplace, on the white carpet in his townhouse living room. She had teased him about the cookie-cutter townhouse, and he accepted the ribbing with good humor. They had watched a thriller on the VCR, and Ellenberg had made mental notes during one section where a horse was forced to dive off a high cliff. The movie studio was not one of the majors, and Ellenberg wanted to pass a note along to the national organizations, to see if the studio had signed any agreements about not abusing animals. There was no disclaimer with the credits.

"You gotta get your butt back up here and deal with her," said Grumley. "I sure as hell ain't doing your dirty work. You gotta put a scare in her or something, figure out if she's going to nail your ass. That is, unless you want it to get nailed."

"What the hell?"

"Who is it?" asked Ellenberg again, a hand gently stroking his back.

"It's okay," said Dean again, feeling torn. What could he do? How could he not expose himself if he did *anything*. "I can't," he said to Grumley.

"I'm sitting here looking at your rifle. Nice one. Maybe the cops will enjoy a peek, too."

Fucker, thought Applegate. "She can't have anything worthwhile, can't put anything together."

"You haven't seen nosy until you've seen this bitch."

Grumley hung up without any good-byes.

"What was it?" asked Ellenberg.

"Nothing," said Applegate. "At first, I thought it was somebody I knew. But I was wrong. Wrong number."

* * * *

The rapidly dimming orange dot of fire was her reference point. She trained on it as she spun.

Her ankles were tightly lashed. She could manage a half sit-up, to the point that she could grasp her knees with her good arm and dangle there, but the position didn't accomplish much, and her weak arm, the left, wanted nothing to do with helping hold her weight.

The cold, surreal aftershock of the man's departure was settling in. Especially the cold, which was getting a grip on her insides.

She shimmied up again and hooked her right elbow around her right knee, then talked her left arm into enduring the pain, too. She wanted to howl, but fear urged her to keep quiet. In the dark, she couldn't see the knots that bound her ankles.

An upside-down toe-touch. Accomplished.

Her left arm bore the weight, complaining to the point of agony, while her right lunged quickly for a new grip, higher up. Her fingers brushed rope where her hand landed.

Her back creaked. Not much time. The knots on the back of her legs, behind, were farther out of reach. Until she could get some weight off the ropes, the knots would stay snug.

The orange dot was right-side up as she peered off. She shook the rope with her body gyrating and tried to do a pull-up, like eighth-grade gym class, and remembered she was not one of the three girls who could. She ignored the pang of her complaining shoulder and shook and inched up, knowing there was no future in dangling. She rattled the rope around her legs, searching for the strength to lift herself above the knots, knots that gained the cinching power of her own weight.

Up. An inch.

Endure the pain.

Her toes wiggled. The bottoms of her heels came up—down—from the inside of her boots. She pointed her toes and scraped for another inch; her instep strained. He had lashed her boots. Not her legs. There was room to wiggle, but no bootjack for leverage.

She clawed up, her right foot finding more leeway, and her arm now above her boots, gripping the ropes. Her right foot came free.

The orange dot was fading.

Her left foot came free.

Her legs flopped down, and her back sighed as she gripped the rope. And before she could give it too much thought, she let go and dropped through the dark, wondering if she should come up swimming.

11

Pete Weaver had her wrapped unnecessarily in a colorful serape, and she was sitting on the floral-pattern couch in his huge farmhouse, a hundred yards from the barn where she had arrived, obviously injured. She sipped tea and stared into the huge fireplace, which was roaring full-bore.

"I called Sandstrom," said Weaver. "He said either he or someone else will meet you in his office late this afternoon, or as soon as you can make it down."

She stared at the fire, looking for answers.

Why hadn't he killed her? Had he meant to give her a chance to survive? If so, why?

"You've got to report it," said Weaver, his kindly old eyes unwavering. "I've never heard of anything like this."

"There's not much they can do," said Coil.

"Hell there isn't," said Weaver.

"There's nothing to look at, the camp site is trampled all over. I'll report it, but don't think it'll exactly fire 'em up."

"What about Mr. Forest Service?"

The thought of repeating the story more than once was agony. She wanted to tell David, maybe Trudy, and then sleep the whole thing off.

"I'll tell him. I'm sure Sandstrom will play Big Foot on it, keep all the other forms of government footprints away."

"They still oughta know, Slater and Bridgers."

"It's not like they need to warn everybody who goes into the back-country. It was me he was after."

"This whole business, I don't know," said Weaver.

"It seemed like everything was fine in this valley until the mother of all protests," said Coil.

"That's not—"

"What?"

"What I meant. But you're right, everyone in the valley has been on edge. This won't help."

"It doesn't have to get out."

"Doesn't *have* to. It just *does*."

"How much tranquilizer would it take to kill an elk?"

Weaver, who had taken up a cozy spot on a recliner and started to light a pipe, stopped and gave her a funny look.

"Excuse me?" he asked.

"Would two shots do it?"

"I have no idea," said Weaver, "or what you're talking about."

As soon as she talked to Sandstrom and grabbed a good night's sleep, she'd go get answers to her own questions.

Why hadn't he killed her?

"I'll need a couple days' R and R."

"It's okay," said Weaver. "We'll make do."

* * * *

"Big like football-linebacker big . . . or somebody, you know, bigger than your petite self?"

A few flecks of spit flew as Sandstrom hammered the t's in puh-teet.

Coil lowered her tender left arm onto the sheriff's steel desk. It wasn't her whole arm that stung, but the throbbing strain in the bicep made the entire limb flash messages of anger every time she moved it.

"Big, strong. Lumberjack. Paul Bunyan."

"You didn't get a good look at his face?"

"No."

"Didn't hear or see anything else all day?"

"At one point, I thought I heard a horse, you know, off in the distance. That was in the morning. Maybe behind me."

Slater, who had escorted her over, sat on the couch in Sandstrom's office. He was busy taking notes as if she'd come in off the street, and they had never met, and he was hearing the whole thing blow-by-blow for the first time. In fact, he'd had her run it down several times and asked lots of good questions, including questions displaying lots of concern about how her toes had fared and what she would have done if the fire had gone out completely.

"No other indications?"

"Another time I saw tracks, heading up the trail and then splitting off. I didn't think much—"

"Obviously, you were being followed," said Slater, cutting to the quick.

Sandstrom cast a look at Slater that said kids in college calculus classes shouldn't demonstrate their ability with adding fractions.

"But no visual contact?"

"No. Oh, this," said Coil. "I almost forgot." She pulled a long length of rope from a plastic bag and plopped it on his desk.

"Standard issue," said Sandstrom. "Hardware store variety. Plus, this one's already served a lifetime. But that's appreciated, and quite smart of you." Sandstrom put the rope on a shelf next to him, as if it was something she was returning.

"And your assailant said, again, the part about fucking around."

"Where I don't belong," said Coil. "Fucking around where I don't belong."

Coil slid another glance at Slater, who had his mind on the back side of a distant planet. There wasn't much Slater could do now. This was her pickle.

"So some guy comes and strings you up upside down in the middle of nowhere because you've been doing nothing, asking around about *nothing*."

She had seen this slightly difficult problem before deciding to report the incident, but hadn't resolved how to deal with it. Slater had urged her to get it on the record, at least, and softly dodge questions about her level of involvement.

"Any particular individuals you'd care to mention who might have had their feathers ruffled?" asked Sandstrom.

"I was simply reporting the assault. I really didn't think there was much you could do about it, unless I had more of an idea who did it."

"Then consider it reported," said Sandstrom. "But that doesn't mean we're not interested. We'll need you to show us where this happened."

"There's nothing there."

"He might have dropped something."

"Doubt it."

"We'd like to see."

"Take the east trail to Buffalo Peak. Halfway to Wall Lake, you'll see the remnants of my camp. If you get to one of our campsites, you've gone too far by about a mile and a half. There's two couples staying there now. The tracks around should explain everything."

"I know where it is," said Slater. "Our people can show you."

Standing up, Coil winced as her arm again came under its own weight.

"You know, whatever it was I saw—originally . . . "

Coil let the thought hang, to see if Sandstrom bit.

"Yes?"

". . . is connected with this."

Slater took a breath and cocked his head, as if his neck had a painful kink.

"You've stirred the bees off the honey pot, if that's what you mean. Although I don't think you've come clean with me, young lady. Speaking for myself and not the official government record, I believe one thing. When we find the brainless piece of particulate matter that killed Ray Stern, and if we get a confession, you'll discover that what you saw was Ray Stern's killer, trying to hide things away. I don't think you were exactly where you thought you were, with all due respect for your guide skills, and I think you saw the spineless idiot who killed Ray Stern trying to clean up his mess. You were, after all, a city girl until recently, were you not? Those mountains, I mean, really. How many varieties of shapes, bowls, peaks, and ridges can there be? Don't they all look alike after awhile?"

"Then where the hell is Rocky Carnivitas?" she said sharply.

"Whoa," said Slater, standing up, reaching out. Coil stepped away, but kept staring at Sandstrom.

"Off following some oversized hoof prints in the next county. There was nothing tying him down, nothing. Talk about your transient business, wrangling is one fleeting way of life."

"Find him," said Coil. "Put out the word. Ask why his truck's been parked at George Grumley's barn in the same spot for a couple weeks now. I drive by it all the time."

"It was a huge storm. He could have been trapped," said Slater. "It's possible."

Coil shot Slater a stare, upset that he'd try to derail her train. "Me or you," said Coil. "Not Rocky, no way."

Slater offered back a weak smile. Coil felt her heart begin to thump hard, felt a bit of confusion clog her throat.

"Track Rocky," said Coil. Although he won't be much use when you find him, she thought. Then she did the one thing she'd been sure she wouldn't do; she wiped a sobless tear from her cheek. At least neither one of them came to comfort her. That would really have pissed her off.

"We'll see what we can do," said Sandstrom.

"Thanks," said Coil and stood to leave without saying good-bye. "If you don't find him, I will."

Coil waited for Slater in her Blazer, thinking of spending a day scrubbing the cabin down within an inch of its life or giving Bear a thorough groom for the heck of it. But both activities involved her shoulder. She wouldn't mind a day of not thinking about it, of not trying to force the puzzle together. The view through the binoculars had seemed, at first, like it would remain clear forever. When had the image started to wobble? Who was responsible for that? Could the moment she heard the shot really have coincided with the last moments of a human being's life? One she knew? Was that possible?

Slater ambled out and stood by her rolled-down window.

"You think the report amounts to anything, really? Telling Sandstrom?"

"A chance for him to talk in football lingo," said Slater.

"It's the season," said Coil.

"You hit a nerve, anyway. Somebody went to a whole lot of trouble up there, chasing you around. But when you get a minute, think about it. It might have been the protesters."

"What?"

"Whoa now. A thought. This guy was suicidal."

"So?"

"So maybe he had help with his wish and now, because of what you saw, maybe it wouldn't look so good anymore. I'm trying to say it may not be the obvious."

The idea was hollow, offered no substance as she unwrapped it in her head. It was a strange world—but not that strange. Not worth debating.

"You think Sandstrom will do anything?"

"Depending on what there is to do, yeah, he'll take a look. Maybe somebody else saw this guy, can give them a description."

"Maybe," said Coil.

He leaned down, kissed her briskly, and then she started to roll up the window with her left hand by reflex, but her arm issued a yelp of agony. She reached across with her right and awkwardly cranked the glass up as Slater watched, offered an exaggerated frown, turned on his heels, and headed to his own truck at a jog.

As she pulled out onto the highway, she noticed that Glenwood Canyon was draped in its late-fall garb. The canyon's cliffs were dressed in their finest, butterscotch brown. She let her eyes go soft-focus, and it looked as if a painter had come through with a brush full of water that forced the colors to run together. A long freight train picked its way along the opposite bank, and she briefly thought she spotted a hobo poking his head out of an empty green boxcar. But the road veered sharply in front of her, and by the time she flicked her eyes back he was gone, even though she could now see deep inside the boxcar. She sped up to see if she had the right car, but there were no other green ones on that whole section of the train.

There was no giving up.

Now, as she headed home, the thought of being alone wasn't unpleasant. Her mind swirled between Sandstrom's odd interview style, almost too carefree, and the snapshots of sounds and images—snorts and strange horse tracks—leading up to the assault by the fire.

How long would it have taken for somebody to find her body hanging from a tree? Her brain zipped through the events like an endless loop on a film projector, like a mental mobius strip, where she was forced to re-live each frame again and again, sometimes in slow motion.

She had lain awake in her sleeping bag, gingerly avoiding putting any weight on her stinging arm, and turned every creak of a tree branch into the return of her attacker. She had fed the fire every hour, and, just after dawn, she'd hopped over to Bear in her socks, her feet in frozen agony. Climbing up on the saddle, she had guided him around to her boots, stood on his back to undo the rope, and retrieved them. She had warmed both the boots and her feet by the fire, staring into the flames, replaying the attack as if it had been a movie. She had to watch the movie over and over. It was the only theater in town, and there was only one person in the audience. There was nowhere else to go.

* * * *

It was the same space. Same cats, same plants, same everything, except the constant presence of another person, whoever it was on any given day, altered the state of the air and the attitude of her environment. Trudy felt shaky. She could not adjust to the sensation of being a prisoner. Her mind ran wild with theories and speculation. She kicked herself for giving in to George and leaving Allison there on the riverbank after only putting up a minor fuss.

Trudy tried to bury herself in her chores and routines, attempting to let the small stuff soak her up. She made herself busy repotting plants and cooking and the usual, but nothing freed her mind, let her relax. She made a game out of trying to be nice with her half-hearted captors, those switched temporarily out of "Trudy Duty" to "Jail Guard." Every morning they passed the baton. Once or twice they had even overlapped for a few hours, and she could hear them both in the living room, laughing and shooting the breeze while they ate their coffee cake and worked their way through a pot of good French Roast, not that they knew the difference. It was all very civilized.

George hadn't said much of anything. The point was clearly to stay put and mind her business, but how was that possible? Her mind often tried to slash its way through a thicket of anger and uncertainty. She felt trapped, even more than usual, by the facts from Allison. It all made sense except for the sheer scale of the hole George had dug for her, a hole from which she hadn't been able to see much of anything but a pinprick-size glimpse of his whole dealings. Rocky must have gotten caught up, somehow, in the tangle of money and illegal junk. Trudy half wondered if it was something she had said that might have given Rocky the feeling that he could be more bold confronting George. She wondered what Allison would do with the information, where it all might lead. She knew that it wouldn't work to sit back and wait. Someone had to make a move.

* * * *

The trail was now trampled, mucky in spots, and the snow was beginning to yield to the steady power of the sun. The dead elk had been gnawed and picked over by more than a few predators. They had picked their favorite parts. It was not a cheerful sight. Nature's version of an autopsy wasn't attractive.

The landscape was lifeless, as she had feared. She didn't want to go another step, but she climbed off Bear gingerly, cautious with her tender arm. She took in the sounds of wind and air and her own breathing.

"Rocky?" she asked out loud. "Where are you?"

She had seen Rocky and Grumley confronting each other, in her mind, over and over. Maybe it was over Grumley's wife. Or the business. Or both. Poor Rocky, trying to stand up to a gruff boss and yet soft enough, on the inside, to want to care for Trudy.

It was Rocky, more than anyone except Weaver, who had accepted the city girl into the fold, showed her the ropes, literally, and never let on that he expected her to fail.

Failure. An interesting word. Wings fail to provide lift, and the result is a flying machine in the cold, salty drink, and dead bodies bobbing all around. Whose failure? And why? And why did it happen when it did? Failure? Or nature? Meant to be? A matter of fact? Just deal with it? Which question led to the best chance of your brain accepting what it was being asked to absorb—and live with forever? Would blame ease things? Could you really assign it to the winds of fate? Did that make it any easier?

Human beings can be propped up and strapped down in rows six seats across with an aisle down the middle one second, and then tumble, through external forces and events way beyond their control, into mess and fury the next. She had learned that from personal experience. One moment, events are calm and peaceful and the world functions in an orderly fashion. The next moment, life—right down to the molecules—comes unglued, and you cannot reach out with your hands and put any of it back together, even though you want to and think you can. Once the egg starts cracking, it cannot be made whole again. Since the airplane flopped into the water, in fact, she realized that a thin, fragile shell bubble-wrapped each waking moment. Life, for people or animals, could be shattered apart at any moment. And here it was again, that feeling, now, more distinct than ever in the stark, snowy landscape. The plastic bubbles were right there, all around her, and they were starting to pop, one at a time.

You're here on the side of the mountain, Coil thought, breathing fresh air. And somebody else is long gone—simply because of a seat number. There was no time to prepare for the lifeless bodies in the water next to her. They were all so recently alive. And there really was no good way, no sure-fire way, to absorb the loss after it was over, after the survivors had been rounded up and counted, after the dead had been lined up and counted, after the crash had been folded into the wrinkles and warps of history.

"Stay here, Bear," she said, eyeing an out-of-place lump, down off the steep slope, up against a tree. She trudged down, but lost track of which tree she thought displayed something irregular, once her angle changed on the plummet down. At the bottom, she had trouble resetting her bearings. The trees were all similar in size, build, and stature. The snow was packed, less conducive to somebody wading through. It was like gooey gelatin, not yet set. She picked a tree, more or less at random, and headed for it. Whatever had been semi-clear from the trail was murky here, down at snow level. Coil stepped slowly. The base of one tree was smooth, ordinary, and so was the second. Should she go north or south? She took a glance back at Bear, who wasn't even watching.

Her heart went for a brief sprint in her chest, looking for a safe rhythm to run a marathon.

From a few paces away, the shape suddenly appeared, a snow-covered, sitting-up shape. Her chest tightened, and she gulped for air.

There was nothing to fear, nothing that could hurt her, just acres of snow and mute trees. But her brain wasn't finding a way to connect up and get in gear. Coil kneeled down and dug through the snow at the top of the sizable lump, where no rock should be.

She brushed at the snow, and instantly something non-white appeared, something light brown. A hat.

Her stomach had time to register its opinion by slamming itself up inside the back of her throat and trying to crawl out on its own. She buckled in the snow, spitting slime and trying to get the blood back in her head. She scooped a glove full of soft snow and patted it on her cheeks and stumbled off a few yards, stood up, and inhaled some deep, long drags of the mountain air.

"Rocky," she said. "Shit."

But she had to make sure, scraping off the snow and thinking of all the times Slater and Sandstrom had dismissed her, what she had seen and heard.

There was a good side to his face, and another that hardly existed— shattered bone and muscle and a blown-out eye socket. His entire face was white and stiff, hardly facial at all.

There was no need to dig any further. There would be no lifting him up to the slope and then to the trail, no way to flop him over the back of Bear, no way to even budge him more than a few feet with only one good arm.

She reached for his hat, as good as his fingerprints, but then thought to herself, no, this is a crime scene.

Everything had fallen into place, as she'd hoped it wouldn't.

* * * *

"Hey, why would I be worried about the gun?"

"If I was you, I'd make sure it was really disappeared."

"I've told you three times what I told them; I hiked it back up into the mountains and gave it a good heave."

"She's onto something. Sniffing hard."

There was always a good steady background buzz of clatter and chat and bustle at FATE headquarters, so agreeing to meet at the office with a Grumley pal, in this case Bobby "Fishy" Marcovicci, seemed at first like a low-risk proposition, especially in the partitioned cubicle which served as his office.

"You think she's onto something?" asked Applegate. "There's nothing to be on to."

"Earnest little kid, I must say. Lot of experience in a meager frame. Although she's got a sweet little rack on her."

"Please," said Applegate.

"Oh, Mr. Sensitive now. Sorry."

"So what did you do?"

"I called George, of course."

"And—"

"He didn't like the idea of getting tangled up in all this mess any more than I did. And that's why I called you, because she was mentioning your name quite a bit, too."

"Thanks. She's wasting her time, whatever it is she's trying to do."

Suddenly Applegate realized that he didn't want any more contact with the people who knew him as his previous self.

"So this anti-hunting thing," said Marcovicci, "it's real?"

"Of course."

"What I mean is, you believe this stuff? It's got you on television and in every newspaper from here to Podunk, but—"

"But what? I changed my mind. It's about as simple as that."

There was an unbending silence in the space between them.

"Excuse me?"

Marcovicci cranked his head at the sound of the female voice at the opening to Applegate's partition. Ellenberg stepped in, not waiting for permission. The office was like that, free flowing. Applegate had grown to like its loose feel. Applegate introduced them but only mentioned Marcovicci's profession: nothing to do with the hunting. Ellenberg didn't seem interested in small talk.

"Pleasure to meet you," she said curtly. Marcovicci had stood at her entrance.

"We need to talk schedule when you get a minute," said Ellenberg. "Local morning show here wants you to debate the author of that new, disgusting book that says, you know the one, that hunting is in our genes and can't be suppressed."

"The guy that says hunting is loving yourself," said Marcovicci. "Interesting premise. Yeah, what's the title? *Born To Gather, Dying To Hunt.*"

"Gives me the creeps," said Ellenberg.

"Actually," said Marcovicci, "he's a reputable scientist, or theorist."

"Like how our brains can't possibly control some little impulse stuck in our genes," said Ellenberg.

"Stuck—or built up, developed over the centuries," said Marcovicci.

"Perhaps you'd like to debate your friend here," Ellenberg said to Applegate.

"He'd eat me alive," said Applegate. "So to speak."

"Yeah," said Marcovicci. "Bet the cannibalism metaphors don't go too far around here."

Applegate thought he saw Ellenberg give Marcovicci a faint sneer.

"We've got a big fundraiser and everyone wants you there for a few words. The next weekend we have a little stunt up our sleeves for the people breaking ground on that new aquarium. So when you get a chance . . ."

Ellenberg smiled and was gone, casting a curt glance in Marcovicci's direction.

"You're doing the horizontal bop with the queen bitch," said Marcovicci.

"What do you mean?"

"What do you mean what do I mean?"

"Jesus—"

"Jesus, what? Christ, Applegate, you're a fucking mess. War paint camouflage and looking for a big elk one week, boinking Mrs. Fucking Doolittle the next. And I mean *do little* but make a fuss and raise a stink for her goddamn political purposes. She'll probably run for Congress or mayor some day, and all her minions will have laid the groundwork. And you, you ride in like Mr. Cowboy who suddenly decides to engineer the fucking peace train. I hope you're getting plenty and I hope it's good, but there's nobody out there who believes a blessed word of what you're saying."

Two pulsing veins flanked Marcovicci's throat. Applegate thought he felt the cubicles nearby go hush. He wanted to somehow signal Fishy to cool it.

"You got problems or a rifle or whatever you left behind up in the mountains, then I'm sorry I even bothered. Christ, screwing her."

"Wait, Fishy, it isn't that simple."

"Then what's complicated about you standing in the middle of FATE headquarters like the last great talking head? You guys and Operation Rescue and all the strident one-issue groups. It must be nice to see the world in such black and white terms. Later," said Marcovicci, turning to leave. "Or maybe never. One thing for sure, more room in the tent next year."

"Fishy, look."

What was there to say?

It might not matter. There was plenty to do.

The rifle. He'd need to drop things for a few days, maybe only one or two, and get back with Grumley, somehow. He'd have to go up there and do with the rifle what he'd said he'd already done.

Fishy was gone. What excuse would he give Dawn?

He couldn't afford to let things wait. The rifle. Maybe Grumley had destroyed it. Maybe he needed to make a phone call to find out. Could he risk a phone call? Life was confusing, just when he was starting to believe in something.

* * * *

"You can't honestly think," said Trudy, "that I'm really and seriously a threat."

Popeye Boyles sat at the kitchen table, gun propped precariously over his knee.

"Like physical threat? No, I don't suppose," he said.

"You're letting me fix us a decent lunch, perhaps we can at least be civil about this prison thing."

"Just following orders."

Trudy stirred the homemade clam chowder in her cast iron pot, added some milk, and set the flame on low. She wanted to stretch things out.

"Clam chowder. Don't ask where a Colorado mountain girl comes up with a taste for slimy old seafood, but it's possible. Always made me feel kind of warm and cozy."

"Only chowder we got in the U.S. Navy was corn with canned ham, and baking soda biscuits. Surrounded by an ocean, and never clam chowder—well, maybe twice a year. Go figure."

She half wondered if this leathery old man had an eye for her. It crossed her mind that if she couldn't go through with the mushroom plan, which had kept her awake most of the night—the idea appearing crystal clear and foolproof—she might at least make herself available for something physical. The age difference between them was, maybe, fifteen years. She could live with that. And his gruff way of talking didn't bother her as much as his dull musty odor. It was like the back of a damp basement closet, and she wasn't sure what might be growing there.

"There's no ham in the house. But I do have tomatoes and cucumbers and this wonderful seven-grain bread. With a bit of Dijon and a pinch of mayo, not the imitation stuff, you'll never crave a pork product again in your life."

"Sounds a little veggie," said Boyles.

"And we mustn't forget my secret little zing."

Boyles stood up as Trudy skipped quickly into the greenhouse and pushed aside the massive glass top that covered her own private piece of forest floor. She had thought about trying to secretly pocket a couple of the fly agarics or orange clitocybes, which studded the loamy bottom of her terrarium along with the dependable chanterelles and yummy oyster mushrooms, but she couldn't imagine herself slipping them into the sandwiches so slyly. The rich, humid, mossy, and slightly lemony air filled her nostrils. She took a moment to savor it.

"Whoa, whoa, whoa," said Boyles, right behind her. "I ain't eating nothing out of there."

"I suppose you like all your food wrapped in plastic and shipped half way around the country for a couple of weeks before you take a bite."

Trudy pushed back some ferns. The irregular, vise-like 'shrooms looked healthy and prime, the salmon-orange caps giving way to a brown base.

"Mushrooms?" said Boyles.

"You've never tasted a mushroom until you've had a chanterelle fried in butter with a dash of nutmeg."

She grabbed the impostor clitocybe by the base, the fattest of the six she could see, and pulled the root free. The clitocybes also had gills that extended far down the stalk, but the chanterelle's trunk was stubbier. The cap on this clitocybe was puffy and full blown, but the whole thing barely created any weight in her palm.

Boyles took a step backward.

"They grow from dead things, dead things that have energy." She spoke calmly, or tried to. She wanted to hold the clitocybe up for Boyles' inspection but realized her hand might betray her fear.

"A dead insect, rotting wood, anything with some left-over energy. The mushroom is the fruit, sort of. But it doesn't need chlorophyll to capture energy from the sun. Mushrooms, in fact, mostly avoid the sun. People pay top dollar for chanterelles in hot-shot grocery stores, and we've got our own right here."

"Curse of the Navy right there. If you know your history. Disaster for oak-hulled ships up until the American Civil War. The mushrooms were packing a punch—dry rot. Nothing but a headache that meant constant repair. Couple of ships, I think with the British Royal, even had their hulls rotted clear through. At sea. Entire crews gone."

"I think we need two," said Trudy. "I wasn't aware they were such a problem." She plucked another mushroom, this one a nutritious chanterelle.

She built the sandwiches, sliced each mushroom neatly into two separate piles on her cutting board.

Think ahead. Keys to the car. Grab his gun. Slit open a 20-pound bag of cat food, good for a couple of weeks, perhaps. Pack some clothes. He might writhe and gasp; he might not go all the way out.

"Cut diagonal or straight across?" she asked.

"What?" he said.

"Your sandwich," she said.

"Whole's fine," said Boyles.

She spooned the soup into a bowl, thinking a broth base might have been better, because all the thick milk might coat his stomach if he ate the chowder first, and the mushroom might not as easily find his blood-stream. Maybe he'd get sick. She started on her own sandwich while he peppered the hell out of his soup, stirred it around, and peppered it again.

He tested the soup, too hot, and packed his mouth with a bite from the sandwich.

Her heart fluttered and went light.

And then another bite. And three more.

"Beer to go with that?" she offered, wanting to be out of reach when it hit.

"Sure," he said, through a mouthful.

She spent longer than she needed, digging in the refrigerator. She couldn't turn around. How could she look? She listened for sounds of anything behind her, the clink of a spoon on the soup bowl. Nothing.

She pulled out two cans of Coors as the kitchen table careened up and crashed down. She scampered for the far corner of the kitchen and crouched by the garbage can and the bowls for cat water. Somewhere one of the cats meowed like a dull howl, and she thought she saw a bundle of black fur go flying as the table came to rest on its side. Then she heard a human grunt and half a cough—a cough like gagging. He was moving, crawling toward her. She stood up, thinking she should have planned to head the other way, because now she had to go around him or over him and through the mess. And she would probably have to look. Slowly she went along the counter, her back to the cabinets, keeping an eye on the table that shielded her view of him. Maybe he was pretending. Maybe he had tasted the poison. One of the two Siamese, Pookette, lapped peacefully at a pool of clam chowder on the floor. Bliss.

She leaped across a thrown chair, and his arm came flailing from behind the table. She screamed and then scrambled free, not looking back.

Put the clothes in a suitcase, especially the heavy stuff, she thought to herself. Her heart was beating wildly. Why wouldn't her hands calm down? How long did she have? She'd have to drive, at least a few miles down the road. She needed his gun and realized she should have grabbed it first, right away. Put the suitcase in George's old 4-Runner. God, did she even know how to work the clutch? Could she? Don't forget her purse and credit cards. Anything else? The table moved; it sounded like the table moving. Did the table move? The cats seemed to be watching her, unsettled. Take a big winter coat, the wool one. The gun. She couldn't look. She covered her eyes so there was only a small gap to see.

Bless her brain, it was hanging in there.

She stepped to the kitchen and tried not to see too much. The gun. The evidence! Down the disposal? The telephone—911? She would make that the last thing. The gun, where was the gun? He was keeled over sideways and wrapped around a chair, hugging its legs. He wasn't moving, but his chest heaved. The gun—it had to be here. There it was—the barrel underneath his leg. She squatted down, gave up on the idea of not looking, reached around to where the grip should be, and dug for it under his grimy jeans.

A hand clasped her forearm, locked on and dug for blood. She grabbed the gun by the muzzle and whacked the knuckles hard. The hand bounced off quickly, and she sprung away, shuddering.

She and the gun sat in the front seat of the 4-Runner. Now make that 911 call. Two rings. She spewed out something and gave directions, then let the phone dangle, off the hook, after saying she was heading out to look for help.

The clutch went in too fast the first time and killed the engine. She thought smooth, smooth and almost managed to keep it running the second time. The truck, at least, had started to roll. The third pop with the clutch, it jerked backward but kept rolling. She cranked the wheel once the car was outside, to turn it around. With the clutch down, she practiced finding the four gears, keeping a nervous eye on the door to the house.

First gear. A lurch, and off, down the driveway hill. She would get better at it. She was free.

"Meow," came the high-pitched whine, before she realized it was an echo in her head.

She took the main road back to the interstate. Third gear, fourth. Keeping her mind alert, supple, focused, relaxed. Relaxed? Impossible. The world was vivid and alive and coming at her in a Technicolor rush.

"Meow," came the sound again, and she risked a look around.

"Good Lord, Fossil."

Two yellow eyes peeked out from a ball of black fur that had found a bed on her suede coat, the big winter job. The cat didn't move, but answered politely with the only word it knew.

12

C oil's A-Frame looked friendless and neglected, an untended orphan, in the dusk-lit clearing. But she wouldn't be alone.

A boxy station wagon was parked off to the side of her house. The car was broadside to her view from the top of the road leading down. She couldn't make out the car's color, just the shape, and its odd parking place off to the side, as if it knew it didn't belong.

A figure moved from her front stoop to the car.

She stood with Bear for a second in the road, kept an eye peeled on the car, then headed down.

The man drifted back to her front porch. Something about his gait and build seemed familiar, but she couldn't connect her gut with good or bad.

A match made a gentle arc from somewhere up to his face and then was gone, replaced by a hot red dot that repeated the arc back down. There was a quick glimpse of skin, no meaning to it, even though she was much closer now.

One gentle turn remained in the road to the A-Frame. Now at least she knew he wanted to be seen. Bear snorted on cue.

The man was tucked half in the shadows. The orange cigarette tip bounced down her front steps, and suddenly she recognized his froggy frame and pug-like profile.

Fishy Marcovicci was dressed in full winter padding and stood off to the side of her porch, not smiling.

"I was going to give you another ten minutes, then I would have had enough of listening to my toes go pop, pop, pop," he said.

"Supposed to be five below zero by dawn," said Coil, hitching Bear up to the porch. "Something that couldn't wait, I suppose?"

"Damn right about that," said Marcovicci.

His puffy white cheeks were locked up tightly. He shifted his weight on the gravel driveway, and the noise, the only sound in the deadly cold, seemed hooked to an amplifier.

It wasn't hard to figure out that the over-sized shadow with the threatening words and the rope had materialized at her campsite shortly after her chat with Marcovicci.

So, Coil thought, he might still be sniffing around, chasing a trail. Working both sides.

"You still after Applegate's rifle?"

"Nothing has changed," she said.

"Tomorrow," he said. "You and me. Let's go find it."

His look was maniacal and cock-sure.

"You know where it is?"

"I didn't say that."

"Then why are you suggesting it's possible?"

"I just know we can get it. Just as long as there's no—what might be the appropriate word?—involvement of those parties that now, um, possess it."

"You mean I can't squeal on whoever has it now."

"Precisely."

"But I get the rifle?"

"You get it."

"But you can't tell me where it is?"

"Can't," he said.

"You have to show me?"

Marcovicci thought this over.

"It'd be like looking for a chunk of fool's gold in Fort Knox. You'll need help."

"Just a personal favor to me?" she asked.

"Something like that," he said.

"Where you staying?"

She couldn't reveal any slight mistrust, not if what he was promising was true.

"Man," he said, already stepping off into the darkness toward his own car. "I thought you'd never ask."

"I gotta make a few calls," she said. "I found something. Uh, some-body."

"Body?" said Marcovicci, pronouncing it like buddy, not the street word for corpse.

She opened the door for Marcovicci, then headed for the phone. Sometime soon, she'd have to take Bear back to the barn.

"Yes," said Coil. "Now there's two."

* * * *

"You two were eating lunch. Cozy."

"She offered. It seemed—"

"Don't tell me. Harmless."

"Yeah. I suppose."

"A sentimental jailer," said Grumley. "Just what I needed."

Boyles' face was sunken. It carried a gold, unhealthy sheen. Grumley wondered if there was a plug somewhere he could pull, make the face turn the color of death.

"Felt like my innards were on fucking fire."

A nurse giving a sponge bath to an old guy in the next bed glanced up and over.

"I gotta find Trudy," said Grumley.

"I'll bet she's long gone."

"I doubt it."

"Because she doesn't have any friends."

"This is what she knows. Around here."

George stewed. Should he make a beeline to Alaska, right now? File a flight plan for Alamagordo but head to Juneau?

He had every refueling stop planned out, and a friend of a friend who would trade him for a Mooney with a rebuilt engine, outside of Spokane. For years, however, the images in his mind about the day he'd disappear were all calm: an ordinary day in the summer, chatting with all the usual people, doing all the usual things; cash from the private and quiet sale of the store; cash from the private and quiet sale of the outfitting business; cash from the routine sale of his car and horses.

He had never figured out about the house. He supposed somewhere in his head and heart he had always pictured leaving it to Trudy, so she could decide if she wanted to liquidate it, or part of it, to pay for her operation on her own. Now it might be possible to sell the house, too, if Trudy truly disappeared.

There'd be another couple hundred grand. If Trudy truly disappeared. Another couple hundred grand, minimum a hundred and a half if he was in a hurry to cut a deal. If she truly disappeared.

* * * *

The Sulphur Inn carried CNN, free of charge. It wasn't an extra, at least. The inn, with its neon steam rising off the sign, was tucked between a new Wal-Mart and a lumberyard out on the road to Carbondale, south of Glenwood Springs. The road provided a plateau of commerce in the otherwise steep canyon formed by the Crystal River.

The motel was laid out like a sideways H, and Trudy asked the grandmotherly clerk for a room around in the back, and then for a different room when the cable didn't work in the first. She hadn't even bothered to unpack before checking the cable. The sign out front had said "Vacancy, Free Cable, No Pets," but she smuggled in Fossil when they weren't looking. She bought cat food, kitty litter, and air freshener at Wal-Mart. She hid the litter box under her suitcase during the day, until after the maid finished her rounds.

She timed her brief trips to the grocery store to coincide with local news on the radio, but there had been no mention of the authorities finding a dead man at their house. A good sign. Perhaps Boyles had regained consciousness before the ambulance made it out there. Finally it dawned on her to call the medical center and ask for Boyles by name. The operator patched her through without so much as a verbal blink. He was alive.

She wanted to drive back home and feed the cats, but she couldn't work up the courage and couldn't imagine what would happen if she ran into trouble like, say, George. In the rush, she had forgotten the plan of slitting open a bag of cat food. Maybe she'd call into the barn and ask one of George's helpers to swing by and look after them. It wasn't as if they could trace her call or even know if she was nearby.

Everything pointed to going to the cops, but now there was an obvious problem. They would first want to talk to her about Boyles' trip to the medical center, and about why his stomach had to be pumped. She supposed if Boyles pressed charges, it would not be too difficult for any prosecutor to show that she should know, given all her plants, what ground vegetation to throw into a sandwich. There seemed a possibility the cops had already scooped up a few slivers or scraps from where she had made the lunches. She wanted to try Allison Coil: ring her up. But she had probably already asked too much, then had given in so easily when George had shown up at the riverbank. She didn't feel she had any right to lean on her again, to ask any favors.

Maybe in a day or two, but not right away.

* * * *

Marcovicci cleared his throat, sipped some coffee.

"We had a deal, remember? You don't get to care who owns the gun now."

"Grumley."

"So you're a genius. You think of the crew up there hunting, and you figure I'm here, in Ripplecreek, and there's not too many other possibilities."

"It's Grumley."

Marcovicci took a long slurp of coffee and then bit off a chunk of bagel to slop around in his mouth. Coil, standing by the sink, imagined a sponge in a warm bucket.

Coil had been standing by the sink. In Marcovicci's paw, and disappearing in his mouth, the bagel seemed like the beginnings of a snack.

Marcovicci had slept on the spare bed, snoring deeply off and on all night. She had stayed awake for an hour, wide-eyed in bed, and worked on figuring out why George Grumley would have destroyed Applegate's rifle. Then she spent a minute imagining how Rocky died, followed by a minute of picturing Slater, relaying the news she'd given him, over the phone, to Sandstrom.

How soon would they head up and get Rocky off the mountain?

She wanted to tell Sandstrom herself, to rub it in, but she'd let the "Boy Scout" handle it. Perhaps they were already putting a team together, to be ready at daylight. A red bandanna was stuck on a stick off the trail where Rocky was. Her footprints would lead them the rest of the way. Then she spent another minute imagining what Marcovicci might say, and then it was back around again to Rocky. At one point during the night, she didn't know when, she sobbed and imagined Trudy being told, and it wasn't hard to picture Trudy weeping. And she cried some more.

Marcovicci's mention of the "arsenal" had clicked. She remembered her job interview and the racks of rifles that lined his room in the barn, the definition of overkill.

"You think your pal Applegate could have slipped up?"

"Let's put it this way. Now Applegate's another one of the millions in this country looking for the fastest route up Moral Mountain to stake out a big piece of turf on one issue or another and to point accusing fingers down the slope at anybody who dares to disagree. Makes me sick."

"Agreed," said Coil. "But he's your buddy."

"Sort of. You trying to talk me out of helping you?" asked Marcovicci. Coil sat down next to him.

"Not at all. Who else did you tell that I had come asking around?"

"What's the difference? You're leaving him out of this. The deal, you know?"

"Couple days after you and I talked down in Denver, I was up with a couple horses doing my rounds, checking on our camps. Coming down at dusk, I pitched a tent and built a fire in the snow. Nobody around, right? Out in the middle of nowhere. Except this guy appears, jams my face in the snow, tells me to mind my own business. And strings me up—upside down off a tree."

Marcovicci seemed to feel the pain.

"So Grumley has Applegate's rifle."

"I didn't say that. I said I'd help find it."

"Okay. You assume he's got it."

"A guy shoots somebody, I think they should be a man, step forward. *Confess.* You imagine walking away from a person dying in the snow? A person you shot, let's hope, accidentally? Leave him to die?"

"You don't need to go with me," said Coil. "I can poke around over there. I've got a friend or two, if it comes to that. Just tell me what I'm looking for."

Marcovicci seemed focused on a distant planet, decision in his eyes.

"What am I looking for?" she repeated.

"It's a Sako. The sight is chipped in spots, and underneath, around the trigger housing. But on the butt of the rifle, my initials. RM. R for Robert, what my father called me. Engraved. It's one of a kind."

"Your rifle?"

"Yeah," said Marcovicci. "Four years back, Applegate said he liked it. We were out target shooting. I had bought myself a new one, so I sold it to him."

* * * *

Applegate's hands flipped about and his chest rumbled, rattled by temperature and fear. He would have let the engine run to keep warm, but the fuel gauge said a shade below one-quarter. The gas station, the one he'd been banking on in Eagle, had been closed for repairs.

The barn was a dull hulk in the pre-dawn starlight. He gripped the door handle and tugged it open. It didn't seem possible that the outside air was even colder, but he could tell the difference. It was twenty or thirty steps across the compacted, frozen snow to the side entry, a people-sized door within a horse-sized door.

Warmth? The rich, steamy smell of heat, at least. Animal heat. Horse heads still. Sleeping, worry free. They made him nervous.

A flap of wings bore down on him, and Applegate ducked away from the bird, which had to be bigger than some damn barn swallow. And then the sputtering was gone, but his heart had picked up on the rhythm. Light blasted through the window next to the door, and he bounced back, out of the way. He watched the beam, made square by the window, flicker across horse heads and then climb the far wall and switch off. The next second there was the sound of a car or truck, chewing up the road, gone. Applegate slumped against the inside of the door, mentally wracked.

Fishy's voice drove him on. Among all the things he couldn't imagine, having the rifle linked to him was about the last. The world would laugh, in unison.

To the office. He'd seen Grumley, dozens of times, dig for the key in a saddlebag hanging in the tack room, near the front. Why would he have changed the location? The saddlebag was there, and so was the key. The padlock snapped on command, and Applegate put the key back.

Flick on the light.

A few rifles? Maybe fifty. Maybe a hundred. Maybe more. All lined up neatly, stock down, side by side around the walls, in racks. He scanned them all up close, at trigger level. He picked up a few, and held them to his shoulder, looking for a feel. One, and then another, and then back to the first. Different, but similar. One felt close; they all felt the same. The weight? The length? All were within a narrow range. It was too subtle.

Finally, one felt right, or at least he wanted to believe it did. He flipped the rifle around in his hands. He sighted the rifle again and then forced himself to touch each of the others in the racks. The process was like trouble-shooting a computer program. You had to scrutinize each comma and parenthesis. Study them: each barrel, each trigger.

He heard a thud and a slow whine, which echoed in his head. Somewhere nearby there was a shuffle of boots. He heard a soft snort from a horse, then the doorframe filled back up.

"Whoa Jesus, thought I heard something."

The kid had his hands stuffed in his jean-jacket pockets.

"Who the hell? Christ. I know you."

Applegate recognized the kid. He was one of Grumley's helpers, Bobby Alvin.

"You've been on TV. What the fuck you doing?"

"Looking for George."

"Tad early to be rousting him."

"Don't," said Applegate, wondering if by any chance the kid might know one rifle from the next.

"You're the one that's working for all them animal groups. I remember you."

"Grumley is a friend, for Chrissakes."

"Some pretty weird shit going on here lately. Boyles in the hospital with his stomach all ripped apart. That Allison babe asking all those questions. You ain't supposed to be here. I can smell it. The fuck . . . I will wake up George."

He headed for the desk.

"Don't," said Applegate, standing between Alvin and the telephone.

"Get the fuck outta my way," said Alvin, giving him a shove.

Applegate pushed him back, and Alvin took it off-guard and stumbled, rattling a couple of rifles as he clutched for a grip to break his fall.

"Asshole," said Alvin, charging back.

Applegate remembered to follow through and connected on the fuzzy and freckled jaw. Alvin moaned something unintelligible and fell to his knees, spitting blood from his low-slung head.

Applegate grabbed the still-gagging Alvin up off the floor and shoved him against the desk, body-checked him against the wall, and let his hands fly into Alvin's stomach and up around his head, frustration and anger pouring from his whole being. He punched and flailed until he felt his arms grow weak, and Alvin was reduced to a sputtering mass of self-protection.

Applegate stumbled from the barn with tears and anger all over his face, wondering, where to? And what now? The cold didn't register. The car seats were like blocks of ice—no spring, no give, just cold—and the engine turned over with a snarl.

* * * *

She heard the scuffle, the solid whack, and the sound of one of them coughing and gagging. Coil stepped back into the stall, a horse's stiff belly wedging her against the wall. She hoped he didn't spook. She stroked his flank with one hand and patted his cheek, almost out of reach, with the other.

One of the two had headed out. She recognized Bobby's attitude as much as the sound of his voice, but the shadowy shape that drifted past, inches away, seemed too tall to be Bobby.

The door crashed to a close. Her adopted horse shook its head like a dog with fleas, stretched out its neck, then shifted around as if to see, in the dark, what person was crowding his space without giving him the benefit of a brush. Then she heard the sound of a car revving up.

Coil followed her horse to its head, found the chest-high stall door, then the latch, and pushed it open. Light poured from the office, but it wasn't making much of a dent in the barn's main cavern. The car rumbled off, and the quiet left in its wake inhaled every remaining particle of sound. Coil stepped toward the light, wracking her brain for a decent excuse if she needed one, for her presence in Grumley's barn.

Glancing around the barn, her eyes were riveted to the door, looking for any movement, and she pricked her ears to detect even a whisper of sound. She heard a shuffle, like something being dragged nearby, then it seemed to be accompanied by a low, human moan.

And then a voice, Bobby's voice. She thought for a second she had badly miscalculated, that there was somebody else in there, too.

"It's Bobby . . ."

Coil stepped away from her secure hold in the stalls and into the broad open space, halfway to the office. No protection. She stopped to listen.

" . . . It was him . . ."

And moved closer, smack behind the open door.

" . . . Him. One of your old buddies . . ."

Bobby took a second to cough and gag.

She peered through the crack between the door and the jamb. He was on his knees, clutching the desk with one hand, propping up the telephone with the other.

" . . . The one that joined up with what's-her-name, the animal queen . . ."

Bobby's voice was trembling and weak.

"Applegate . . . at the barn, going through your stuff."

Applegate?

" . . . Took off. Somewhere . . ."

Long pause. Bobby listening, touching his jaw.

" . . . Couple minutes ago. Didn't have nothing when he left here . . ."

On the dirt floor, Coil back-pedaled lightly. She waited a minute. She could still hear some of Bobby's mumbles.

She counted to twenty, slowly, like a careful kindergartener, then reached behind her, opened the door, and shut it again. Nice and loud, with a bang.

There was no decent excuse for being here. It was not her barn, and not the time of year to go chit-chatting. That was summer on break days when the creeks gurgled, and the sun offered up warmth all day. She plopped her boots on the dirt floor with some extra shuffling, but they didn't make enough noise.

And then Alvin stepped out into his own light, holding the door for stability.

"It's me, Allison," she called.

"Christ," said Alvin, turning back inside the office as she got there.

"What's up?" she asked, as innocently as possible. She turned and saw Alvin back on the couch, a streak of blood across his cheek.

"Hey, you okay?" she asked.

"Christ, yes," said Alvin. "Caught me off guard."

"Who did?"

"What are you doing here?"

"Looking for someone who knows the trails south to Deep Lake, the ones that cut up over McKenna's Ridge."

"Christ, that's the only way to go, on horseback anyway, from here. The only other decent route from this end turns into old scree at the top." Bobby sighed and moaned. "You're going up there, what, now? God, it hurts to talk."

"Later today," she said, in case he ended up seeing Bear, who was packed for nothing better than a stroll around a corral in one of those "horse ride" rip-offs by the interstate.

"You okay? Your jaw?"

He rubbed it, rolled it around, and while he did she blinked, and the rifles were suddenly there. All the rifles, in their racks, were at arm's reach.

"I've gotta meet George back at his cabin," said Alvin, standing up to go. "We're gonna track that pesky little mother down."

"Who?" said Coil, wondering if he'd tell.

"One of his used-to-be friends."

"I think he has more than a couple."

"Probably true."

He wasn't going to say.

"Business friends?"

"Not exactly."

But he wanted to.

"Old buddy?"

"Say 'former.'"

"Not that guy, the one who flopped over with the animal nuts?"

"Bingo," said Alvin.

"Applegate," said Coil, as if it was no big deal.

She kept thinking about the rifles, sneaking a glance, trying to avoid looking too interested, too studious.

"Surprised the heck out of me," said Alvin.

"No shit," said Coil. "But he's not supposed to be doing any fighting. Bad boy."

"Guy was fucking desperate."

Now Coil needed to drop it, before it got to be too obvious.

"You don't need help?"

"How do you tell if a jaw is broken?"

"X-rays," said Coil. She sat down next to him. He seemed to recoil at her closeness and sat up straight. She pressed two fingers along his chin.

"Ouch," he said, as she pressed a spot halfway up to his ear. "A definite 'ouch' right there."

"There's a doctor in your future," said Coil. "Of course, there's nothing they can do for a broken jaw other than give you a bottle of pain pills and a box of straws."

Alvin shook his head in disgust. "Fuck," he said. "I'm going to get that fucker."

"So where do I pick up the trail?"

She stood up as if to leave and hoped Alvin would take her cue.

He stood too, describing where to find the trail, and she half-listened, working to spot the Sako, thinking it might, might, jump out. Alvin locked the door before she saw anything of distinction. He slipped the key into the saddlebag to the left of the office and they strolled out.

She climbed onto Bear and watched as Alvin headed to his pick-up.

"Thanks," she said. "Hope you find him. You really oughta get that checked out."

Coil thought she heard him mumble another "fucker," oblivious to her concern, and he was gone, not looking around. She circled Bear around to the opposite side of the barn, tied him up loosely, and headed back inside.

She retrieved the key from the saddlebag. There was already so much more light in the barn itself, coming in through the high windows. How much time did she really have?

It took a second to lift each rifle out of the rack, drop it down and around and look, hoping and praying that the next one was it, while listening hard in the background for any noise, anything that might be a problem.

Ten rifles, fifteen, and more to the end of the first rack. Nothing. Turn the corner at the wall and keep on chugging. Down, flip, look, back, balancing speed with quiet.

And then, getting really good at the routine, thinking it would never appear . . .

There, waiting patiently for its turn: R.M.

Lights off. Lock on. Horses watching. Stoic masters. It didn't feel wrong to have it in her hands, but this wasn't proper procedure, and she had to concede it felt weird somehow. But it would have felt self-conscious and out of the ordinary to stand up from her seat on the airplane, too, while the jet engines roared down the runway. And nothing would have been wrong about that.

The rifle felt good in her hands as she reached the door near where Bear was parked and turned around to look things over. It was her sixth grade math teacher who made a big deal out of reading through word problems twice. That's what this was: one big word problem, some things so obvious you could skip over them.

Like the key in the lock. She hadn't put it back.

She propped the Sako by the door and scooted back, eyes focused on the padlock and telling herself she should have kept going, what difference did it really make? The sun was too high now, so high that she wouldn't be alone much longer. Why was the office so far away?

And, of course, a truck or car, most likely a truck, right on cue.

Five steps from the lock, so close, her momentum and brain following through.

It could have been an angry truck, now that the sound of its quick-skid stop was finding a foothold in her head. She didn't know why she reached for the key in the padlock until she was about to drop it in the saddlebag, and then, without hesitation, she stopped and put the slim slice of metal into a high-arcing orbit that carried it up to the loft above the stalls next to her. The piles of loose hay and dirt and junk swallowed the key with a silent gulp.

She was halfway back to the rifle when she heard the door begin to open behind her, and heard two guys talking or arguing, the sound already muffled by the size of the barn and her inability to listen for detail and run at the same time.

Coil scooped Fishy's rifle back up in her hands, the shouting growing in her head, until she was about to open the door and then realized she probably blended in with the generally brown and dark scenery. But the crack of the door, the sound and the shot of light, would change all that. There was no clear harm in stopping a second or two to see what she was up against and who was doing all the shouting, except every fiber in her felt compelled to keep going and run, as if her subconscious almost knew that this weapon in her grip would do the trick, would be the first pick-up stick nobody could touch without making all the others rattle.

Stepping more slowly, Coil backed away from the door and crouched low to fashion herself as a smaller target. She worked to keep her mind from sinking into the swamp of chaos and panic where her heart had already gone.

"Christ," came the distinctive Alvin voice, in a shout, and she wondered why he hadn't left like he had promised.

During the second or so she had risked a glance back, they had arrvied. There were two figures standing close to the office, and now one, the one who hadn't yelled, extended a gun at shoulder height, the weapon in profile and pointed, it seemed, at nothing.

Boom.

They had shot at the lock. She reached for the door, hoping for cover from the pistol crack.

Boom.

Something zinged by her head, and she wondered when she might first feel the pain and how bad it would be.

She ducked and was through.

Bear looked like an impatient dad, waiting for the teenagers to come home.

Rifle in the scabbard.

Ties off.

Turning Bear before she had climbed all the way up, she kicked him into gear as the door crashed open again.

She was already weaving behind some trees that lined the road in the direction she didn't want to go, away from her house, on a dead run.

Fishy's rifle was in reach where she could touch it for reassurance.

13

Applegate sat on the banks of the river at the Grizzly Creek rest area, deep in the heart of the canyon. He choked and sobbed, replaying the tangle with Alvin, half wishing he had wiped out the little fucker, half thinking he should have stayed to keep looking for his rifle, and knowing full well it wouldn't have made any difference if he had. So close to the rifle, so damn close. So close, his salvation, but so far away.

Earlier, he had gone out of his way to the closest spot to fill his tank. He had pumped gasoline and used the station's pay phone to leave an upbeat everything-is-fine message on Ellenberg's voice mail. Said he'd be back in Denver for lunch and was sorry he'd missed a night with her.

He fidgeted in the downtown pool, and he sat in the steamier section with all the morning regulars, the locals, who avoided the mid-day tourists and late-day skiers. His puffy toes floated off in the distance, through the fog, and he hid his celebrity in the steam. Nobody said a lick, but he felt disoriented, constantly watching each thought.

He drove back through the canyon and spotted the rest stop pullout, realized he needed to get his head screwed back on right before driving back, and realized he needed to think things through as an important player in the FATE camp, not as Dean Applegate, loser.

He sat and watched the white caps bubble, stared high up at the cliff tops, far overhead. He tried to figure out what impulse had overtaken him to mix it up with Alvin, and to allow his anger to boil.

And then it occurred to him out of the fucking blue; the rifle was Marcovicci's. Fishy's. Why had it taken so long to realize that the rifle, if it was found and turned over, would lead straight to the guy who had been trying to get him all alarmed? Fishy had been trying to save his own fat-laden skin.

A smile percolated through his brain, subjecting all other clouds in his head to a bit of sunshine. Whose word against whose? Fishy would say he had sold the rifle to him. Where's the paperwork? Fishy would say he wasn't hunting the day Ray Stern was killed. He might have an alibi. But between naps and drinking, were the others rock sure of every single minute and who was where the day Ray Stern strapped on his suit of felt? Applegate would say he'd gone for a hike. Besides, he was known among them as easily the least likely to hunt alone.

Bobby Alvin was a problem. He'd already thought of that. Alvin, at some trumped-up trial, saying Applegate had come looking for the rifle, would be a big problem. Maybe he could blame Fishy for spooking him, getting him all worked up. It sounded good in his head. It was a detail to be sorted out. There had to be a rational blip of logic, some nugget somewhere that would make everything come clear.

In the meantime, forget the brick wall. Think of the distant vista.

Fishy's rifle. His initials were even on it, for Chrissakes.

Applegate leaned back on the cold grass next to the river and stared up again at the steep canyon walls, flipping his mind back around to the struggles of Ellenberg's crew to follow through on the success of their anti-hunting protest. And then another idea began to grow in his head, and by the time it had begun to fully develop, he was back behind the wheel of his car, almost without thinking about it, driving back to Denver with a growing smile on his face.

* * * *

Coil looked behind her, straight down several hundred yards of Bear's tracks. The grade was steep, and the vegetation thick, so somebody on horseback could easily be scampering up that section right now and she wouldn't know it. But beyond that was a long slow incline where the trail she had followed hugged the edge of an aspen grove surrounded on three sides by snow-draped field. Empty.

Bear steamed hard, his chest white and wet.

She didn't think she knew the valley any better than Grumley. Did she have a five-minute start? Ten?

Glenwood Springs was too far, in snow, on horseback. On a good day in summer, maybe.

"Stay in your own tracks," she told Bear, guiding him back across the clearing.

The snow was light and fluffy, their first set of tracks more like the damage from an ineffective snowplow, not the work of an animal. It would take a careful eye to see the snow had been re-churned on the double back. Just a hundred yards across the clearing, using the same steady gallop as the first time. But it seemed like double that, because she could run right into one of them. She was half expecting her view to be filled at any second with Grumley or Alvin or both, a killing look on their faces.

Finally. She stopped Bear stock-still in his tracks at the base of an enormous fir, with the bows draped low, and pointed him to walk slowly around its base, stepping now. Eight steps. Ten. Twelve. Around the other side of the tree. She dismounted and plunked her way back to the junction of Bear's tracks, wiped out and smoothed-over the first few prints so there was nothing obvious. Nothing terribly obvious. She back-pedaled and listened for the clank of a harness, the crack of a rein. From her spot, it appeared that Bear had been on a beeline to the ridge top. And by the time one or two more horses chewed up Bear's original tracks and they saw the trail flat-out ended . . .

She got back up onto Bear. They made a straight shot up the ridge, at a right angle to her old heading. She tapped Fishy's rifle to check again, to make sure, wondering if she had wasted five minutes too many. Or perhaps the stunt would piss them off.

Up, bouncing on her feet in the stirrups as Bear climbed and crested a ridge, the wind smacked her in the face as quickly as she realized Bear was standing on grass. They were making tracks, of course, but they wouldn't be visible to someone in a hurry.

A gift.

Onward to the very top of the ridge itself, not daring to or wanting to linger on a high spot too long. She feared throwing her own silhouette against the sluggish winter sun.

Coil guided Bear in a dance along the edge of the snow line until they ran out of rocks, and the barren, snow-free stuff came to an unceremonious end.

* * * *

"I tell you she was asking about how to get to Deep Lake. Seemed innocent enough."

"'Seemed'," said Grumley.

"Hard to believe she circled back," said Alvin.

"Fuck it," said Grumley.

The tracks that dead-ended set them back fifteen minutes at least, and all the while Alvin hadn't stopped with his endless theorizing, coughing up globs of wet cement. Grumley hoped a chunk would harden. Now up on the ridge top where she could have taken any direction back down, and off, he was at it again. It was small minds like Alvin's that made it difficult to trust anyone.

That was why he hadn't waited for the little runt to come to the cabin; he had decided to get on top of things himself. There had been one other set of headlights on the road before he reached the barn. And he couldn't figure out if he would have been better off running them off the road because now he knew, through Alvin's eleventh monologue about the sequence of events, that the headlights hid Applegate. They were too far down the road to have been Alvin's. Instead he had flashed his lights at the second set of lights, Alvin's, and the two of them had headed back to the barn, although at the time he was thinking nobody should see how desperate he was to make sure Applegate's rifle was still in place.

What Grumley couldn't figure out was how Coil knew to lift the Sako, the only one missing from the rack.

"Maybe you gave her the rifle," said Grumley. "Maybe you want into her pants."

"Right," said Alvin. "I'm sure."

"The second you get off the phone with me, she happens along."

"Like I said."

"Yeah, yeah, the bit about Deep Lake."

"What she told me."

"Casual conversation at six fucking thirty. She strolls up."

Alvin thought for a second. Maybe it was just now clicking together.

"That's what happened," he said.

They were walking the long perimeter of the windblown ridge top, looking for tracks. Every minute it was more of a joke.

"We're cooked," said Grumley.

"She had to go somewhere," said Alvin. "Let's do another circuit of the ridge top, only in the snow, say thirty or forty yards down off the top here. You go one way, I'll go the other."

"How the fuck we going to find each other if one of us sniffs her drawers?"

"Together then."

"It'll take twice as long. Meantime, she's making tracks."

"One nosy bitch," said Alvin. His fake sympathy.

"How the fucking hell did she know which rifle?"

Alvin paused too long. A flinch.

"Not me, no way," he said, the words coming out in a funny, splattered jumble.

"You screwin' her?"

"She wouldn't have me."

There was a touch of fear in the kid's voice now, sensing this line of questions might keep up.

Who really cared about Bobby Alvin, either? Would he be missed?

Grumley couldn't stop thinking of the rifle in Coil's hands, and how soon she might get it in the hands of the cops. Would they believe her story that it might have something to do with Mr. Elk Suit? With Trudy gone and that whole mess, too, and fucking Applegate on the loose.

He had given Trudy's trail to Popeye, but the guy spent a few hours driving around, grew queasy, and gave it up. Still suffering the effects, he said. More likely he was too overwhelmed with the fucking prospect of not being able to find something he shouldn't have lost in the first fucking place. Why did he suffer losers? Grumley's mind swirled, but he couldn't figure the advantage now of leaving Alvin here to think about his mistakes forever.

"Where we going?" asked Alvin, as Grumley turned his horse around and headed down.

On the other hand . . .

He pictured a bullet in Bobby's forehead.

"You okay?" Bobby asked.

"Never better," said Grumley. He pulled out his pistol, the '58 New Army Texas, a .44. A replica, but it should do the job.

"Hey," said Alvin, as he started to dive. But it wasn't a dive. Some invisible force separated him from his saddle. And he landed in the snow in a lump, on his side.

The sound of the shot echoed in Grumley's head. There was something satisfying about making a decision.

* * * *

A week after her taste of the harbor, Coil had been in decent enough shape to ask for the newspapers that covered the accident. Her parents had flown in from Denver, and her dad, a chronic newspaper hound, brought the stack of *New York Times* from the hotel. She glanced at the pictures and scanned the copy, grating at the notion that some see-it-all-writer looking down from above could use the verb "flopped," as if the jet was a human form that could choose between a cannonball or a head-first dive on its entry into the water. "Flopped" wasn't what had happened inside the cabin. "Flopped" had a fun and frolicking tone to it, almost carefree. The newspaper headline was the first time she had known how many had died, but she certainly hadn't needed to be told that many had, in fact, perished.

Walking now with Bear, she thought of Peter McBride, one of those naturally open, relaxed people who were always seconds away from a comfortable smile. He wore round wire-rims, sported short but tousled hair, and was about her size—compact, trim and lean. He had bright, clear eyes, like blueberries in a pool of milk. They were talking like good, old friends in the terminal long before they boarded. Their flight was late departing because the plane hadn't even left Baltimore at boarding time. Within a few minutes, she recalled, he had mentioned Zen. And she had pressed him a bit, discovering he had spent a week in the equivalent of a closet, meditating on the trouble his life and his being had caused his parents and others around him. He told her they were asked to break their lives down into three-year blocks and consider all the ways their mere existence had impacted the lives of those around them, right down to the nitty-gritty details of contemplating the number of diapers their parents had to change, no questions asked, before they could deal with their own shit.

Her mind had jumped at the exercise. Even as they continued to chat, her mind had gone busy scouring the memory banks, and she scraped together bits and pieces of things she hadn't thought about in years. At four, she had pretended that a neighbor girlfriend had fallen from the roof of the house, and they had poured ketchup around where she had "fallen" to give her mother a jolt, at least from a distance. She recalled old tantrums, battles with her mom over not wanting to waste time in the stupid grocery store, and fights with her brothers over who knew what.

When she had the stack of newspapers, she felt it before she read it. And her parents probably assumed, when she started to bawl, that it was the overwhelming reality of reading about the accident that had caught up with her. But it was the name in newspaper ink. Too real. Too painful. *PETER McBRIDE, 28, Boulder, Colo.*

It didn't seem possible then—it didn't seem possible now—as Bear picked his way in the general direction that would dump them out somewhere on the road, perhaps a mile or two down from her A-Frame. It was three o'clock and going on dusk in the ravines. They had slurped water from creek beds, and she had found an old granola bar in the otherwise empty saddlebag. Bear won the snack. She felt hungry, but couldn't imagine depriving him a morsel.

Trying to work on Peter's problem, she thought of the rooms in the houses where she had lived, and how memories were mostly place. Nothing could happen without a place for it to occur. She remembered Peter tapping her on the shoulder. He boarded last, a stand-by. He could have been in this place, this space, this airplane. Or inside the terminal, bumped from the flight. What if each city had a dozen more good jobs for traveling businessmen, through a slightly better economy, and there had been no room for stand-bys on that flight? Peter would have stayed behind, safe and dry.

The woods thinned out. The grade turned gentle. The day's light was being given a brief reprieve as they moved out and away from the darkened north face of the ridge and through an expanse of aspens, spaced like somebody had planted them all a horse-width apart. They wound their way to the edge of a broad clearing that fell away, not so gently. The pitch was dotted with bush-size evergreens and scrub oak. The ravine ended a few hundred yards down, but so steeply she couldn't see the bottom. The other side climbed as quickly, but was topped by a small section of familiar looking guardrail. A stretch of no more than a few dozen feet was all she could see. And down to the right, to the east, a cherry-red house, a farmhouse, basked in the soft glow of the setting sun. It was a mile off, maybe more.

Behind her, someone was following.

She dug her heels into Bear. No coaxing, no time to be choosy. Bear lowered himself down on his hindquarters as his front legs paddled and scraped and pranced, hoping for footing and braking when they started to slide. She tapped Fishy's rifle, scooted low in the saddle and kept her weight back to help Bear stabilize. The guardrail disappeared and so did the farmhouse as they burrowed down in the hole, too steep. Bear angled off on his own compass, sensing an extra degree or two of grade that was beyond his capabilities.

She risked a glance back up . . . and saw the three-quarter silhouette of a man on horseback. He was a big man, Grumley-size. He watched her, standing where Bear had just stood.

She and Bear were halfway down. She was aware the other side of the ravine was better lit. It wouldn't climb fast enough to do her much good, provide any cover. Nobody would think twice about a couple of gunshots, if there was anything left to hear after the ravine swallowed up the noise.

She turned her head around to look back up the hill as Bear reached the gully. Her pursuer was halfway down, making it look easy. She let Bear take a few strides in the relatively gentle pitch of the ravine bottom, no creek or trail, but so rocky under the snow that even Bear preferred the switch to climbing. She worked to keep a straight line and hoped the cherry farmhouse would come into view when they crested the top.

The sound of the rifle shot had been in her head all along. She flinched at the crack and waited. Bear kept his stride, what was left of it. She took a second to find her breath again and wished she could meld into the saddle. She couldn't find a clear thought. She just hoped for the farmhouse.

Boom.

And Bear's nose plunged into the snow. She waited for her own flick of pain as his front legs buckled and his rear rolled sideways and the snow came up to smack her. Suddenly, the background of farmhouse and dog pens and sky came tumbling through her vision. As soon as he was down, Bear struggled to bounce back up, worked to right himself out of instinct, snorted and growled at his own frustration. And agony. Coil wound up splayed across his neck staring into his skyward eye. She rolled off and buried herself behind his shoulders, already starting to mourn before she saw the wound and the blood gushing from his haunch. Bear's head settled down onto the cool snow, and she tried to think of something to say, anything. Then the look in his eyes turned milky and distant.

The rifle. She slid the rifle from the scabbard, thinking it had been fifty-fifty that she would have been able to reach it at all. If it had wound up under Bear, no way. She held it up to show the bastard what she had, in case that alone would make him scram, then propped it on Bear's sweaty chest and lined up the man's—was it Grumley's?—frame in her sights. She turned the rifle over, found the safety, hoped for ammunition, and put him back in her sights. He stood there.

She aimed at his head and then an inch to the west, her finger still hesitating. And then not.

The blast of her rifle created a steady ring in her ear. The man on horseback spun instantly on the spot, realizing now that he was the wide-open target, and scampered off. She stood and placed the rifle at the back of Bear's skull, between the ears, wasting no time for a good-bye with the next shot. Bear seemed to sink another inch lower into the snow, and she didn't linger before she turned and ran through the calf-deep snow. Toward the dogs.

Her legs churned on an untapped source of power and fear. Two large pens flanked the farmhouse. A dozen or more doghouses were scattered around both pens, and each dog was linked by rope to its own house. Other than the dogs, she hoped nobody was worried about the sight of a strange, rifle-toting woman sprinting toward the house, although the tears on her face and fright in her eyes might convince anyone that she was hardly the fearless agitator. The dogs howled and scraped the dirt, desperate for a ring-side seat, as she dashed up between the house and the pens, now starting to see that the farmhouse sprawled up the hill. She followed a beaten-down path along the side of the structure and around to the front.

A woman stood on the front steps, holding a bundled-up toddler in her arms. An older child, a daughter, stood wide-eyed next to her mom. Long red hair poked out from the hood of the toddler's jacket. A sack of groceries stood by itself in the driveway, plunked down in the mud. There were more groceries in the back of a Subaru station wagon, the rear door up and open.

"Oh my," said the woman, clutching her daughter more tightly.

"No, no. Don't worry," said Coil. She held up her free hand like she was stopping traffic. "It's over."

"We pulled up, started to unload the food."

"Sorry about that," said Coil.

"They were shooting at you?"

"Killed my horse," she said.

Her breath was a draining search for oxygen.

"Oh my, oh my," said the woman, putting the toddler down, panic on her face. The girl stood studying her, inches away. "Valerie, you take care of her while I get a glass of water."

Coil studied the kid. Valerie stared back. Her stone expression didn't crack.

"I need a phone," said Coil. "If you don't mind."

"Of course, this way."

The woman introduced herself, Stacy Burnett, and led Coil and her offspring inside the massive farmhouse, with its wood-plank floors and bright braided rugs. Stacy showed her to a telephone, a rotary dial, on the wall next to the kitchen table, and Valerie tracked every move like an indifferent guard.

Coil dialed Slater's office number. Her world wobbled crazily, off-kilter, and her breathing was deep and unsettled. From the kitchen window, she scanned the wide field that swooped down and away toward the ravine. She could make out Bear's inert, prone hulk in the snow.

Slater was out, checking on a few stray buffalo that came from a farm up toward Craig. She didn't feel like telling anyone else.

Sandstrom? Trudy? Weaver—to tell him about Bear?

Sandstrom. The female receptionist on the phone took notes, composed all the way, then decided after a minute to relay her to a deputy, who also took notes for a minute, and then put Coil on hold while he tried to patch her through to Sandstrom in his sheriff's car.

"Ms. Coil," said Sandstrom, when he came on. "What's this—a shooting?"

"At me," she said, then started to go over the whole thing again, ignoring the part where the chase started, and why.

"Jesus H.," said Sandstrom, when she finished the sketch. "You staying put for a few minutes? Never mind the question. You are staying put."

"Cops are on their way up," Coil said to Stacy, cupping the mouthpiece.

"No problem," said Stacy. "They have to come."

At least Sandstrom's concern seemed true. She'd ask later about Rocky. Coil relayed the address; Sandstrom said he knew the kennels.

Stacy brought homemade chicken soup and wheatberry bread while they waited. Connecting with the authorities offered a touch of calm, along with the steaming broth. She tried Trudy's number while she waited. No answer; a strange no answer, one she didn't expect. She tried Slater's trailer, just in case he was home, and she got his message machine but didn't know what to say except, "Call me when you resurface, there's a lot going on." Then she tried Trudy's number again and still it rang on and on, into the void.

Sandstrom and two deputies arrived more quickly than she'd expected, in three separate cars. Gerard, who gave her a wink, followed her boot prints down to Bear, after she pointed him out. The other one, a green-looking kid, and Sandstrom sat in the living room with her going over it all. The kid took the notes.

"I don't get why someone tracked you down clear over here," said Sandstrom, after she had finished.

"May I show you something? In private?"

The deputy and Sandstrom exchanged glances. Stacy said they could use the kitchen, she'd keep Valerie out of the way, or even better, they could use the walk-in pantry. Coil picked up Fishy's rifle from the kitchen, where she had propped it, and led Sandstrom to the well-stocked food closet, shutting the door behind her.

"Dramatic," said Sandstrom.

"Necessary," said Coil.

"Whose is this?" he asked.

"You got Rocky down yet?"

"We're getting to it, we're getting to it. Jesus . . . I'm not into tricks." Sandstrom stared at the rifle.

"Then I'm here to cut a deal."

"Everybody always is. That's life. What's yours?"

"First, I wanna hear you say I wasn't crazy."

"We get the body down, I'll give you that."

"It's there."

"If it is, you're not."

Coil found that a bit of steam and energy were mixing in naturally with her anger over Bear and Grumley and Rocky. She hadn't mentioned Grumley yet by name, and couldn't, but wanted to light a fire somewhere, somehow, that would jack-up all the issues at once.

"What's with the rifle?"

"I stole the rifle. As a kid, though, we used to call it 'borrowing back.' I went over to get some trail information from Grumley's place. I was talking to Bobby Alvin. He'll tell you all of this." The words were coming easily. She could also clearly see the spot where she could nail Sandstrom. "I spotted this Sako. I took it, and some folks chased me. I have a pretty good idea who, but I'm not sure, so I'm not saying. This rifle's a bit unusual, I think you'll agree. But check the initials here. A guy named Bobby Marcovicci sold it to Dean Applegate."

"Mr. Turncoat."

"Correct. A few years back. Chances are it'll match up like a bad recurring nightmare with the bullet you pulled from Ray Stern."

She waited a second to see if Sandstrom could soak this up.

"Now you can decide if you want to book me on some sort of theft charge, make a nuisance out of that. Or, if you agree to let it go, and if you agree to make a very concerted effort to find out who shot Rocky Carnivitas, then I'll give you the rifle, and you can do some experiments and see if you can solve this nasty little migraine called the media that's been tormenting you for weeks."

Coil decided she would hold the Sako until Sandstrom made his choice clear.

"Theft?" he said.

His jowls quivered, and his eyes flicked around.

"Hey, I'll return it, through you. Unless you want to test it first."

"How do you know this is the one?" asked Sandstrom.

Coil thought for a few seconds, wondered if there was any chance that she'd been set up, that Fishy was in on something, that this was all a fancy charade to make her feel better.

"Call it a hunch," she said. "Call it one big, fat hunch."

14

"What loose ends?"

"Things I had to deal with—there's no point in boring you with the details."

"We don't like you gone. I missed you, you big lug. Plus, secrets. They make me queasy."

"It's over, done with. History," said Applegate.

It was early evening. They were strolling the cool, wet streets of lower downtown Denver, post-dinner. There had been waves of food with hummus and eggplant, all laced with garlic. And two bottles of wine had been safely tucked away as stew for their brains. The alcohol had erased any chance Applegate had of connecting all the dots from the bizarre journey.

"Another circle-the-parking-lot protest isn't going to cut it," said Ellenberg. "Makes us both look unimaginative, anyway."

The new plan skip-rocked through his head, from thinking cells to pools of confusion and across to solid ground. He hadn't been able to find a flaw since he first thought it up, lying on the grass in the canyon.

"What you need is a major non-violent disruption, right?"

"Sure."

"You need a surprise attack, something that will again get national attention. And you need something soon."

"Tomorrow would do."

She pulled up and sat down on a street bench, pulling him down with her, to snuggle, for warmth.

"Caravan goes up the interstate. Say twenty cars, unmarked. No banners, no nothing. Not obviously together. Maybe there's a news crew with you—one, so it's not that obvious. You drive into the canyon two across, ten deep, all going the same speed. The cars come to a halt, cap the breakdown lanes, too, and then pull out the banners and stuff. March down the highway, do whatever you want. Fifteen minutes. Thirty. However long it might take to draw some response, make the point, make sure there's good video and one helluva long traffic jam behind you. For a half-hour, you clog the only major east-west artery in the state and give old Sandstrom another stroke."

"It's brilliant," she gushed. "I love it."

The scheme turned her giddy, in fact. They ran it through a few times to test for trouble spots, but it seemed foolproof.

"Maybe we should cut off the highway in both directions at the same point."

"You'll make it too difficult for the sheriff to reach you," countered Applegate. "And then he'll be really pissed. Plus, you want the cops, lots of 'em, to make for a confrontation."

A fine mist of snow had begun, almost unnoticed. Breathing felt like drinking. She hugged him around the chest as they walked, mostly to balance herself, and buried her head against his coat. They weaved through a crowd of kids hanging out around a late-night dance club, but otherwise the streets and sidewalks were nearly empty. Applegate felt the solid buzz from the wine as they negotiated their way back to her place, nearly their place.

Ellenberg jumped on the phone, starting to spread the idea around, her face lighting up at the response. The word came back quickly: tomorrow. He heard her say "Dean's idea" and "Dean thought it up." Applegate poked around her brick loft, feeling useless as she chatted on the phone. Suddenly he felt very sober.

People would take the day off from work and would do whatever it took to make a difference. Mention doing something in the name of Ray

Stern, it seemed, and an instant army was at your disposal.

They all wanted to get it going immediately, the next day. No questions asked. Ellenberg had a news editor friend who was sympathetic, and the friend checked the advance log for the following day's scheduled news. It was a slow news day, or appeared to be. That cinched it. The phone tree, dry timber, was on fire.

When she was done, and the phone stopped ringing, Ellenberg lit a dozen candles. Applegate had to stop and think if it was still the same day he'd wailed on Bobby Alvin. It was.

"Come here," said Ellenberg. She stood in the glow she'd created, unbuttoning her white cotton blouse, the one with the red and blue flowers embroidered on the pockets. Braless. She hooked her pants down and off, pulled back the quilt comforter, and stood there in her powder blue short cut panties, trim and lean.

"You just going to stand there?"

"Enjoying it," said Applegate.

"Hurry up and get naked," she said. "We gotta get to sleep. Tomorrow's a big day."

* * * *

The garage door was open; so was the door that led from the garage to inside the house. The door clattered something back as Coil pushed it.

She heard one soft meow off in the distance, and another, lower pitched and more like a siren. She shut the door behind her, stepped over a chair lying on its side, and sprayed the room with the beam from her flashlight.

"Trudy?" she called out, half-scaring herself. Scampering cat feet everywhere made it worse. Add trespassing to the list of charges, thought Coil, as if the cops don't have enough to worry about. This last piece, finding Trudy, was simply a matter of closing the loop with the only other person who seemed to care about Rocky. And now she was beginning to wonder if anything was simple.

Coil stood in a ransacked kitchen. The table was turned over, there were smashed plates, and a skid of food or slime covered the floor. Bits of broken glass and a bottle of mustard had smashed and exploded, leaving brown-yellow shrapnel everywhere. The light caught a pair of green eyes staring back at her from the floor. Another feline, this one jet black, crouched low in the middle of the mess. Careful of putting her footprints in any gobs of food, she picked her way around the clutter and upended table to the other side of the kitchen.

More meows. More cat eyes, pairs by the dozen.

She took the stairs up to the bedrooms. One bed was a mess, with squirming balls of fur in the middle of it, on the spread. A mother and her new brood, hours old at most.

A bathroom was empty; a second bedroom empty, too.

Coil went to the greenhouse, then poked her flashlight down the basement stairs. The chorus of meows grew in strength as she stepped down, with one cat doing a figure-8 between her feet. She found the light switch and snapped it on. A cat sprinted up as she cautiously stepped down.

Coil found the tub of cat food and gently slipped the plastic cover off the giant vat. It didn't seem to make much of a sound, but the stairs behind her were quickly cluttered with cats. They pounded their way down and assembled at her feet like an alluvial fan of bubbling fur. They rubbed their chins on her ankles and on each others'. There were five bowls, some with nothing more than crumbs left. The cats jostled for position, spreading out and around until every munching station was full and the pecking order established.

"Knock yourselves out," she told them, and sneezed.

She went back upstairs. The house was clearly empty, but the mess didn't look good. Finding Trudy would depend upon how far she had decided to go, and how long ago she left. Coil found herself standing next to a leafy fern-like plant in the living room, and she jabbed a finger down into the potting soil, to the first knuckle. The surface was dry, but the dirt below stuck to her skin. No more than a few days without water, she guessed. Trudy wouldn't have gone too far, wouldn't have left her cats and plants to the winds.

* * * *

The motel room bugged her. There was so little room to move that it felt like a cell. All the surfaces were hard. There was nothing green. The only activity was on the TV. Worse than that, there was no news. CNN, sure, but no real news or developments. There was nothing on the local channels, either. The crest of the wave of hyper news was passing. The media needed a real slice of something meaty now for the next chapter to begin; anything but another loosely hinged sidebar about some remote aspect of animal rights, creative suicide, or the history of Ray Stern.

She needed Coil but wondered if she would still want to help. There hadn't been any answer at Coil's house, the few times she had called. She left a message at Pete Weaver's barn, but the mumbling guide seemed unreliable, at best. Then she decided to go right to the top. If anybody could find Allison Coil, it was Pete Weaver. The phone at his farmhouse rang uselessly the first four times she tried it, on the hour, until after dusk.

"Weaver," he answered.

"Hi, Peter. It's Trudy Grumley," she said, trying to sound casual. The Grumley-Weaver tension had always been polite, but real. They were competitors after the same market in the same valley showing off the same wilderness, hunting the same herds.

"What can I do for you?" asked Weaver.

"I'm looking for one of your guides, Allison Coil."

"Popular girl," said Weaver. "Been plenty busy, anyway. I'll leave her a note on the message board down at the barn. You tried her home?"

"Yes. No answer."

"Probably up on her routes," said Weaver. "How about her boyfriend? The ranger?"

"Don't know him."

"Everybody else does. David Slater. National Forest ranger. Lives down in Glenwood Springs somewheres."

Trudy said goodbye quickly, checked the directory for Slater, found a D Slater, no address, and dialed the number. She let it ring until she heard the message machine start, then hung up.

She had moved from one stuck place to another stuck place.

But she hadn't left her house, taken such a risk, to just lie low.

There was nothing that said she couldn't find the National Forest Service office, ask around, or even drive out to Slater's place, just for a look. It was a matter of working up the nerve, and then convincing herself it would be worth it.

* * * *

Slater was waiting for Coil at the Waffle Hut, not too far from downtown, and was deep into his second or third cup of coffee, judging by the disheveled newspaper in the booth. During the drive down from Ripplecreek, fatigue had briefly unbundled itself from her fears, but it was all back together now in a troublesome cocktail. Her mind was trapped in a box where the name George Grumley echoed with more and more volume.

"Hi," she said, having snuck up behind him, a fearless man with his back to the door. "Breakfast for supper?"

"First meal of the day," said Slater. "Got trapped dealing with some unlicensed hunters from Indiana."

"You mean poachers."

"They hadn't shot anything. Yet. Fine line. We talked. And talked. Aren't you joining me?"

"I can't decide."

"Why?"

"I don't want to sit still."

"I can imagine, but now you're with me. Besides, I want to hear it all again from start to finish."

Over coffee and waffles? It seemed too every-day. She wanted his undivided attention at some place where she could be held. It was like being back in the harbor, floating and bobbing with airplane parts and suitcase stuffing. She'd never forget the bear hug clutch of the anonymous firefighter as he wrapped her in a blanket. Slater took a sip of coffee, moved over, and urged her to sit down on the same bench with him. Not quite the same, but . . .

"No idea who it was? Chasing you?"

"Yeah. But nothing I could prove."

"Who?"

"Saying it would make it real in your head too. And I might be wrong."

"So?"

"It looked a helluva lot like George Grumley."

"The guy who owns the barn where you picked up the rifle?"

"You don't have to add two and two so quickly."

"Comes up four every time," said Slater. "Cops take good care of you?"

"More thorough than I had the patience for."

"What kind of rifle was it?"

"Which?"

"The one you lifted."

"A Sako."

A waitress drifted by with a pot of coffee. Slater ordered waffles; Coil some juice.

"Finnish."

"Huh?"

"The rifle. Good precision. Should be easy to match up."

"Especially with Marcovicci's initials."

"They'll need proof of ownership. Or they can pick up Applegate, pretend they've got the goods, tell him they found the rifle and all, and get him to confess on the guarantee of some lesser charge. Have the rifle right there, see if he flinches, see if he does a good, solid double take and then spews it all out. No lab work needed."

"How about photographs of Applegate holding the Sako over the last few years?"

"If they're available. And very clear."

"Or maybe there's somebody who witnessed the sale. That would do, too."

"Jesus," said Slater. "You don't give up."

"What was I supposed to do?"

"What?"

"Nobody believed me. And now there's Rocky. I never saw anything that had to do with Ray Stern. Trudy Grumley calls and says Rocky is missing. All I did was a favor, running by his place. Speaking of which, now Trudy is out somewhere. I went up to look for her, tell her what I knew, and her place was trashed. Tables turned over, mess on the floor."

Slater cocked an eye. "Not good," he said.

"Tell me," said Coil.

"But that would explain the name on the message on my desk," said Slater. "It was only the first name, Trudy, and a phone number."

"Did you call?"

"No, I didn't know there was any need or rush. It's on my desk."

"Can you call and get it?"

"Closed up for the night. But we can go back when we're done. Or it can wait."

"Tonight."

"Fine," said Slater, a slight hint of irritation on his face.

Coil put a hand on his thigh underneath the table and slumped into his shoulder, letting weariness take another run at her. She drank her juice in a few long gulps and tried to suppress her desire to get going, to at least talk with Trudy.

"Do you know if they got Rocky down yet?"

"Don't," said Slater. "I've been out of the loop. Or out on the loop, depending on your point of view."

"You don't think that the dead elk, and finding the GPS, meant . . . ?"

"Researchers?"

"Yeah."

"Not likely. I've already talked to Bridgers. We're putting a task force together to investigate this one, interview all the appropriate people that Rocky worked with and worked for. Should get going here in a day or two. We want to bring in some folks from other districts who don't know all the players, to make it as fair as possible."

Slater wolfed his waffles, whip cream, and a scoop of some sticky blueberry compote. Coil tried not to gag.

They walked three blocks to Slater's office, as a freight train lumbered through downtown. Slater unlocked the front door, and they headed upstairs in the dark to his desk, where he found the message slip among a bunch of others.

Coil dialed the number and asked for the room.

"It's Allison. You all right?"

"Sort of. I'm fine, yeah. Thanks for calling. You got my message?"

"Yes. Your place, what happened?"

"You went there?"

"Of course, when there was no answer."

Slater took a seat and plowed into his paperwork as if it was high noon. He moved letters, files, and memos one at a time from his in-box to the center of his desk, and then either to a metal, vertical sorter or to the circular file.

"There was a bit of a scrap," said Trudy. "I had to get out."

"Where are you?"

"Sulphur Inn, south of downtown."

Coil knew the place, with its fake neon steam on the sign. In fact, Trudy was only a mile away. She didn't want to tell Trudy what she had to tell her over the phone. Since Trudy hadn't brought it up yet, it was entirely possible she didn't know about Rocky, especially if the cops hadn't retrieved his body or released any information. But Coil could not imagine staying awake any longer than the twenty minutes or so that it would require to drive out to Slater's trailer.

"You're okay for the night?" asked Coil. "Can we meet first thing tomorrow?"

She'd have to talk with Weaver. It was hard to imagine going back to routine chores right away. But it was high season, and she knew Weaver's team was thin to begin with.

"I'm okay," said Trudy unconvincingly. "I'll be here. Room 141. Look for the 4-Runner."

"First thing," said Coil. "Count on it." She said good-bye and hung up. "She's okay?"

"Just," said Coil. "Lonesome and scared, for sure."

"Are we done?" asked Slater, looking up from his now-clean desk. Only a stapler, tape dispenser, and pencil cup stood guard.

"Except the crashing part. Your place okay?"

"Alas, no," said Slater. "I have to head over to Grand Junction tonight, big Poo-Bah from Washington is in town for a regional meeting pep talk thing at o-dark thirty in the A.M. I'm afraid you're on your own."

"Again," said Coil.

"Sorry," said Slater. "We're part of the show. Gotta lick some boots."

"That's okay," said Coil. "I expect to be conked out for hours to come."

But already her mind stirred, imagining ahead the conversation with Trudy and trying to think how she'd tell her. Trudy's airplane had crashed, too, only she didn't know it yet. How in the hell did you give somebody that kind of news? She would play the role of co-pilot, drift down the aisle, sport a matter-of-fact tone of voice, and tell everyone, "Hey, we're going down."

* * * *

It was a soft knock, three quick raps, unassuming and weak, no demand involved. Trudy responded instantly, jerked by the string of habit, call and response, to the door.

"Just a minute," she said, looking for her new Wal-Mart robe and feeling her heart start to pump on a bit of adrenaline generated by the steep climb from parked to flying. It was still dark out.

It was only 5:30: too early for Allison, she thought. Or was this what she meant by first thing?

"Yes?" she said at the door in a half-whisper. Probably too soft.

"Miss Trudy."

It was the maid, Mariela. They had chatted twice. Mariela had spotted the cat but didn't mind covering for the violation of house rules. She was a hard-working immigrant from Guadalajara who had taken the time to learn English.

But so early. Perhaps something about the cat; a warning. Her mind was regressively fuzzy now, in the few seconds she had technically been awake. She cinched her robe, tried to remember where she was, and flipped on the bedside lamp.

"Miss Trudy." And again another trio of knocks. Trying not to wake the neighbors.

Trudy unfastened the chain, braced for a blast of cool air and opened the door.

"Miss Trudy. I . . . "

Mariela stepped inside without being invited and then stumbled awkwardly to the bedside chair, challenging Trudy's sense of decorum and hospitality. A worried, fearful look had gripped Mariela's face, only she wasn't looking Trudy in the eye, but at the door.

George. Gun in hand, filling the door frame. He was still pointing the gun at Mariela, but he was looking at Trudy.

"Nice place," he said. "Good help."

"George, what the—she's not involved."

"Is now."

Trudy stayed standing, the back of her knees against the edge of the bed.

"Besides," said George. "I'm no trouble. This here is sort of a glorified key, that's all. Harmless."

George put the gun down gently on the table, grabbed Mariela by the hand, brought her up like a small child, and whisked her out the door, with a fake, forced smile plastered all over his face. Trudy found herself on the other side of the bed now, unsure how all this came to be—this moment and all its bare-bones reality. Did the bathroom lock from the inside? Was it worth a try?

"How did you . . . ?" she started to ask. But why make conversation? It was coming.

"Hell," said George. "You left your number all over the valley. Little thing called a reverse directory. Simple."

He was stepping around her, one hand out and palm up, inviting her to dance. Trudy kept her own hands pressed between her butt and the wall, trying to flatten herself into the paint, or find a handhold on something that would provide a grip, anything. He put a hand around her forearm and squeezed his fingers down, between muscle and bone, into a painful spot she didn't know existed. Then he flipped her onto the bed.

"What the fuck you doin'?"

He was straddling her hips now, in her face.

There was no need to answer.

"Almost killed Popeye, know that?"

She looked away, off to the side, saw Fossil sitting, watching, from a chair by the bedside table. Do something, she thought.

"You fuckin' bitch," said George.

His breath was sour, rotten. He reeked of bourbon.

Hand on her breast, he was mauling her. God, no, she thought.

"Husband and wife," said George. "Motel room. No laws against it. Or maybe you know of one? Just a last fuck. A good-bye fuck. A fuck-you fuck."

She turned her head away as far as was possible.

"Try to show a little affection," he said, sarcasm everywhere. "It's me. Your fucking husband."

He yanked open her robe and leaned back up a bit to undo his pants.

"You pushed way too hard. But now you have nothing to push against. Nothing. Nothing. Because I'm outta here."

Trudy kept her head cranked to the side, looking off and away, feeling the powerful clamp on her legs, caught between deciding whether to struggle, or to just lie still and disassociate herself from what was happening.

"Husband and wife," said George. "Been a long time since we did it in a motel room."

He jerked down her underwear, and Trudy started to shake and buck. George smiled. "Please," he said. "Husband and wife."

He lay down on top of her, smothering her, and what little effort she had mounted seemed of no consequence. He jammed his stinky head against her neck, pawing her breasts, seeking to arouse himself enough to gain a full erection. Laughing? Laughing.

George was laughing so loudly that he didn't hear the small squeak as the door opened. Mariela stepped inside in one smooth motion and grabbed the telephone off the bedside table and brought it up over her head. George turned, either because of the sensation of cold air flooding the room, or because Trudy's eyes were wide and couldn't keep a secret. George turned and stayed turned, surely half in humor at the sight before him, Mariela not much bigger than a large child, even with her arms up. And as the phone came down, Mariela jumping up off the carpet to give her blow more oomph, George was beginning to put up a defensive wrist. But the steel plate of the phone's base caught George on the forehead, and he seemed to rise, up instead of down, before flopping harmlessly in the tight space between the far side of the bed and the wall.

"Mariela!" said Trudy.

"Vamanos," said Mariela. "I mean—"

"I know, I know."

She only had a few things, scooped them off the rack from the doorless closet, and stuffed her feet in her tennis shoes. Mariela grabbed what she could, anything.

"You can come back for some of it," she said. "No time."

George, in fact, was starting to stir.

What about the gun? Trudy picked it up in a bundle of sweaters, jeans, and Fossil. Mariela scampered to the truck, and Trudy dug into her jeans' pocket for the key, found it, tossed everything inside, and started up the 4-Runner, sitting in her robe.

She stared straight ahead and saw nothing but a thick coat of frost on the windshield. She groped for a scraper, knowing she needed a hole, for starters. But it was the worst kind of frost—thick and crusty.

"Drive with your head out," said Mariela. "Out the window."

"Come with me."

"I can't."

"He'll—"

"He won't find me," said Mariela.

Trudy had the window down now. She needed to go a few blocks, and she jerked the car into reverse.

"Did you know him?" asked Mariela.

"Mi esposo," said Trudy, having no idea why she used the Spanish.

Mariela's eyes widened as the door to Trudy's room opened, and George stumbled through. Mariela ducked around behind another pick-up and disappeared into the night. Trudy, lights off, backed up quickly and then jammed the car in gear, head out the window, freezing air blowing in her face.

* * * *

Room 141. Look for the 4-Runner.

Coil had etched the room number in her weary head, but the knock went unanswered. It was after nine. The whole world was up. No 4-Runner. None parked at any of the motel room doors. She circled the parking lot twice, slowly. Should she bother going to the office? What if Trudy hadn't checked in under her own name? Coil sat in her Blazer and waited, radio and heater on, engine running, antenna up. How long should she give her? Coil tried to think it all through.

A maid pushed a cart along between the rooms. She had a pleasant face, youngish. Not trouble-free, not burdenless, but simple and uncomplicated. Wrapped in a down vest, she left the door open to room 140 so she could come and go with her supplies from the cart.

The images kept coming back to Coil: Rocky, Stern, and Bear. She pictured each one going down. Rocky was still a puzzle, in terms of who had killed him. She saw the elk, whole and unblemished, the shell that held life somewhere in the combination of parts. She imagined vessels, organs, veins, and muscles that needed to work together, to keep each other functioning, to provide the host animal with the ability to breathe. Who had brought the elk down?

And what did Rocky really know? How much did he know? And for how long?

Finally she wondered, would anybody else be asking these questions?

There was a knock on her window. The maid had sidled up to her before Coil noticed. Coil rolled down the window.

"Excuse me," she said. Good English, but clearly a second language.

Coil smiled; the maid didn't.

"I'm waiting, is that okay?"

"Yes, of course. For the woman in this room?" Pointing to 141.

"Yes."

"Is your name Allison?"

"Yes." How did she . . .?

"Trudy told me you could find her in the parking lot at City Market." The look on her face was deep worry.

"She's okay?"

"Okay."

The drive was a half-mile at most, two stoplights' worth. Both were red, both urged patience she couldn't locate. She wouldn't even know where to begin to look. It felt as if connections in the whole business were always beyond her grasp, slippery and odd, a world where putting one foot in front of the other meant going zig-zag. The rest hadn't been rest at all, just fitful blips of snoozing with intermittent bouts of stark-awake insomnia that neither chamomile tea nor rye whiskey could snap.

The parking lot was half full. Most were SUVs—Cherokees and Explorers. Coil figured she'd find Trudy on the perimeter of the lot, where she could watch everything, or in the middle, where she could hide. She spotted a 4-Runner in a pack of cars near the center row and parked a few slots away.

Trudy sat in the driver's seat, eyes flicking nervously about. Coil tapped on the window.

"My God," said Trudy, rolling down the window, reaching over to unlock the passenger-side door, invitation enough for Coil to circle around.

"Mariela found you?" said Trudy as Coil hopped in.

"It wasn't hard," said Coil. "I was parked right there. How long you been waiting?"

"Couple hours. Two cups of tea from the bakery. Mariela saved me, literally. George found me." A kitten hopped up on Trudy's shoulder. "Fossil. The refugee."

"Found you?"

"Said something about a reverse directory. Dumb me."

"What happened?"

"Crashed in, stinkin' drunk. He was all over me. Mariela came in, whacked him with a telephone, got me away. I think he's leaving, as in really leaving."

"What do you mean?"

"Alaska. Some godforsaken place like that."

"Just bail out?"

"He called it his trapdoor. Liquidate everything and go. He never wanted to be on any government record anywhere. This was always too much, dealing with permits and wilderness regulations."

"Apparently," said Coil.

"He always wanted to go, live where nobody knew his name and nobody could easily track him down. I think he means it this time."

"The pressure's on," said Coil.

"What do you mean?" asked Trudy.

Coil started with Bobby Marcovicci in Denver and wound through most of the highlights of the days she and Trudy had been separated. When it came to telling about finding Rocky, she needed to breathe. She cracked the window and let her own tears flow in advance, anticipating Trudy's, which came before Coil said his name. They hugged. Trudy said it confirmed what she already knew, asked a few questions about whether they had moved the body, and cried some more, this time alone. Coil went into the store for a box of Kleenex and some cold sodas, keeping her eyes open for Grumley or anybody else.

"It's too weird," said Trudy.

"It's all tied up," said Coil. "What if your George stumbled across Applegate? The trail down from where Rocky ended up would put him in the same area. Applegate is dazed and a mess, mentally, from having killed Ray Stern. George gets him squared away, maybe even takes his rifle, but tells Applegate to keep quiet about them ever hooking up. Now the police have Applegate's rifle, and George knows it."

"The Mooney," said Trudy.

"I don't follow."

"We need to keep him here," said Trudy. "His plane. He'd be stuck without it. Well, it'd cost him a day or two."

"What are we going to do, fly it away and hide it somewhere?"

"No," said Trudy. "But maybe we can make it difficult to start."

15

Three hundred cars were strung out behind them. Ellenberg drove with a giddy sensation of power, right at 65, the mouth of the canyon ahead, around a wide curve.

"Here we go," said Ellenberg.

The valley closed down. The road dropped slightly. The roadside climbed up, way up, and out of sight, as they plunged down into the canyon.

Applegate looked back. In the mix behind them, there were semi trucks and other commercial vehicles, including one UPS van. Surely the drivers of those not involved must be wondering about the knots of traffic, the caravan growing tighter with each mile, unaware that they were bees in amber.

Five miles down the canyon, Ellenberg eased up on the gas. A BMW, two snowboards strapped to the top, shot around them. A 1970's-era station wagon pulled up alongside and matched their speed, fifty and dropping. The woman with long blonde braids in the shotgun seat flashed Ellenberg two Vs with both hands and smiled. And then an old red Volkswagen pulled up in the breakdown lane on the right, and it slowed, too. The exit veered off to the right from the bridge as the interstate banked on a turn right where the canyon opened up.

Ellenberg brought her car to a crawl, jogging speed, and then to a stop in the middle of the bridge about twenty yards beyond the exit. The station wagon and VW did the same, the VW squeezing in tight to make room for a fourth car, a brand new model Jeep Cherokee, all shiny and buffed. The driver climbed out, hopped around to the back, flipped open the gate and held up two long sticks, material wrapped around one.

Applegate climbed out, and so did Ellenberg. He could hear a bit of honking off in the distance. The banner was unspooled straight across the lanes of interstate, giant bright red letters on a white sheet: WHO KILLED RAY STERN? Ellenberg stood up on her car and looked back. Applegate glanced back, too. Gridlock, but no grid. People were standing around, banners everywhere, cheering and chanting.

"Beautiful," said Ellenberg. "Let's see how long it takes 'em." She checked her watch.

From out of nowhere, it seemed, two television crews, on foot, jogged up through the traffic and started recording everything that didn't move. A third and a fourth crew drove up the exit ramp onto the highway and started to set up. A short, fifty-ish reporter named Kirkwood, a tailored suit under his winter parka, came straight over to Ellenberg.

"You promise, you deliver," he said to her.

"Thought you'd be interested," she said.

"We've got a helicopter rented, too. No way to shoot a sucker like this from the ground. You get all three hundred?"

"Maybe double that," Ellenberg lied.

"And Dean Applegate to boot, quite the display here," said the reporter.

"I understand this was your idea," the reporter said, film crew already taping over the reporter's shoulder.

"The point is nobody seems to care about the death of Ray Stern," said Applegate. "We can't let society forget the price he paid."

A helicopter screamed above them, heading east. A cameraman leaned out of the open side door, his feet on the skids.

"Who the fuck is in charge of this goddam mess?"

The booming voice broke through the din as the helicopter's drone waned. The cameraman kept rolling as Dawn turned to look at the man, several hundred pounds of frustration. He wore a dirty white T-shirt and grease-stained jeans, oblivious to the mountain air. Long dark hair flowed from underneath a yellow baseball cap, but the youthful elements masked a man in his mid-forties.

"You can't fucking stop in the middle of the goddam interstate," he yelled. First he approached Ellenberg, and then Applegate, who flinched as the man stormed over. "I'm half an hour late as it fucking is," he yelled. "I got zero time for any political bullshit. Is this your stupid idea of a joke?"

"We won't be here all day," said Applegate.

"I don't have time for anything, never mind all day."

"You must have cared about something in your life, believed something needed changing," said Ellenberg. Her tone was cool, non-threatening.

"Like the fucking Vietnam War."

"Exactly. You go, or did you protest?"

"Fuck. Both. Went first. Came back and joined the other army that marched on D.C."

He was inches away from Ellenberg, glaring down at her calm, centered expression.

"You helped save thousands of human lives by protesting. By voicing your opinion, standing up for it. It's on your record. And you deserve credit. We've got an issue with the police work up here in Glenwood Springs and an issue with hunters and hunting. Somebody shot and killed—"

"Yeah, yeah, I remember hearing about that." His tone had eased.

"We are trying to exert a little pressure on the local government here, so somebody will decide to deal with whoever took down Ray Stern."

"Okay, okay. Christ," said the driver. "Ten minutes?"

"Max," said Ellenberg. "Unless the cops are even slower than we think."

The man turned sheepishly and departed. One news crew followed him, probably to get his name and more of his story.

Ellenberg smiled.

"This is our day, our day," she said, "I can feel it."

Good, thought Applegate, as long as that includes both of us.

* * * *

Trudy showed her driver's license to a man who controlled a buzzered door that led out to the tarmac, and Coil followed right behind. The man didn't realize George had the plane on the market but told them if Mrs. Ferguson—Coil's made-up name—needed any technical questions answered that he would be glad to come out and poke around with them, though he didn't think you could really judge a plane until you took it up.

It seemed colder out on the concrete apron, walking around the couple of dozen or so planes tied down to their moorings, following the man's directions. The wind picked up, and the loose tethers on a few of them snapped in the breeze.

"Now pretend you're doing lots of talking, the good sales pitch routine, in case old Mr. Anal Airport Security Man happens to be watching," said Coil, getting a feeling that this little bout of sabotage might feel pretty good.

Coil dug in her coat for the all-purpose Leatherman and folded out the needle nose pliers. Trudy opened the doors on both sides, and Coil reached around underneath the dash and pulled down a few wires, unsure of what was what, but remembering an old trick—to not cut the middle but instead excise a whole long section to make patching more difficult, or make it hard to see what was cut. She took out a foot-long piece of blue wire and a couple of yellows, then lifted up the side flaps of the cowling and did the same to some wires that seemed to go in and out around the distributor. The pliers lopped off a couple of sections of vacuum tubing, too.

"Nice plane you've got here, Ms. Grumley," said Coil, "but its value seems to be dropping as we speak."

"This should hold him up a bit," said Trudy. She seemed to be hiding a smile. "How much?"

"You're the one in the pilot's seat," said Coil. "Say when."

"'When,'" said Trudy. "We need time for Sandstrom to put everything together."

They were sitting in the cockpit, side by side.

"While we're here . . ." said Coil.

"What?"

"Just want to take a peek, see if there's anything of interest."

The rear of the Mooney was seatless and spotless, an open area with two built-in storage bins.

"What's to find?" asked Trudy.

"Just worth a look," said Coil, on her hands and knees, lifting up one of the lids on the bin to find a flashlight, rope, mess kit, dried food, a gallon of water, a gallon of fuel mix, a box of shotgun shells, and a funny-looking insulated orange hat with ear flaps.

"Hardly George's style," said Trudy, trying it on.

"Hardly been used," said Coil.

Trudy had the other bin open. "Nothing," she reported, "unless you count an empty cardboard box."

"We could use it to carry our parts," said Coil, referring to the pile of wires and tubes by the front seats.

Trudy lifted the box out.

"Slater?" she asked.

"Huh?"

"Isn't that your boyfriend's name?"

"You must be . . ."

Trudy had the label in her face, a bright red business name on the return address and then, in smaller black ink, the typed name, D. Slater.

Coil's eyes blinked involuntarily, perhaps hoping to erase the moment.

"Mercy," said Coil. "Plain old fucking mercy."

* * * *

Two state patrol cars, blue lights flashing, cruised toward them, eastbound in the empty westbound lane. The exit ramp filled simultaneously with police cars.

Applegate counted four. It was as if they had been waiting together. Weird. Ellenberg scooted over as the state patrol cars parked nose to nose, to prevent anybody from going anywhere.

"Don't worry, we've got lawyers standing by," she said. "How many can they arrest?"

Dozens of people had worked their way forward to the front of the line of cars and had joined hands, chanting: "Who killed Ray Stern? Who killed Ray Stern? Cops don't care, does anyone care? Who killed Ray Stern?"

The state patrol deferred to the local cops, who were already cuffing the couple with the largest banner, out front.

"So they arrest 'em, how are they going to move all the cars?" Applegate asked.

"I don't think they've thought it through," said Ellenberg.

The cops left the couple in cuffs leaning against the side of one car.

The news crews sandwiched in as the cops strolled up.

Sandstrom hooked his thumbs in his belt buckle, waited for a few more cycles of the chant, then held his hands up like a preacher encouraging quiet and order from the congregation.

The chant went to full shout. Ellenberg was right with it, shrill and piercing. Ellenberg stepped forward, turned and waved her hands overhead, and the chorus broke down quickly to weak fragments and then stopped.

"Any car without a driver will be impounded," Sandstrom announced. "We have tow trucks standing by." A few more police cars zipped up the exit ramp. "Return to your cars now. Your point has been made."

Some people skittered away, but most stayed put and then sat down on the pavement, linking elbows together. Ellenberg sat down with the others across the highway. Applegate stood.

"We have an announcement on this very matter," said Sandstrom.

Kirkwood snapped his fingers at his crew, who was busy doing close-ups of those sitting on the highway. The crew spun around, and it seemed like even Sandstrom knew to wait for the cue.

"We have a suspect."

A gasp went up. Somebody whistled. Another started clapping.

"It has taken lots of hard work by the staff, but we have a suspect," said Sandstrom.

"How about an arrest?" someone shouted.

It was possible somebody had tipped the cops. One bad twig on the phone tree.

"Yeah, an arrest," shouted another.

"We can make that happen," said Sandstrom, but only loud enough for those in the front row to hear.

Sandstrom stepped out from the growing brigade of cops.

Applegate's legs said spring, in sync with his heart and mind. A dive off the bridge? His legs flinched to go, enough that Ellenberg stood up, sensing it all as Sandstrom stood in front of Applegate's face.

"Dean Applegate," said Sandstrom.

The others stood up, too, gathered closer around. Sandstrom watched from a distance.

"You are under arrest—"

Cameras were right there.

"Dean," Ellenberg cried out, "what is going on?"

"—On suspicion . . . of first degree murder in the death of—"

"Dean?"

"—Ray Stern."

His legs wanted to bolt as Sandstrom, vice-gripping his arm, spun him around and clamped a pair of handcuffs on his wrists.

Applegate forced a look of confidence, leaned down to whisper in her ear.

"Don't worry, Ellenberg," he said. "It's a little mix-up. It was Fishy's rifle."

"Who?" she said. "What?"

* * * *

A wobbling whirl of possibilities spun through Coil's head. She imagined Slater doing business with the man who had chased her down, killed

Bear, tried to kill her, and who probably had something to do with the death of Mr. Deer Suit and Rocky.

She piled up stuff as she fought the tears. She opened the closets and dug under the bed, winging things into a laundry basket as she went, wanting every scrap of her stuff out of his place. And her life.

Coil found a beer, took four or five long pulls off of it, and started combing through the rest of the place. Pictures, letters, phone numbers— anything might help. She wanted to find the obvious thing she had missed, something about him that had been right under her nose all along.

Coil had already swung by 101 East Creek, the address on the label. It was at the very eastern edge of a relatively empty street. 101 sat off by itself, a few city blocks from any other trailers, tucked down a bit in some old-forest aspens. There were no trailers down there, just one prefab concrete building, maybe 30-yards square with a light green exterior, no signs, and no windows. Just "101" in cheap stick-on lettering on the door, and a large, plastic storage bin propped out front. Probably a mail drop. There were three boxes inside the bin, labeled and ready: two for Hong Kong, one for Taipei. Waiting for UPS.

The building stayed with her as she dug around Slater's trailer: a stack of letters in a straw box, bills, gas station credit cards, phone, electric, and Visa statements, a few scraps of paper with names and numbers. Nothing sinister. In the bedroom, she dug through the built-in dresser, four draw-ers in a stack. All clothes and no surprises. She had met lots of hunters in the campgrounds and out on the trail. His type was rare. Too soft, right? Too with-it, right? Too complex. No. She had mistaken terse for complex. Boy Scout? Right.

She ripped through a closet, trying to think back to whether she'd been manipulated and thinking about times he'd talked about his phi-losophy. She steamed about how she'd been duped and started to cry, frustrated by her lack of ability to see him. She wondered how she could have bound herself up with his veneer and not seen beneath. She knew herself even less and felt ripped open again, needing a new set of stitches across her head in the place where things had begun to heal. And she wondered how she and Slater had connected, if she would have picked him out of a crowd in a busy airport, and why creeps like him, mysterious creeps like him, never seemed to die in messy accidents.

In the kitchen, checking the cupboards for the hell of it, she felt the urge to bolt. In fact, she found herself fighting the compulsion to bolt. Trudy had said she'd follow in an hour, after swinging by to check the cats. But how long would she really be? What if she had a seizure? What if George somehow found her?

Dangling on a nail on the inside of a cupboard, she found a round paper tag the size of a quarter, with a metal rim. "101" was written in pencil, and a key was attached.

Coil was back in her car without remembering how she got there. Her world was doing that flippity-flop thing again, and she thought she tasted saltwater. She took a quick breath, unconsciously, and tried to bring things back into focus.

David Slater. A screwed-up ranger. She had heard stories about antler dust, rumors that you could move the stuff if you wanted, rumors you could pad your income. But nobody really knew how or where. It was one of those whispers in the wind, nothing she had ever tried to pin down. Jesus, the money. Where were the profits stashed? Why the cheap trailer housing?

The key fit; she was half hoping it wouldn't. The room was dark, and her fingers groped for the light switch along the cool concrete wall.

The interior was like somebody's messy, unorganized basement, except for the scale of the operation. From inside, the building seemed even larger. There was more open space, plain old room, than stuff. The work area was confined to a corner of the interior, maybe a tenth of all the space available. Tall steel shelving defined the work space on one side, stacks of what looked to be empty boxes, not much bigger than needed to mail a wristwatch, were stacked on the shelves. On a lone workbench she found spools of twine and other threads, straight needles and round ones, and a series of knives and heavy-duty scissors. Coil squatted down in the middle of the room, picked up a clump of brown hair. Straight hair, tipped white. Deer fur.

In the middle of the work space, there was a piece of industrial machinery with a motor at the bottom of a huge steel bowl, like a baker's mixer for bread. Through a fist-sized hole at the bottom of the bowl, two gears with sharp teeth were hooked to the motor, and below it a collection bin. Light tan dust coated both the bowl and the bin. In the other corner, there was a shelf full of plastic vials, nothing special. Also empty. There was also a giant plastic bag full of Styrofoam peanuts, strung upside down from the ceiling. A flexible tube at the bottom of the bag worked as a dispenser. From somewhere, she kept getting whiffs of her high school biology class, formaldehyde or something. And she realized Slater saw more profits in the pieces than in the whole. Her head buzzed with fury, equipment went toppling and flying, and her vision blurred with tears and anger.

* * * *

"You got a rifle. It wasn't mine. Isn't mine."

"We've also got Mr. Marcovicci waiting and willing to testify that he sold it to you, three years ago, during another one of your annual trips up here. Where were you the day Ray Stern died?"

Sandstrom had his foot hitched up on a chair. Another cop, nameless, stood by the door the entire time. Didn't someone usually take notes at these things?

"Off on a hike," said Applegate.

"Oh right," said Sandstrom. "All the other boys are cooling their heels in the tent, and you decide to go out and take a stroll. We're supposed to buy that one, special discount for stupidity? Wouldn't take a rifle along, in case? Wouldn't decide to sling a rifle over your shoulder, maybe in the back of your mind thinking you might stumble across something? What if your luck changed while you were out there, and you saw this good looking animal, and you didn't have your rifle? What then? You'd feel kind of silly, wouldn't you?"

They had been at it for over an hour, in an empty office somewhere near the building where they had held that one parking lot protest. The trip from the highway had been a blur. He couldn't wipe Ellenberg's puzzled look from his mind.

The rifle was supposed to have been right there, in the barn. Now they had it? Or *said* they did. He wanted to appear relaxed, but couldn't begin to find that gear.

"I took a hike."

"We got everybody else accounted for at the time Ray Stern was killed, about noon. He was shot before it started snowing. And the route he took, it must've taken three or four hours for him to get from his tent to there. It ain't like auto mechanics, figuring this stuff out. So we got everybody else accounted for, every other person in Ripplecreek, except you. And you're out for a stroll."

"Except Grumley."

Sandstrom stopped, straightened up, hitched up his belt, walked around in a small circle, and leaned back against the wall.

"And how exactly do you know *this*?" asked Sandstrom, stepping up.

"He left that morning, too."

"And didn't come back?"

"Nope."

"At all?"

"No—"

"But you're off on a hike, smelling the pine cones."

"I ran into him."

Applegate didn't quite know where this would lead, couldn't quite determine if mentioning this would make a difference.

"Where?"

"On the main trail."

"What time?"

"It was snowing pretty good by then, two or three maybe."

"And where was he going?"

"I don't know."

"Or coming from?"

"Farther up on top, I suppose."

"And what difference does any of this make?" asked Sandstrom.

"He seemed agitated."

"Okay," said Sandstrom. "we'll talk to the world class hunter and see what he knows."

"No, really."

"Look," said Sandstrom. He opened the door, disappeared for a count of no more than five. He stepped back in the room and swung the butt end of the rifle in Applegate's face. "We got Marovicci's testimony he sold it to you. We got him in the tent. All the guys in the tent remembered—*guess what*—all the guys in the tent. Hours in a stinking tent together, it's not hard to remember. George Grumley uses a different caliber rifle, a .270. The caliber on this Sako matches exactly the caliber of the bullet we pulled from Ray Stern's body. It was resting against his spine. It plugged. It matches. You gave us this yarn about walking with your rifle back up the hill and tossing it off some unknown cliff, and now we know it's bullshit. Fucking wasted our time. Your whole charade. Joining the animal rights bozos because you had a change of *heart*? How about the guilt factor bursting your head? Imagine walking up to a dead deer or elk in the woods, you think you've got some beauty, and it's got fingers instead of a hoof, and you poke around a little bit and realize what you've done. Imagine I'd feel slightly whacko, you know, a bit out of sorts."

From somewhere deep inside him, the stored-up fear was unshackled. It floated up from a dark interior holding tank, an underwater cave where the air bubbles had fought for years for a path to the surface, and trickled down both cheeks. There was a point in keeping up the fight, but it meant nothing more than prolonging the inevitable.

He had done what Ray Stern wanted him to do.

It wasn't cold-blooded murder. More like entrapment or assisted suicide. He knew that. But now, Jesus, now. The embarrassment.

"Okay," Applegate blubbered. "Can we make a deal?"

* * * *

No question that Coil had the Sako. Couldn't figure out why her nose had to be shoved so far into it. Was it a thrill? Couldn't imagine that now she'd return to her A-Frame any time soon, and he knew the Sako was already in the hands of the cops, or worse, the state or federal assholes, who might think it was a really big deal.

Time to go. All-the-way go. He should have put the screws to Coil when he'd had a chance. And Applegate. And Popeye. Like he did with Alvin.

His own house was too depressing, with Trudy's cats in charge. The chorus of meows was non-stop. He couldn't believe he had bothered to check to see if they had enough food, and it really pissed him off to see that their bowls were topped-off. Who? When?

He needed the fucking banks and his lawyers to get the properties sold, to liquidate. The thought of all the fucking paperwork to sell property was a headache, the government making it so complicated, sticking their mitts fucking everywhere. Grumley picked up the phone and dialed his lawyer. He waited through two whole songs and part of a third. How could his own boot-licking lawyer put him on hold?

"George?"

Finally.

"I don't pay you for the privilege of listening to elevator music on the fucking telephone."

Bennie Murdock was small-time, barely legal, and on a tidy retainer to advise him on the side about shady transactions.

"Sorry," said Murdock. "Practically everybody down here's been watching the activity over on the interstate." Murdock's office was above a restaurant near downtown. "We were up on the roof. Looked like something out of the goddam movies. Don't see that too much."

"What's that?"

"They busted this guy out in the middle of the highway, this big traffic jam, some sort of protest. Only the cops busted one of 'em, carted his butt away. Carried the whole thing live on CNN."

Applegate. Gone. And he'd be singing soon.

"It's time," said Grumley. He'd have to swing by the barn, grab some of his favorite rifles.

"Time for what?"

"Bennie—"

"Oh man, punch-out time?"

"Gotta go." There was an old Winchester somewhere that had been very reliable.

"All the account numbers the same? Nothing's changed?"

"Yes."

"Prices?"

"I could get more for the store, of course, if it was on the open market. But a deal's a deal."

"I'd give it 120 days for the money to show up in the accounts, once all the deeds get recorded, and the closing dates, all that stuff."

"And you can sell the house, too," said Grumley.

"Your wife going with?" Murdock asked, as if all he was planning was a vacation at the beach.

"She's got her own plans," said Grumley. "Besides, to you it doesn't matter where I'm going, right? I could be right here watching you the whole time, a member of the ethics panel of the Colorado Bar Association, here to make sure you ain't fucking your clients."

Grumley heard a snort-like laugh, a cautious one.

"And how will I know I've got the right buyer?" Murdock asked.

"Because he'll walk in one day soon, probably within a week, and his checkbook will be wide open and he'll know the exact price. He'll be the only one. I guarantee it."

"Well, safe travels."

He slammed down the phone, dialed another number, and told who-ever answered, as calmly as he could, to get David Slater.

"Can I help you?" answered Slater.

"Hey little buddy, you fuck."

"Always nice to hear your voice, Grumley. You hear your good friend, the animal rights prince, got picked up?"

"Yeah, yeah, what's he saying?"

"I'd have to be a cop to know the answer to that one."

"Thought you had access."

"Only when I need it."

"The kid's clueless."

"What did you have against Rocky Carnivitas?"

"He came up to blow my fucking head off. Thought he was standing up for Trudy, for Chrissakes, and wanted a piece of the action for his troubles. Totally self-defense."

"I'm sure the world's a better place."

"Where's my wife?" asked Grumley.

"Wouldn't have a clue," said Slater. "You're out of here?"

"See Bennie Murdock in about a week. Money goes into the right accounts, it's all yours."

Slater would be king: all the custom hunts, all the hot shots, and all the antler traffic. He'd practically control the market.

"Sandstrom cool?"

"More than likely. He's got his plum. Media boys have the picture of the sheriff getting his man."

He thought about mentioning how pissed off he was at Slater's little buddy, Coil. But let him find out on his own that she was piecing things together. By then, he'd be trading in his plane for scrap in Spokane, Alaska-bound.

Grumley wildly packed some clothes in a big old laundry bag and dug out a small stash of twenties from a cigar box where he'd been building up a supply. Last time he'd checked, it was $15,000, enough to keep him liquid for a few months, pay for plane fuel, and cover whatever else would come up. He climbed into his truck and sped first to the barn, and then to the airport, riding the line between too-fast and driving with an edge. Only a matter of minutes now, he told himself, and he would be soaring above this mess.

Grumley bolted through the doors to the tarmac, jogged out and could see from a distance that the cowling was up and wide open to the sky.

"Fuck," he yelled.

Back to the terminal. The asshole, the meek little airport man, stood by the door, quaking.

"Your best mechanic. Now."

"His day off."

"Now," said Grumley.

"He doesn't live too far—"

"And I'm leaving a pile of stuff here. I want it loaded when he's done. I'll call in a couple hours, when it's finished."

"Couple?"

"Yeah, two. Couple. One, two. Who fucked with my plane?"

"Nobody. Your wife came by, wanted to show it to this other woman. Didn't know you had it for sale."

"How long ago was all this?"

"Few hours ago."

"I'll be back in two hours," said Grumley. "An extra hundred for you if it's fixed by then. Whatever it takes. Fix it. Good as fucking new, okay?"

Back in his pick-up, he concentrated on the loose ends, trying to imagine Applegate talking and wondering if anybody would make anything of it if he did. And who was there to hear it?

At some point, though, Applegate would think clearly enough to hire a decent lawyer and then offer a trade of information. Even Applegate would have to take that bait, tell 'em how his old pal George helped eat the dead guy's lunch and then took the Sako off his hands.

His truck skidded and bounced as he flew. He would leave it all behind, that was for sure. One little delay, but manageable. At a gas station, Grumley slammed the truck to a stop near the phone booth, out under the big sign with the prices, put two quarters in, and dialed.

"Slater, please."

"Just left. Can I take a message?"

He crunched the phone back in the cradle, dug for more quarters, dialed Slater's home number, listened to it ring and then to the message-machine beep. He recognized it.

"My wife's going back in the bottle. I think I know how to find her. She's not going to like the fit. You might wanna take care of that little Coil chick. Okay?"

The second he hung up, he realized he should never have left such a stupid message anywhere. He kicked the truck door once with his boot, good enough to make a dent and rattle his ankle. It would cost him an hour, to and from Slater's place, to fix the mistake.

* * * *

The radio switched from Dwight Yoakam to national network news. Top of the hour. Trudy tweaked the dial to improve the reception as she maneuvered through the canyon, probably going a bit too slowly for all the others behind her.

Bombing in Tel Aviv, floods in Virginia, President worried about unemployment numbers. And then the announcer said there was an arrest, an update on the case of that "odd, somewhat bizarre, so-called creative suicide by the animal rights activist last month in Glenwood Springs, Colorado."

Trudy reached for the volume.

". . . Police here in Glenwood Springs are now questioning 38-year-old Dean Applegate, arrested during a massive protest on the Interstate right near downtown. The one-time hunter turned activist was leading the demonstration for FATE when he was arrested. Police have not yet indicated if he is cooperating. Other activists said they were sure it was some unfortunate mix-up, but Dawn Ellenberg, who has not usually been difficult to find, was not available for comment tonight in Glenwood Springs."

Allison's rifle, no doubt, thought Trudy. It paid off. She wondered if the pieces would come around and grab up George, too, in Applegate's mess and in Stern's death. If they could find him. The key now was to hook back up with Allison; it was unsafe hanging around the house, alone.

The first stop was Wal-Mart. Trudy had checked George's gun, which was curiously empty.

"I need some ammunition for this," said Trudy. She looked around, not wanting anyone, other than the salesman back in sporting goods, a rounded young man with a dark, bristly mustache, to see. She lifted up the handgun from her pocket a bit, so the kid could get a look at it.

"Ma'am, really, it's not a good idea to be walking around with a concealed—"

"Tell me what I need, please." She smiled as calmly as she could manage.

"It's not, in Colorado, legal to—"

"Help me, please," said Trudy.

The kid eyed it. "44 mag. Jesus. I could get in trouble; just remember I never saw that."

Back in the 4-Runner, she loaded the gun down by the gearshift, keeping an eye on shoppers coming and going nearby. Her hands shook a bit, but her head felt clear and serene. She felt like she'd swallowed a large stone, growing now in her stomach, but that things were coming to a head.

* * * *

On top of the television, held down by the remote control, there was an envelope, ragged at the seam and open. Coil plucked it off the TV, stood there jittery, looking for what she had missed, determined to uncover any scrap in the trailer. She read the return address. She had to read it again before it sank in.

Pete Weaver. The Weaver Ranch. 40 Ripplecreek.

"Mr. Slater."

Her eyes flicked down to the signature, recognized it from her pay-checks.

"This letter is to confirm acceptance of your offer."

Her eyes absorbed the date. The letter was a month old.

". . . I know it's been six months since we broke off talks. If you are still interested . . ."

Her brain would not let her read every word.

". . . purchasing my property. I'm ready . . . The last price you offered is acceptable . . ."

Her eyes leapt to the only figure on the page.

". . . $1.5 million . . ."

Some discussion of earnest money, ten percent. How to deliver it and when. And if not delivered in two weeks, "I'll put the property on the open market . . . Let me know . . . Sincerely . . ."

And the signature.

Weaver? Turning over the largest property in the valley to the man with the antler dust factory? Coil thought of Weaver's prime property, and the fact that permits for guides were not held by individuals; they were sold with property, part of the package. It was the way it worked. Weaver would have no idea about Slater's real business, would he?

She dialed Weaver's number while she stared at the blinking light of the answering machine, a blinking light that wasn't there earlier, before she'd headed down to the factory. She stood in the kitchen, getting a whiff of something moldy from the sink, steadying herself for an answer she couldn't stand to hear and trying to find the words to ask the question.

Three blinks of the little red light for each ring in her ear. Another ring. Blink . . . blink . . . blink. No answer. Hang up. Blink.

She pressed play.

"My wife's going back in the bottle."

The unmistakable voice.

"I think I know how to find her. She's not going to like the fit . . ."

She shuddered at the venom in the words.

"You might wanna take care of that little Coil chick. Okay?"

The door opened behind her and she spun.

"David! I was just . . ."

She was trying for an easy-going tone and failing, as she stood and stepped around, anticipating.

"You were just."

Grumley, dripping ugly.

"Finding anything?" he asked, looking at the pile of stuff on the bedroom floor.

"I was just . . ." She'd already said that. There was no back door on these trailers. A window? She looked around, giving herself away. She wondered if he'd even notice if she threw her full weight up around his neck, going for a take-down that would be just enough for her to scramble past him and out the door.

"What did you see?"

"You. Dragging Rocky."

"Rocky was a loser. The biggest reason he was an asshole. But just one."

"You killed Bear."

"Just another animal."

"So it's any animal, any old day? You and Slater both?"

"So what?"

"All the land and all the animals, there for you, and you alone."

"No. For whoever gets 'em first. Winter gets 'em. A wolf gets 'em. Or I do."

"I think you got more problems than me seeing you dragging Rocky. There's Applegate. Between us . . ."

· "The fuck I care."

He kept coming. She backed up to the bedroom, thinking weapon or windows? The options were nonexistent.

16

topped at a traffic light, second in line, snug up behind a big RV, Trudy
tapped the steering wheel and studied the stickers on the bumper in
front of her. *My Family Dug The Grand Canyon. You'll Feel Peachy In Georgia.*
And others: *Carmel, Seattle, Juneau, and Parris Island.* The RV's plates were
from Arkansas.

She couldn't quite imagine a life on the road yet, a home on the highway. Too much dread blurred that vision.

The lane of cars next to her started to move, and the large land yacht
didn't budge. Now its flashers came on. Trudy slapped the wheel with her
palm and checked the rearview mirror as the line behind her began to peel
off from the rear forward. Eight cars to go.

Trudy felt a cloud trying to push its way into her brain, the swirl of
excitement loading up. She couldn't quite tell if this was the brink of a
seizure, or if she was seeing things more clearly. Not likely. One blink
brought light, the next darkness.

Her breath came in small gulps. Why? On what basis?

Five cars.

Her mind tried to leap ahead, anticipate what was next, but she
worked to stay with the moment. There was a funny taste in her mouth
that was either working its way down her throat or working its way up.

Three cars.

She checked the gun again, sitting on the seat next to her underneath
a T-Shirt.

One car.

Finally she backed up enough to give herself room to maneuver and came up alongside the RV, ready to gun it, but the light was red again. The elderly man had the hood up and was poking around the engine, a bit of white smoke drifting up from where it wasn't supposed to be. The man's wife caught Trudy's eyes and, arms folded tightly across her jacket, scowled.

Finally the light cycled around again, and Trudy pulled out as quickly as she could manage without causing a stir. The 4-Runner whined up, a fine blue mist of exhaust chasing her down the highway.

As she turned off toward the Blue Sky Trailer Park, the car shuddered over a cattle guard, hit the dirt road, and the rear window was coated with a swirl of red-rock dust. In the distance, she could see the entrance to the trailer park. She tried to picture staying focused, tried to picture staying focused, tried to picture staying focused.

* * * *

Grumley stepped up and swatted her down, one sweep of his arm knocking her off balance, and she grappled for a soft landing on the couch. But her head went first, and her neck jammed.

The gun was in his right hand by the time she looked back up, and she grabbed the side of her neck as it pulsed in agony. The gun came across the air, and Coil heard a grunt, stared at the butt end of the grip and then ducked and rolled, trying again to jab his leg with hers. She bounced up off the couch, still on the wrong side of him from the door. A lit lamp on a side table next to the couch crashed over as she knocked around, eluding his grasp and dodging another windmilling arm. Watching his momentum, she helped him follow-through. A bear, standing one-legged on a rock in the river, swatting a bee. She pushed up on his ribs from underneath, bumping him with a shoulder, and he went with his own momentum, head on line with a shelf that propped an air conditioner up to a window.

The gun went off, so there was no sound of his head whacking the appliance. Her ears rang, and they were both underwater, slow motion and flipperless, unable to find a new center of gravity.

She checked herself for bullet holes, thoroughly aware that major body parts could be punctured without, at first, major pain. No blood.

He climbed to his knees. She turned and scampered for the door, thinking to grab her coat, then realizing she had never taken it off. She felt her legs bound up in his grasp, kicked, and felt some body part behind her go smack.

"Fucker," yelled Grumley behind her.

She leapt for the door and bounded through, to a beautiful sight.

* * * *

Trudy fired one shot into the ground the second after Allison got behind her, as George stepped out.

He stopped.

"What the f—"

She moved the gun up so his nose was square over the muzzle.

"Trudy."

He said it with disdain.

"You've been sticking your nose where it doesn't belong."

The gun sounded good. The force in her hands. Control, power. And his response. She liked his response. Frozen. But he was shifting now, moving away, egging her to try another.

"Shit, Trudy, whatchya' doing?"

"The obvious."

"Nobody saw nothing," he spewed.

A tear shuddered up inside her, with anger and images of Rocky.

"For a scrap you could have fixed me up," she said. "A little scrap. And you'd be on your way, outta here. Gone. Do you believe that? Do you know that?"

"Always knew it was an option. And Rocky pressed the point, although he wanted a huge chunk of cash for his troubles, to keep quiet about something or other."

"So you saw—"

"Never said I saw anybody anywhere."

"A scrap, George."

"Shit," said Grumley. "You have it easy. What you gonna do?" He turned and headed to his truck. "Nothing is what you're going to do."

Aiming was easy, and so was pulling the trigger. She watched him reel and flop down to the dirt, and she kept the gun on him as he crumpled down and yelled in agony.

"Don't worry," she explained, "it's only an ankle."

She stepped over to where Grumley scraped his way along in the dirt. He was wincing in pain, digging into the ground with his hands and good leg, trying to cover the space to his truck, trying briefly to stand, then collapsing back down. There was blood and ooze all over the ankle.

"*A scrap*," Trudy yelled at him.

"Shit," said Grumley. "My leg."

"A scrap," said Trudy.

Her husband spread himself out on the ground, one hand looking for a grip on the tread of the truck tire, his face turned upward, pleading.

Coil pulled up beside her.

A visible look of concern edged its way across her husband's face. It was a look she'd never seen before.

"You're going where I've been," said Trudy. "Only yours will have real guards and lots of barbed-wire."

* * * *

The beauty of it, Slater told himself, was that he would be able to clear out without too much trouble. Weaver had the money. Slater would need the money.

There were four cop cars jammed in around his fucking trailer. They had passed him on his casual drive home, just after he turned off the paved road, and plugged the road down to his trailer. The hoods of Grumley's truck, and Allison's, told him everything he needed to know. He slowly turned around, like a lost tourist. Invisible, that's what he wanted to be. The police vehicles' flashing cherry tops refelcted in red flickers off the surrounding trailers everywhere. He fidgeted and puttered about, trying to look aimless and loose, and made his way back out of the fray.

He didn't need a plan like Grumley's, with complicated plane swaps and fake flight plans. He would make his up as he went along. It would be creative, spontaneous. The beauty of it was that he had the money. Weaver had the money and wouldn't have any reason to keep it.

There weren't too many other positives. Everything else was about to crumble. It would have worked. Well, was working, just fine. Nobody was really being hurt. The government's "concern," was entirely unwarranted. Always the fucking government, the thing you're supposed to work hard for, pay taxes to, so they can fucking give it away to other people in other countries. What a weak-ass nation.

The police radio hadn't stopped squawking. They were at his place, tearing his world apart. The authorities. Immoral assholes, dealing out their bits of justice in such a haphazard fashion, whatever and however it fit into their schedules and needs. The same government that could clean you out, swipe your land. Eminent domain. The phrase alone implied the government thought of itself as superior, thought of itself as prominent. Eminence. The real overlord who knows what's best, assumes what's best, decides what's best. Hadn't the government been designed to serve, not swipe?

He would start over somewhere else, for the third time, as soon as he got the money back from Weaver. That was the beauty of it; at least he had some funds to start.

Two more cop cars flew out of downtown Glenwood Springs. What was the rush now?

He thumped the steering wheel to some unheard beat, waiting at the lights, cursing for the hell of it at the slowpoke cars crossing in front of him. He wondered which way he should head, after he stopped to see Weaver.

Spin the compass and go.

* * * *

The neighbors stood around, including one grizzled old man in a tight white T-shirt who tried to take charge, fetching bandages for Grumley and telling other neighbors to go down to the entrance and point the way for the cops and the ambulance to make it in as quickly as possible. The man smoked as he worked, keeping others at a distance, barking out his orders like he'd seen it all before. The cops had split into two groups—the other group at 101 East Table, starting to get the whole picture, with Sandstrom overseeing the search.

Coil leaned on Trudy's 4-Runner and looked back into the eyes of neighbors who were staring at them and the scene, and who were probably wondering what all this could be about.

Trudy was inside her truck, sobbing quietly off and on, and Allison went to join her. Coil kept thinking about Pete Weaver. She'd tried his number right after she'd called 911. No answer.

"You heard they arrested Applegate?" asked Trudy. "And the reporter said he was cooperating."

"Sandstrom mentioned it," said Coil. "I don't think he's too happy with this happening now, drawing attention from his big bust. You okay?"

"I suppose. How's George?"

"He's hurting. You did what you had to do."

"I could have let the cops chase him, catch him. It felt so easy, shooting him. Too easy."

"George would be long gone if you hadn't shot him, and it might have ended up being a bigger mess."

"What about your David?"

"That's next," said Coil. "Finding him."

Sandstrom arrived an hour later and went over the statements, realizing there would be no way to charge Trudy Grumley anything, realizing that Coil had fought in self-defense and that George would probably face attempted murder, at the very least.

Bridgers arrived after the ambulance left, and Sandstrom asked Coil to go over again how she had found out about the secret factory. Nothing about the factory needed explaining. Bridgers had four other rangers in tow, and they were quickly on their own radio, calling for an evidence crew of their own. After the tour of the antler dust factory, Bridgers seemed exasperated, beyond disappointment.

"Check the Polaroids," said Coil, pointing to the bulletin board. "Couple shots of him grinning with hunters."

"This day is like a sack of woe," said Sandstrom. The neighbors had all drifted away, and the unnecessary cops had gone back to their other assignments. "Trouble follows me wherever I go."

"Been a busy one," said Coil.

They were all huddled around Sandstrom's car, wondering what Sandstrom would do next.

"You gotta find Slater, too," said Trudy.

"Check," said Sandstrom. "We call it an APB. Slater's probably listening on his own damn radio, but I don't know how else to alert the others."

Sandstrom barked into his radio. To Coil, it seemed that Sandstrom's limits had finally been reached. He was pissed. Sandstrom spoke in code and numbers, but they all got the gist of his message to the others: find and stop David Slater.

"I've got something else to show you," said Coil to Sandstrom.

She led him inside Slater's trailer and pulled the letter from Weaver out of her pocket.

"I found this sitting on the television," she said, "this afternoon. It was open."

Sandstrom scanned the letter.

"So Slater's profits from his exports were going to buy a base for his empire?" he asked.

"I've been trying to call Pete Weaver on the telephone," said Coil. "I'm worried. I'm positive Weaver has no clue as to what Slater is really involved in."

"You'd have an easier time getting a bird to stop flying than you would corrupting Pete Weaver," said Sandstrom. "Everybody knows that."

"Something doesn't feel right," said Coil. "Can we go up there?"

"Well," said Sandstrom, "I think we're done here anyway. Hard to believe this day has one more surprise, but right about now I wouldn't bet more than a nickel on that."

Coil took a minute to tell Trudy they were going to check on something back up in the valley and that she'd catch up with her soon. Trudy said she'd head back home, and they hugged. Trudy started to cry, then patted her heart as if she might be able to find the handle to the faucet. But it wasn't anywhere to be found. In fact, it had the opposite effect and Coil gave her another hug.

"I'm not sure I did the right thing," sobbed Trudy.

"When it comes time to hurt somebody, I don't think most good people do know if they did," said Coil.

Coil climbed into Sandstrom's police car, slowly letting go of Trudy's hand, knowing there was at least one person she could trust.

* * * *

The police radio hadn't stopped squawking. Sandstrom made a reference to the National Forest crew, and they all agreed to switch to the same frequency. David Slater could hear the whole back-and-forth as his world started blowing apart at the core. He used his own radio to call the medical center, identified himself as Officer Joe Krabb, tweaked his voice up a notch, a bit higher, and insisted on knowing the identity of the victim they'd picked up from the trailer park. Nobody would suspect a thing with the question coming in on the police frequency, and a real officer asking it.

And the answer came back. George Grumley.

Slater raced his pick-up along the dirt road up into Ripplecreek. It was dusk now, and only a faint band of yellow lit up the distant ridge. The pick-up skittered around the washboard corners, fishtailed a bit, and he tried to calculate how much time he'd need to find Weaver and get his money back. Would they take cash for a ticket at the airport in Denver? Why didn't he always carry his passport? Why hadn't he foreseen this? There was a customer in Hong Kong, one distributor he knew, who wouldn't be afraid to put him to work. Maybe he could make the Mexican border. Or the Canadian. He'd always heard Vancouver was wonderful, home to the second largest Asian population on the West Coast.

The pick-up gobbled up the road as he drew close to Weaver's place and imagined how it could have gone so very differently: putting Weaver's spread together with Grumley's and running the whole shootin' match. The best camps, the top permits in the whole state for prime elk, the most under-patrolled wilderness areas for a steady flow of customized hunts during the season, and off. It was the best valley to say "fuck you" to the world of government work and shit jobs, the best place to sit back while the teams of guides earned him his millions.

He stopped at Weaver's barn and let the engine idle as he hopped out. Some grunt was shoveling out a stall as he walked inside.

"Seen your boss around?"

"Who, Pete?"

No, the fucking man in the moon. Slater let his expression say it.

"Probably at the house. Left here to go get some dinner."

"Thank you," he said politely.

Up the driveway to Weaver's, a quarter-mile from the valley road. The light was on in the glassed-in porch, and it looked like lights were on in the kitchen, too, closer to the back. The house was a two-story, old clapboard job—white with green shutters and trim. It was a big, rambling, but neatly kept house that was way too much room for a single, never-married, old ranch owner on the verge of retirement.

Who would now have to keep working? Oh, well. Slater opened the door through the porch and then opened the main door and slipped inside. Fool, he thought. Careless fool.

Hunched-over, Pete Weaver stood in the kitchen, stirring a pot of beans or some shit. The look on Weaver's face was frozen.

"Nobody . . ."

"Nobody what, grandpa?"

He stopped stirring the pot, stood up a little straighter.

"I thought we had this settled. You look . . ."

"I look what?"

"Agitated, I suppose."

"Not for long. Only uniti I get my money back."

"Whoa," said Weaver.

"'Whoa' is for fucking horses," said Slater. "Cash back. Now. The deal's over. I miscalculated, let's say."

"Can't."

"Can't what?"

"Can't return it," said Weaver, slipping around the side of a big butcher block table.

Slater stepped up close to him, to get the point across.

"I haven't got much time. You and I both know you haven't put the money in the bank. You and I both know it's too much money to put in the bank all at once. Too many questions."

"Where did you get all that cash?" asked Weaver. "My Lord, it took me a couple days to count it."

"Fuck you, Weaver. The money? I'll find it myself if I have to."

"It's a mighty big ranch. I don't think you'll have much luck," said Weaver. "Besides, a deal's a deal. I got plans now. Plans I didn't have before. It's opened a whole new world of possibilities."

"Possibility this." said Slater. He stuck the gun in Weaver's face and, for the first time, saw Weaver flash some fear.

* * * *

Sandstrom drove within the limits. Coil wanted him to dig his spurs in and give it a kick. They were turning off the interstate, heading up toward Ripplecreek.

"I say you go up to Lizard's Tongue next spring and dig around after the snow's melted. Look where Rocky landed. Near where that elk was, you'll find the shells from the bullets that killed Rocky. They'll be Grumley's," said Coil.

"We got Applegate," said Sandstrom. "One step at a time."

Coil had tried her how-Grumley-and-Applegate-might-have-hooked-up theory on Sandstrom, and he had mused it over. He said it might be worth exploring more with Applegate, because he sure was a steady fountain of interesting information.

"I'm having trouble trying to figure out David Slater."

"We can form a club," said Coil. "I'll be president."

"Ranger wages aren't much, but forest rangers are usually straight arrows who love the outdoors. You're more likely to encounter a corrupt cop in the city."

"Never been tempted?"

"Sweetie, the world is full of people who try to influence you. Some days you feel like nailing every speeder going a whisker over the limit. The next you couldn't care less if they're turning Main Street into the Indy 500. I can't say I've looked as hard into every questionable allegation as maybe I should have. But you can only do so much. Government in general, it can only do so much. People like Slater, flaunting it, doing their own trip, clearly operating outside the law. That's a different story altogether."

Coil leaned forward and took a deep breath, wishing she could will Sandstrom into picking up the pace and wondering if she was being given a line.

* * * *

Slater held the gun to Weaver's temple, pushed him with the muzzle, and pointed him from room to room. Slater kicked open dish cabinets and cedar chests and dug through bookcases, yelling at Weaver that if he so much as tried anything tricky, he'd blow his brains out. And it was all so useless, time slipping away. Weaver kept mumbling about the deal, about how they couldn't go back.

"You made the mistake of making it clear that it's here somewhere, asshole," said Slater. "Big mistake."

They stood upstairs in Weaver's bedroom, which was fixed up like some old lady's. Neat comforter, four-poster bed, and a big mirror over the dresser. Fussy little lampshade with fringe next to the bed. Everything in its place. The money had to be somewhere.

"I'm tired of these fucking games," said Slater. "We're going to get down to business. You got one minute left."

There was fear in Weaver's eyes, but not as much as there should be.

"Kill me and I guarantee you'll never find it. Give me a couple days and maybe I'll loan you back some cash, if that's what you need. As for now, I've already made plans for just how I'm gonna wind down my life."

"Where is it?" Slater asked, shifting the gun around to between Weaver's eyes.

Weaver was in shape, perhaps, but not enough for what he tried, which was running to the top of the stairs.

Perhaps thinking that Slater didn't have the guts.

Perhaps thinking that Slater had bought his story about never being able to find the money.

Nobody could hide something forever.

Everything could be found.

Weaver was halfway down the stairs, one hand steadying himself on the banister as his feet worked and tripped and skidded down, probably thinking he was home free, probably one half of his brain thinking see, he didn't have the guts, and the other half thinking it had been a nice life . . .

It felt good knowing some things could be controlled, even if the "something" was a lazy old man who really should have known better.

Weaver's shoulder exploded in a burst of red, and the old man went tumbling, his head crashing into the wall at the bottom of the stairs. Slater pumped two more bullets into the body for an extra kick and then told himself, the sound of the gunshots ringing in his ears, that the money had to be somewhere upstairs. People kept valuables close to where they slept. It gave them comfort.

* * * *

"It's Slater's pick-up," said Coil.

"Forest Service, at least," said Sandstrom. "No jumping to conclusions."

"Shit," said Coil, hopping out.

"Wait," said Sandstrom, grabbing his shotgun off the rack.

Sandstrom had parked forty yards away from where the skirt of light flared out from the house.

Coil bounded ahead, then waited a few moments while Sandstrom ambled out, thinking it might not be a bad idea, at this point, to work together. Sandstrom put his hand on the hood of Slater's pick-up and shook his head to say 'yes.' It was still warm.

From where they stood, the house looked empty. Sandstrom led them around to the kitchen, and they peered inside. There was no movement, but there were some lights on upstairs.

Sandstrom led the way into the glassed-in porch, set up like a living room, with wicker chairs, wicker couches, a few large plants, and a hammock. The door to the house was slightly ajar, and Sandstrom pushed it open a bit more before it stuck, blocked by something.

"Christ," said Sandstrom, giving it a heave so she could squeeze under his arm and in. She peered around, wanting to see what the problem was with getting the door open, thinking that the key was to simply warn Weaver, that at worst they would catch the two of them working on the deal, negotiating, figuring things out.

Pete Weaver stared back at her from the floor on the landing to the stairs, his legs climbing up the wall, his forehead blown off, and his arms tied up in a contortion.

Coil backpedaled and went faint, somehow realizing deep inside herself that she couldn't utter a sound, couldn't say a thing, but must somehow communicate what she'd seen, and the danger, to Sandstrom.

And then they both heard the sound of feet scuffling somewhere, a door or a drawer being slammed shut, and maybe even a muffled shout. She couldn't be sure. The cry came from deep within the giant house. Sandstrom held her by the arm and eased them both over to the large window from the porch into the living room. They could see dishes and books piled up on the floor, tossed haphazardly. Junk was everywhere.

"Weaver's behind the door. Dead." Each word was a struggle.

"I'm going in," said Sandstrom, backing up to the door and pushing hard. Coil waited this time, while Sandstrom looked at the body.

They heard scuffling upstairs, and their eyes gazed up at the ceiling, as if they suddenly had x-ray vision. Coil couldn't be sure what she was hearing with her heart pounding so loudly. And then there were the sounds of a door being slammed and a man cursing, too distant to hear clearly.

Down the hall, from the kitchen, they could hear a bubbling sound, like a steady gurgle. Sandstrom went first, shotgun at his waist. He could move quietly for a big guy, and Coil stayed in the shadow of his frame.

"Something on the stove," said Sandstrom. "Beans."

Sandstrom crossed the kitchen quickly to turn off the gas fire. "Basic fire prevention there," he whispered, and stepped over to what, in the dark, looked like a walk-in pantry, some sort of back room, to double check. As he did so, David Slater stepped out of the shadow, reached back and let the rifle fly, swinging it with a grip on the barrel. The stock clocked Sandstrom's head, sending him hurtling down in a heap.

"Allison." He on one side of the butcher block table, she on the other. "Love these big houses with the back staircases."

Sandstrom lay in a lump. Allison backed away from the table that separated them.

"And nothing like a guide's house to find yourself a baseball bat," said Slater, admiring the rifle. Slater plucked the shotgun from Sandstrom's hands and put it up on the counter behind him.

"I had it all set up for us," he said. "We were going to be set."

"We?"

She looked for an escape route, seeing he had flipped the rifle around in his hands.

"You and I. The whole valley. We would have run the whole valley."

"There never were any biologists. Or researchers."

"Probably not," said Slater. "But how do you know? Know for sure? That's government information."

"You know who strung me up?"

"No. But Grumley would probably have an idea."

Taste of seawater in her mouth; was that possible? And a wet sensation from her clothes, but maybe this time she wouldn't be able to swim, keep her head screwed on straight. It would be okay if they could race ahead to where it all got resolved.

"Why?"

"Why what?"

"Why all this?"

"Oh, I could tell you a story little missy, make your hair curl."

"Try me."

Hands behind her, fingers feeling for something, anything.

"Story about the government."

"Writes your paycheck."

"Fuckers, that's who. The government. Govern nothing, fuck everything. Swiped my parents' land. Section 9 of the Endangered Species Act of 1973, as amended. But the government wouldn't issue a special rule pursuant to Section 4-d. No 4-d, land gone. Here's your compensation, your land is gone, and they pay a nickel for every dollar it's worth.

Timberland. Ten thousand acres of prime timberland, a retirement bank account, ready to sell for harvest. Land that climbed a gorgeous hillside in the western Cascades. Everything mortgaged to the hilt for this tidy little investment. Little, hell. Gone. The owls won. The government won."

"Jesus," said Allison. "Revenge?"

"Revenge, shit," said Slater. "Just playing within the same bendable rules. They rip off my family for their political needs, and that's money. I play with the wilderness, hurt nobody, and that's money. My parents had the bad luck, God rest their weary souls, to buy land in what became a SEA, a Special Emphasis Area. Where the fucking Forest Service had determined that it was necessary and advisable, based on God knows whose advice, to apply broad protection—"

He stopped, seething, a sneer coming over his face, his already sweaty skin pumping out fresh perspiration. Coil let her hands drift behind her on the counter, wondering if there might be a knife rack.

"—from incidental take. Incidental take to protect a few spotted owls."

"No different than a little incidental take in Flat Tops?"

"Where there's plenty of deer and elk and nothing's endangered. Nothing."

"Jesus," said Allison again. "Rocky was 'incidental take'?"

"Ask Grumley about his own damn sense on that one. I wouldn't say the victim was innocent, based on what I know."

"Hunting anything anywhere, anytime?"

"You're a stickler like old Mr. Weaver, I suppose."

"Selling antler dust to the Asians?"

"Easy as waking up every morning, milking the cash cow," he said with a growling, sneering look in his eyes.

"And illegal."

"Nobody gets hurt."

"As far as you're concerned."

"Not a soul."

Her fingers were coming up empty. She needed a weapon, something, and she scooted a couple of inches over to the stove.

"It's all come apart. You're done."

"I'm going to find my cash and be gone. You're my last problem."

"Problem?"

"You're certainly not part of the solution, showing up here with this oaf."

"You betrayed everything."

"I was waiting until it was all mine."

Feeling the handle of the pot of beans behind her, the question in her mind was whether it had boiled down too much, whether it would be too gloppy. But the mess flew before he got the rifle up, and he yelped and screamed as it coated his face. She half-hurdled, half-scrambled over the corner of the butcher block and scampered for the door, hoping she could avoid looking at Weaver again, but there was no way around it. Weaver's weight had pushed the door shut, and his body blocked the door. She had to struggle to pull it all the way open: his corpse a perfect doorstop.

"Allison!"

Slater was running from the kitchen, screaming for her as she squeezed through.

She ran down the steps and outside. Checking Slater's pick-up for keys, she found none. Then she checked Sandstrom's. Ditto. But there was a gun, gleaming chrome in a holster next to the shifter. She grabbed the whole thing, letting the holster drop as she started to run.

She ran down the driveway, thinking she might be able to out-hoof him to Weaver's barn. Her legs churned on their own, fueled by fear, and she gasped for breath but her legs worked as if they didn't really care if they got oxygen or not. The driveway turned dark where it ran out of light: the glow of Weaver's place fading. As she was swallowed up by the night, she heard a familiar sound, a rifle shot, and she kept moving, waiting for the next as she dodged, two steps this way, three that way.

"Allison!"

A distant cry.

No second shot.

She slowed, putting the pace back in fifth gear. She had a healthy head start. And then she heard a car start up, probably his. Risking a glance around, she could see the headlights blazing toward the house, then spinning around.

The barn loomed ahead, her feet digging harder once more. And the headlights came up behind her. She tried to outrun the edge of them. Her lungs started to burn, and she knew there was no shortcut through the woods

The pick-up roared behind her, and the lights flicked up on high beam and spattered her shadow across the side of the barn. She had entered a space where it was the barn or nothing, the woods had drifted too far away to be of any use. Coil reached the side door, flipped the latch, and fell inside.

A light from the office cast a faint glow on the far side of the cavern. A horse snorted. She could see the horses in their stalls and briefly wondered if one could spirit her away, bareback. Coil scooted along the stalls, wondered about hiding and figured that was of no use. The horses would give her away. Hayloft? No way out. Tack room. Shit. She kept moving, searching.

Hanging close to the stalls, thinking one of the horses might whisper an offer of protection, Coil scampered along, none of the options seemingly viable. She reached the far door and threw it open, fleetingly wondering if he might think she'd gone on out through it if she left it open. He might think she had doubled back and looked for a place to hide. She would try misdirection.

His car came skidding to a stop in the dirt, and she heard him shout something muffled, her name in there somewhere. As she moved further into the room, she saw five elk sleeping on the floor in a corner. She jumped, terrified that the animals would startle, stand up, give her away. Then she realized . . .

Skins. There were hides spread out in heaps, probably drying for a hunter who liked standing mounts.

"Allison!"

She heard the sound of the door opening and ducked down, lying flat on the floor. Then she rolled over between the first and second skin and yanked the clumpy wrinkles of one of them over her body.

"Allison!"

The warm, fleshy feel of the hide and the light odor of salt enveloped Coil as she froze, urging Slater in her mind to sprint through the door she had deliberately left open and to chase madly after her into the darkness.

"Allison?"

Slater's voice was close, too close. She kept a vise-like grip on the gun. She could hear him stepping through the barn and tried to let her weight sink into the straw beneath the skin.

"I know you're here," he said. "Because I saw you, saw you, saw you." A little sing-song voice, rising higher.

Coil clutched the gun at her knees.

One door opened and slammed shut, perhaps the closet where they hung the rain gear. Next it would be the tack room.

"Nice saddles," said Slater. "Good condition. I'd say it was a fair price."

Coil's heart throbbed and she worked to keep its shock waves from rippling out through her body.

She heard him rustling around. Two minutes or two seconds, she couldn't be sure. Her mind had raced off to some place dark blue and peppered with stray, uncontrollable flashes of purple and black. Her eyes strained for an opening in the dense skin, and she tried not to inhale. She heard the metallic ching, ching of knife on sharpener. The Buck knives, stored in slits in a big chunk of wood in the tack room. Ching ching.

Ching.

But he has a rifle.

What the . . .

Ching.

"Nice blades, too."

Her grip on the gun tightened even more, if that was possible without making a move. Maybe it wasn't.

"Nice skins, too."

Voice above her.

Fuck.

And then he whomped the ground as he dropped to his knees, and it was off to her left, and every muscle in her body wanted to spin up and away from the sudden noise, to react. But she stayed put.

"Nice skins, all salted out."

She heard the sound of knife cutting through fur and skin and drying elk flesh, a soft but violent sound. He gasped and struggled with it.

"I think I smell you. Female mixed with fear," he said. "Very distinct. Well, this one's empty."

Two to go. Or three?

"Damn it, fuck it, we had it all, Allison." He was yelling again, now, practically in her ear.

The next skin was getting carved up. His mouth sounded wet and slobbery.

"I had it all figured."

Was that him sniffling?

One to go?

She heard him stand up, listened to the terrible silence for a long second and hoped he might show some interest in the open door, think he was losing time. Please.

And then he dropped right next to her, plunging the knife into nowhere, jabbing it around, ripping the skin and flailing at it, grunting as he did so.

She aimed in her mind first and then spun inside the elk skin. She stuck her head out at the same time as she poked the gun upwards along with the elk skin. Slater stared at the spot in her elk cover that had come up towards him. His knife was clenched in both hands, up over his head, and he was starting to arc it down for another slash at the empty skin next to her. But he spun and was slicing down toward her when she fired, her mind frighteningly clear. She looked away, and then rolled out, scooted out, as the sound registered deep in her bones and Slater's chest opened up. It seemed for an instant that he might have been blown back over his boots. He was starting to say something. His mouth opened, at least.

Coil dragged herself away, shuddering.

She watched him for a full minute, looking for any movement. She crawled farther away and found the courage to stand up. This time, for once, she realized she wasn't wondering whether all the pieces should be put back together.

17

It was high noon, and the streak of warmish air teased them with spring, still months away. Coil wanted something to melt, something around her to change dramatically, but that would be many moons away.

Trudy sat bundled-up next to her on Coil's front porch. They both sipped giant cups of strong black coffee, an old quilt wrapped around their legs, their heads tipped back against the wall to soak up the low-slanting sun, which added an ounce of warmth to the morning breeze. There was a clear presence to the air in the valley. The day seemed like something tangible, perhaps nothing more than a series of moments.

Coil had shared her bed with Trudy, who had come up to the valley after hearing about the commotion on the news. They both slept the sleep of the dead, which didn't start until the wee hours of the morning. Everyone had come running when Coil called in breathlessly for help from Weaver's house. At that point, Sandstrom was making his way to his feet, groggy and plenty pissed off.

An occasional police car cruised up and down the road. And they'd seen four news trucks, too.

"How are you doing?" asked Coil.

"Okay," said Trudy. "Better. You?"

"Weird. Sad," said Coil. "Mostly sad. Pete Weaver deserved so much better. And it's so hard to understand why I never saw what Slater was up to."

"I want to get back to my animals," said Trudy firmly.

"A good idea," said Coil. "I'll take you there. Can I help?"

"Sure," said Trudy. "I also want to make a few calls down to Denver, see about an appointment to get this brain fixed."

"I don't know," said Coil. "Seems like a reasonable idea to me."

* * * *

In the late spring, when the snows up high had given up their grip on the warming earth, Coil rode up to Black Squirrel Pass. She came up to it the back way, the long way around, and stopped her horse, McCartney, about where she figured she had been when she saw Grumley dragging Rocky's limp body across the rocks.

Coil matched her memory with her current field of view, now on the cusp of green. The air was clear. She imagined Rocky and Grumley tangling on the trail, the shot being fired. Heard it in her head, the dull echo.

She walked McCartney down and around, a faint wisp of apple or pear and muddy earth in the air.

Everything was wrapped up. Grumley's federal trial was a few months off. But nobody argued the resolution of that case, especially with the murder charge tacked on. Bobby Alvin's body had been found by a couple of hikers. Applegate had dealt with a few minor charges, faced a suspended two-year sentence while he was out on probation, and got fined $20,000. Grumley's ranch was sold. Between the two extremes, the poachers and the moral zealots, what was there to choose?

Trudy had made it for two whole months without a seizure. Her house had become a frequent tea stop for Coil, who was starting to learn some of the cats by name. Some of the plants, too, by type. She'd never met anybody who defined the phrase "new lease on life" as much as Trudy. In fact, Coil had taken her on a cool, early spring camping trip on horseback. They wound up around a campfire in a high clearing and shared stories late into the night. Trudy confessed it was her first night out in the open since high school.

Coil stood on Lizard's Tongue, gazed out over the valley, then wound her way down to the picked-over elk carcass. Of course. From a few feet away, the rifle would have been too powerful, too obviously murder. The bulletless elk surely indicated where they had tangled, where Grumley had been confronted.

She stood away from the heart of the bunker, wondering how many paces Grumley might have taken before aiming his rifle at Rocky. She strolled around, her eyes casually glancing down here and there, thinking it would be a small miracle if she spotted anything, but it was possible. The bullet shells that held Rocky's fate were somewhere. Grumley had probably tied him up and then taken his distance.

Coil studied the grass around her boots and pushed aside the leaves on a small bunch of alumroot where she couldn't see the ground. It was possible the earth had swallowed them up. Or a chipmunk had decided to take it back to its den and placed them on a chipmunk mantle, over a chipmunk fireplace. Souvenirs from the big bad world above.

She found nothing, of course nothing. And what difference did it make? Just another piece of the world she couldn't pick up and put back together.

Coil backed up a few paces, stood square, and sighted her rifle down over the elk carcass, imagining Rocky there, pleading for mercy. She checked Black Squirrel Pass and imagined herself coming over the ridge. She looked at McCartney looking back at her and made sure there was nothing in her line of fire.

She fired three rounds and on the last two looked for the shells ejecting and twirling. Both arced up, bounced off a rock, and hopped down and away.

She followed them, studied them, a few feet apart from each other. The third was there, too, and the three shells formed a gold-tipped triangle on a scrap of barren earth. She crouched and picked up each one and let her eyes go soft-focus, trying to discern anything else man-made in her field of view.

There. Worn down by winter. Not so bright. A much larger shell, pointing downhill. The shell with Rocky's name on it. She held it up to the sky between her finger and thumb and wondered about the sound it had generated. Rocky had heard it . . . or maybe not. And George.

And if she had heard it, it would have been the proverbial tree falling and nobody there.

The government could do only so much. She imagined Rocky waiting all winter under the snow, and the animals that would have found him. She tried to imagine justifying in her own mind that the boys in the tower at LaGuardia should be made to feel any worse, or that all the other tax-payers should foot the bill for anything beyond $900,000, nearly half of which was now committed as a hefty down-payment on Weaver's ranch.

Had she sought more, she realized now, studying the beat-up shell, she might actually think the government was the enemy or, at least, a fearful master. She put the bullet in her pocket as a reminder and headed off. She would find a place for it on her own little mantle.